I See You

Also by Molly McAdams

I See You

A Novel

Molly McAdams

WILLIAM MORROW

An Imprint of HarperCollins*Publishers*

I SEE YOU. Copyright © 2016 by Molly Jester. All rights reserved. Printed in the United States of America. No part of this book may be used or reproduced in any manner whatsoever without written permission except in the case of brief quotations embodied in critical articles and reviews. For information address HarperCollins Publishers, 195 Broadway, New York, NY 10007.

HarperCollins books may be purchased for educational, business, or sales promotional use. For information please e-mail the Special Markets Department at SPsales@harpercollins.com.

FIRST EDITION

Designed by Diahann Sturge

Library of Congress Cataloging-in-Publication Data has been applied for.

ISBN 978-0-06-244266-6

16 17 18 19 20   RRD   10 9 8 7 6 5 4 3 2 1

For Tessa.
Three versions later and it totally
isn't what we were originally going for,
but this story will always be for you.

PART I

That Night . . .

MY EYES FOUND his again, as they had often in the two hours I had been here, and I curled my fingers against the back of his neck. Urging, pleading for him to take me away from the crowd of people. Somewhere I could study him and listen to him speak, and not worry about what his touches and teasing mouth were about to make me do.

His full lips made a pass across the line of my jaw until they were at my ear, and his arms tightened around me as he said, "Let's go."

Turning me so he could pull me close to his side, he led us through the packed house and up two flights of stairs. His eyes kept darting down to mine as we walked, but he didn't say a word as we made our way to a locked door and he took out a key. I hadn't taken him for a frat guy, but I wasn't going to question him.

Because I didn't want to know. I wanted tonight with him . . . I didn't want his life.

Or, at least, that was what I was trying to remind myself.

The energy and awareness that swirled between us made it hard to remember what this night was for. Made it hard to remember that it could only be *one* night.

I'd seen him immediately upon entering the house earlier with three of my closest friends. We came up to Duke because we'd heard about this house's parties, and we were looking for a night to be the girls we usually weren't before our senior years began.

For one night, we didn't want to be the good girls everyone knew us to be. For one night, we wanted to let loose, and not have to worry about the consequences tomorrow. Everything we'd avoided the past three years, which was why a party at Duke was so perfect. And I'd found the guy I wanted to remember for years to come.

His presence had filled the room packed with people even though he'd been in the far corner when we walked in, watching the crowd silently by himself. He didn't seem to be looking for anyone—just watching. Studying. Everything about him screamed trouble. The way he stood: tall with hard, lean muscles, and sure of himself. The look on his face, a calm so unnerving, it was like the calm before the storm. All of it paired with dark, sinful eyes that kept finding me until I finally found myself pressed close to him as we danced to the music that poured through the house.

A gasp tore from my chest when we entered the room and the guy quickly pushed me up against the now-closed door. But all coherent thoughts left me when my back settled against the door and I looked up into dark eyes.

He placed his hands on either side of my head and leaned forward until his mouth was at my ear. "Tell me what you want."

My lips parted with a quick exhale even though I tried to keep my composure. But his voice . . . his voice. It fit. The image, the eyes . . . it all fit. Now that we weren't in the middle of a sea of loud people and music that made it nearly impossible to hear anything, I could appreciate the sound of it. It was deep and hoarse. And in those few words, I knew that the sound of his voice would haunt my mind for years to come.

1

One Year Ago

Aurora

R orie!" Taylor yelled over the loud music pulsing through the house—the sound still unable to mask the whine in my best friend's tone. "I'm starving and we've been looking for this mystery guy forever. This would have been so much easier if we'd known who to ask for."

My stomach instantly morphed into a tornado of fluttering wings. I didn't know his real name. God, I didn't even know his name, and that didn't bother me. That made the memory of him more intense—it made my heart beat harder and caused me to feel dizzy for a second as I replayed every second with him.

His lips on my skin. His husky voice in my ear. His intoxicating cologne clouding my mind. His strong hands learning every inch of me, branding me.

My face fell. Not knowing his name *hadn't* bothered me until this afternoon, when I'd decided that I needed to see him again. I hadn't gone more than a few minutes all week without thinking about him, and that had made my decision to come back up to Durham to try to find him. But all I had were memories and an alias.

He let out a long breath and his eyes drifted to the side. "Jay." After a moment's hesitation, those dark pools of obsidian found me again. "Just remember me as Jay."

I had known then that it was a random name to appease me, but hadn't cared. Because I had kind of done the same, and it fit to give each other aliases on a night where we both knew I was trying to be someone I normally wasn't.

"I told you not to come!" I yelled over the music, but Taylor was already turning to raid the table we were near.

I looked around us, hoping to get a glimpse of the only reason we were here. We'd already been here for two hours, and there'd been no sign of him yet. My chest had tightened a few times when I saw closely shaved heads—like the one I'd run the tips of my fingers over—but then the guy would turn and my heart would sink.

An excessively large Jolly Rancher was shoved directly in front of my face, less than an inch from the bridge of my nose, and my eyes crossed as I looked it over before glancing to where Taylor was glaring at me and sucking on her own piece of candy.

"Where did you get that?"

She pointed at the table behind her that was littered with

liquors and cups and candies, and mouthed the word *starving,* but didn't attempt to actually respond over the music.

I forced myself not to roll my eyes as I made one more quick sweep of the area around us, then sighed in defeat as I grabbed the candy. I unwrapped the Jolly Rancher and popped it in my mouth, and turned just as someone barreled into me from behind.

I gasped at the force of the hit, causing the large candy to fly backward and lodge in my throat. Panic instantly set in when I couldn't get it to move.

"Ror—oh my God! She's choking!" Taylor screamed, and her hands fluttered all around me.

I was immediately grabbed from behind, and large, hairy arms crossed over my chest seconds before I was heaved into the air over and over again.

"That's not how you do it! What are you doing?" Taylor screamed, and started punching the guy doing some unknown form of the Heimlich maneuver on me as one of my stilettos flew off my foot.

Taylor's screaming, the partygoers' shocked and worried faces, and my inability to pull in air was taking my panic to another level. I tried to slap the man holding me, but my arms were pinned down to my sides.

Just as the edges of my vision started darkening, my feet hit the ground once again on the guy's downward drive, and the candy went shooting out onto the hardwood floor.

I started gasping wildly, but no one seemed to notice.

"You're going to kill her, you idiot, stop it! Stop!" Taylor continued to scream, her hands still hitting the massive man holding me.

"Stop," I whispered hoarsely. "Stop! *Stop!*"

"It's out, man, stop!" a deep voice yelled from somewhere in front of me.

"Stop!" I yelled one last time as my legs hit the floor. Before I knew it, I was going up in the air again, and my second shoe went flying off.

"Rorie!" Taylor screamed as the guy behind me finally set me down, and forced me to lay on the floor. "Rorie, talk to me!"

I looked over at Taylor to find huge tears streaming down her face. "I'm okay!" I assured her, my voice still rough from having the Jolly Rancher lodged in my throat.

"Girl! Girl, are you okay?"

I jerked against the floor at the booming voice as a massive, mostly naked guy entered my vision. Tighty-whiteys, shoes, and a football helmet. Nothing else.

I nodded, unable to say anything as I tried to get the image of him out of my head even though he was still standing right there.

"I saved your life!" He stood up and lifted his arms in victory, and I covered my face to block things I didn't want to see. "I just saved her life!"

There were loud cheers throughout the house, and the music turned on suddenly, making me jump again. I wasn't sure when they'd turned it off, but knowing that my choking on unusually large candy had stopped a party had my panic subsiding and my mortification kicking in.

"You scared the shit out of me," Taylor sobbed.

"Excuse me, Cinderella?" a deep voice called next to my ear.

Cinderella? I removed my hand from my face to look at the guy who belonged to that voice, then quickly pushed myself up onto my elbows when I took in his face, so close to mine.

My cheeks burned with embarrassed heat, but I didn't know how to look away from him. Despite a large red mark on his forehead, his face was flawless and masculine, with a strong brow and nose, a smirk I knew would've made my knees weak had I been standing, and a lethal stare from green eyes so clear it was as if I could see through the iris.

My gaze had become so fixated on the way his lips moved that it took a few seconds too long to realize he'd said something. "I'm sorry, what?"

The smirk broadened for a brief moment, giving me a glimpse of straight, white teeth. He leaned over me until his lips were at my ear, and if I'd had the capability to breathe around him, I would've stopped then. "I said I think you lost this," he drawled, and I swooned.

Literally . . . *swooned*. As in: all the air left my body in one hard rush, I was unable to keep myself up on my elbows any longer, my head felt light and dizzy, the room spun, and I was pretty sure I'd just entered a romance novel. It really didn't matter that it was from the lingering effects of nearly choking to death, and then unknowingly holding my breath for too long.

"Whoa." He quickly put a hand under my head before it could smack on the hardwood floor.

"I'm fine," I said breathlessly, and internally berated myself for doing everything imaginable to look like an idiot tonight. I tried to sit up, but the guy was still hovering over me, making it impossible to go farther than I'd been.

"Are you sure you're okay?"

"Yes," I promised, and blew out a steadying breath when he sat back.

"Good. I can't have you passing out on me, Cinderella."

"Cin—" My head shook firmly as I corrected him. "No, my name is Rorie."

With another slow smirk, he gestured to the red mark on his forehead for barely a second, then reached behind him and produced my stiletto.

My embarrassment from earlier couldn't compare to the level it was at then as I put it all together. My shoe had flown into his face.

"Oh my God," I whispered so low, the words drifted away with the bass of the music. "I'm so sorry."

He laughed easily, as if he hadn't just taken a five-inch stiletto to the face, and glanced from my shoe to me. "My name is Declan," he provided. "I already know this shoe belongs to you. What I want to know now, *Cinderella,* is if I give this back to you, are you going to run away from me?"

Despite my humiliation, my lips spread into a smile as the

name finally made sense. I reached for the shoe, but Declan held it away from me. His expression showed he was still waiting for an answer. With a raised eyebrow, I said, "I lost both shoes. I don't care what Disney said, a girl can't run away very easily with only one shoe."

His smirk stretched to match my smile, and he dipped his head close. "Then I'm keeping the other one that hit the back of my head."

2
Two Months Ago

Aurora

I released a heavy breath and a wide smile broke free as I took in the sight before me. This was it, what we'd been planning and waiting for . . . we were finally going to be together. Not that thirty minutes away could ever be considered long-distance; but with how crazy both our senior years had been, Declan and I hadn't gotten nearly enough time together in the ten months that we'd been dating. And the time we had spent together had often been filled with other friends or studying. Now? Now it was just us. We'd both graduated a month ago, had debated on where we wanted to live, and then searched for the perfect apartment.

Apartment: *found*. Move everything in: *just finished*. Live out my happy ever after with boyfriend . . .

"Welcome home," Declan murmured into my ear as he wrapped his arms around me and pulled me against his chest.

. . . *definitely working on it.*

"Mmm, I like the sound of that." I felt my body loosen, and my head rolled to the side when his lips moved in a line down the side of my neck. "I need a bath," I said halfheartedly as one of his hands moved under my shirt. "That was code for I'm sweaty and gross."

Declan moved out from behind me and pushed me up against one of the living room walls. "I really don't care," his deep voice rumbled before he captured my lips with his.

His fingers found the hem of my shirt and pulled up, forcing us to break apart for the split second that it took to get the shirt over my head, then his mouth resumed moving against mine.

My breaths came out in short bursts as he moved down my throat and over my chest, his hands gripping and sliding over my hips and bottom as he slowly pushed my yoga pants and underwear down to my thighs. His teeth raked across my nipple over my sports bra, eliciting a gasp that was quickly followed by a low moan when he suddenly pulled up the bra and returned to what he had just been doing as his hand slid between my thighs.

I tore the sports bra off the rest of the way and dropped it to the floor near my shirt as I reached for him. Before I could get to his clothes, he slid his hands back down my thighs and lifted me up. I wrapped my legs around his waist and fused my mouth to his as he walked us down the hall and into the bedroom.

Declan tossed me onto the bed, and was already shrugging out of his shirt by the time I sat back up and reached for him. Grasping the waistband of his athletic shorts, I pulled him onto the bed with me as I lay back, and smiled playfully at the growl that built up in his chest when I grabbed his length.

I'd barely gotten his shorts off before he was pulling my yoga pants and underwear the rest of the way off and climbing back on top of me. His hands ran up my legs and stomach, then continued to my breasts for a teasing moment before they were gone and he was spreading my thighs.

His name was barely more than a whimper as his fingers teased me and his mouth focused on each breast. I ran my hands over his head and secured my fingers in his hair, my body restless as his lips slowly moved from my chest, down my stomach. My eyes fluttered shut when I felt his hot breath against me; a shaky moan climbed up my throat when he leaned forward to taste me.

Within minutes my body felt like it was suspended in air as he relentlessly teased and licked me. Heat pooled low in my stomach, every muscle tensed in preparation of what I knew I was only seconds from.

"I'm—" I cut off when an image flashed through my mind, too real to ignore for the second it was there. But just as quickly it was gone, and suddenly Declan was kneeling between my thighs and pushing inside me, and pushing me over the edge. "Oh God! Dec!"

My toes curled and body trembled as Declan moved

roughly and quickly inside me. Another moan tumbled from my lips.

"Declan Veil, I suggest you get out here this instant!" a very distinct, very frustrated, feminine voice called out from the front of the apartment.

Declan slapped his hand over my mouth to quiet the moan, and we froze in horror for all of two seconds before we scrambled away from each other.

"Crap!" I hissed, and searched the floor for my pants after I got my underwear on. "Crap!"

"Declan!" she called out again.

"Yeah, hold on!" Declan yelled back quickly as he pulled on his shorts. His expression showed every bit of his frustration.

"What is your mother doing here?" I whispered harshly, and covered my bare chest as I looked around for my shirt.

"I gave her a key . . . for emergencies." Declan said the last two words loud enough that I knew his mom could hear. His shirt hit my arms, and I hurried to catch it before it dropped to the floor. "Just put it on; she'll come in here if we don't go out there."

I put the shirt on as we rushed out of our room, and didn't realize it was inside out and backward until we were in the hall. Heat flooded my cheeks, and I wanted to crawl into a corner and die when we walked into the living room, and saw Declan's mom, Linda, holding my shirt and sports bra. Folded.

"I believe you lost this," she said in her thick drawl. Her

wide eyes glanced to Declan, and then she pointed to his shirt on my body. "And I believe *you* lost that, son."

"Mom," Declan said in greeting from where he stood a few feet away from her. "I wasn't expecting to see you today . . . also wasn't expecting you to just walk in."

"Now, is that any way to talk to the woman who spent thirty-seven hours birthing you?" Linda took in a steadying breath as her eyes bounced between the two of us. "I wanted to see what you did with your new place, as any mother would. So why doesn't someone get me a glass of sweet tea before you start showin' me around, and we're gonna pretend like the last few minutes didn't happen." But I could tell from the narrowing of her eyes that she wouldn't forget about what she'd walked in on, what she'd heard—just as we wouldn't.

"I'll get it," I murmured, and hurried into the kitchen to start brewing the tea.

I let loose a shaky breath once I was standing at the counter with my back to both of them, and thanked God for those few minutes to gather myself and clear my mind without Declan or Linda watching me.

Emotions flooded me, threatening to overwhelm me and making it nearly impossible to keep them from my face.

The humiliation of Linda hearing something she shouldn't have was nothing. Nothing compared to the betrayal that sat low and heavy, and burned white hot in my chest. Because for a second while Declan had devoured me, it had been there. . . .

The feel of buzzed hair beneath my fingertips.

Eyes so dark they looked black.

A wicked smirk.

Hard and soft.

Ten months after only one night with him, and *he* still managed to invade my mind. My hands shook as I pulled down a few glasses that I'd unpacked not long before, and guilt ate at me as I forced all thoughts of him away.

Present Day

"Rorie!"

I jerked away from the fingers snapping in my face and looked at my best friend. "Yeah?"

"You just completely zoned out . . . *again.*" Taylor's tone was full of worry, and I hated hearing it. "Do you want to call it for today?"

I looked around at the mass amounts of construction paper, paint, glitter, and letter and number cutouts piled around the living room, and tried to bring myself out of the past and back to the present of prepping for my new kindergarten class. "No, no. Sorry, I must have been daydreaming."

"Or just dreaming," she countered teasingly.

"*Not.* Anyway, thank you for helping me with this. I'm so behind in getting everything ready for my class. I still can't believe school is starting a week from tomorrow."

She waved off my thanks. "That's what best friends are for. Besides, your life is just . . . it's just chaotic right now with everything, and Declan's mom . . ." She trailed off at the mention of Linda, and I groaned. "I'm surprised you have time for anything that doesn't include trying to stay sane."

My mouth curved up in a smile. "That's why I have books. I don't have to try to stay sane; they keep me that way."

Taylor straightened and pointed around the living room of my apartment. "Oh sweet girl, bless your heart," she drawled, imitating Linda. "You just can't go around decorating with your books instead of putting them on shelves."

I huffed a soft laugh and stopped working on the sign to defend myself. "I didn't have money for the shelves I wanted, and I liked the way they looked!"

"Oh sweet girl," Taylor continued, and then dropped her voice down to a whisper. "Did you know that this furniture doesn't match? Maybe you should let me pick out some new furniture for the apartment."

That time I laughed louder. Linda had always been exceedingly opinionated, whether it was about how much time Declan and I spent together, how fast we moved in with each other, the way I decorated, or the way I dressed . . . she had something to say about it. But that was just how Linda was. She had too many opinions about everyone's lives, and she had no problem saying them.

It had become irritating extremely fast, made more so because of the fact that I took every opinion to heart and usually sided with her since I had wanted my boyfriend's mother to like me.

"Only you, Taylor," I said with a laugh. "Only you could make me laugh right now."

"I'll never stop making you laugh. Speaking of Lovely Linda, don't you have—"

A timer went off in the kitchen, and I whipped my head around to look in that direction.

"—family dinner soon?" Taylor finished, and pointed toward the kitchen. "Good thing you remembered that."

"Oh crap!" I dropped the brush I was holding and scrambled to find my phone. "Crap, crap, crap. Linda's going to kill me," I said as I hurried to get up and ran to the kitchen. "Just leave it all here, I'll work on it when I get back."

"Why is she going to kill you? You remembered to bake her . . ." She trailed off, and eventually gave up trying to remember the name of the dish. "Whatever thing."

"Yes, but I'm covered in glitter and paint, and I don't have time to shower."

Like it was nothing at all, like this wasn't a family dinner and this wasn't *Linda* we were talking about, Taylor said, "Just tell her you were working a pole or something. I'm sure she'll understand."

My face fell as I stared at her from across the rooms. "When you say things like that, it makes me question why we're best friends."

"Don't hate me because you don't share my genius way of thinking." She shouldered her bag as she headed toward the front door. "Call me if you aren't hanging out with Declan and need help this week."

"Love you."

"Back!" she called out just before she left.

THIRTY MINUTES LATER I was walking through the doorway into the kitchen to meet up with Declan and his family, and my hands were shaking from holding the dessert that I had made so tightly.

My parents and I had always been casual, not superclose, but not distant, either. We were just . . . there. Declan's family was always in each other's lives and had Sunday night family dinners—something that was important to Declan, so it was important to me. Which had been the huge deciding factor in living here instead of Raleigh.

The family dinners, for the most part, had always gone as expected. With Linda in the kitchen for hours upon hours, cooking enough to feed an army . . .

This time, however, was different.

Because this time I had a dessert. A dessert Linda had given me the recipe for. A dessert that I'd made three days in a row before today, trying to perfect it.

She'd handed me the recipe when she'd randomly stopped by earlier that week, and said, "It's time you start learning how to take care of my son. This is an old family recipe, and is very important to the Veil family. If you want to be a part of that family, you best learn how to make this. I'll be expecting it on Sunday."

I'd learned.

And now I was guarding it as if it were the most precious

thing in the world. As if the dish in my hands were worth millions of dollars, and if I dropped it my world would end. And with Linda expecting the dessert, it just might.

I accepted a hug from Declan's two older sisters, Holly and Lara, smiled at their husbands as they helped Linda set the food out in the massive kitchen, and murmured a quick hello when Declan's dad kissed my cheek on his way out of the kitchen to answer his phone.

"Where can I put this, Linda?" I asked as I checked the full counters.

Linda looked at my dessert-filled hands and raised an eyebrow. "Well, what is it, darling girl?"

"It's . . . it's the white chocolate bread pudding."

"Is that what that awful smell is?" she said with a laugh, and looked over at her daughters and their husbands. They didn't laugh with her. Her wide eyes fell to the dish in my hands again, and she sighed dramatically. "Well, just set it anywhere. Let's see it."

I swallowed past the thickness in my throat, and looked around for a moment before finding a space to set it down. I didn't breathe as she lifted the lid and eyed the dessert like it was going to jump out and eat her.

"Good God," she drawled, then walked away to grab a spoon. When she came back, she moved the spoon through the dessert as if she were dissecting it, and then finally took a bite. After a moment she made a gagging sound and hurried to a trash can.

My jaw was locked tight by the time she'd spit it out.

I'd never been an angry person, but Linda had been pulling it out of me as she'd slowly shown me over the last weeks what it was like to truly despise someone . . . as she'd gone from my boyfriend's too-opinionated mom, to the woman who loathed me with every fiber of her being.

The thought of her stressed me out until I had a headache. Talking about her frustrated me to no end, and usually left me shaking. Being in her presence had me in a constant state of fake smiles, clenched teeth, and hot blood pounding through my veins.

I hated who she was turning me into, and I wanted to hate her. Instead I felt sorry for all the reasons that led to her feeling like she needed to do this to me.

"Rorie, what are we going to do with you? Bless your heart, you don't even know how to bake. Sweet girl, that looked alien." Linda tossed the used spoon on the counter and walked over to grab a casserole dish from the other side of the kitchen. "Well, it's a good thing I was prepared." She placed hers beside mine, and opened it with a wide smile directed at me, and then the other people in the kitchen.

Of course she had made the dessert, too. *Of course.* Because it couldn't be that easy with Linda, to just do what she asked. No, I had to go through some form of embarrassment or harassment first. I felt stupid for even trying, and wanted to go scream and vent to Declan. Instead, I simply nodded as I looked at the nearly identical dishes. The only difference was mine had taken a spoon to it.

"We'll just put this poor thing out of its misery," she mumbled as she grabbed my dish and walked over to the trash. "You know, Madeline can whip up an amazing bread pudding."

I rolled my eyes at the mention of Declan's beloved ex-girlfriend.

I'd heard her name in passing over the months when Declan and I first started dating, but I now couldn't go a day without being reminded about how perfect Linda thought she was.

"Mom," Holly, Declan's oldest sister, began. Her tone was full of frustration, but she didn't finish as we all watched the dessert slide out of the dish and into the trash.

Declan's dad, Kurt, walked back in then. "What are we all standing around for? Let's eat, I'm starved!"

In what looked like an accident, but I knew wasn't, Linda dropped the dish into the trash on top of the dessert, and clapped her hands as she stepped away. "Yes, let's! Food is ready and getting cold. Everyone grab a plate."

I glanced up and caught Declan's sisters watching me. Both wore matching worried expressions, and Holly mouthed that she was sorry. I smiled at them and tried to shake off the horrible feeling Linda always left me with.

Once everyone was serving themselves, I looked over at Declan's plate sitting there untouched. I wondered if I was thankful or upset that he hadn't been there to witness his mom's hatefulness before my thoughts drifted.

Where are you, Dec?

3

One Month Ago

Aurora

Tell me again why I agreed to this?" Taylor grumbled from where she was lying on the floor of a rented beach house a few weeks after Declan and I had moved into our apartment.

I only paused long enough to shoot her an annoyed glance before continuing cleaning. I was trying to make the rental house where we would be spending the weekend with Declan and his brother, Jentry, look perfect.

Dec was currently on his way back from picking Jentry up at Camp Lejeune, and then we were meeting them for dinner before coming back here. And I had found out about thirty minutes before that Declan's parents had decided they were coming in the morning to spend the rest of the weekend with us, and I had been cleaning like a madman ever since.

It didn't matter that this wasn't the apartment that I shared with Declan. I knew if it wasn't spotless that I would get that judgmental look from Linda. The one where she pursed her lips and shook her head just seconds before those words fell from her mouth . . . *"Oh sweet girl, bless your heart."*

Instead of helping me as any friend should, Taylor had spiraled down into a mini meltdown over meeting Jentry—as she had all week after we'd found out that Jentry would for sure be joining us.

I'd heard about Jentry a lot over the course of my relationship with Dec. He was Declan's best friend and adopted brother, and had gone into the Marine Corps after high school. I didn't know all the details of the adoption; only that it had happened when the boys were younger.

Jentry had left for his last tour overseas right before I met Declan, and the last I'd heard was that he planned to get out soon, but I didn't know when that was supposed to happen. Declan had gone over to Camp Lejeune for Jentry's return from Iraq, but hadn't seen him since then and talked about him constantly. So I knew they were both excited about this weekend.

As I had been before I'd found out about our visitors tomorrow.

As Taylor had been before she'd decided that she suddenly had insecurities even though she was the most confident person I knew.

A satisfied smile spread across my face as I looked around the living room. *Just try to find a speck of dust in here, Linda!*

"I think I want to go back home," Taylor continued even though I'd never responded.

With a huff, I turned to look at her. "You're staying here, and you're going to get over yourself. You are the one who was so interested in Jentry whenever Declan mentioned him. And *you* are the one who suggested this weekend, so you can't back out now!"

"But now I realize how awkward it is. This is the worst idea I've ever had." She made a face when I just raised an eyebrow. "Okay, *one* of the worst ideas I've ever had. He just got back from Iraq not long ago; he isn't going to want some stranger intruding on his weekend!"

I groaned and rubbed at my eyes with the backs of my hands so I wouldn't transfer any lingering cleaner. "Taylor, have you forgotten I still haven't met— You know what? I don't have time for this."

"It would just help me if I knew what he looked like." Taylor and I had had this same conversation at least fifteen times by now. I didn't know why she kept going back to it.

"For the hundredth time—"

"Don't exaggerate."

"*I* don't even know what he looks like. You were right there with me when Declan said that Jentry doesn't mess with social media. I already tried talking to Linda to see if there were pictures of the boys, but I bet you can guess how well that went."

"Fabulously, I'm sure." Taylor sighed dramatically. "Why can't guys take pictures of themselves the way we do?"

I studied her for a second, then asked, "Do you really need me to answer that?"

She blinked quickly, then made a face like she'd just eaten something sour. "No. I'm just psyching myself out. In my mind, Jentry is this ripped, sexy badass—but not in a good way. In one of those ways that you're afraid of what he would do to you if you let him get too close. And then in my dreams, he's a scrawny creep who smells. Both kind of make me want to run back home."

I groaned and scrambled to my feet. "I'm sure he'll be average in every way. I'm going to hop in the shower and get ready."

"I don't want him to be average, either!" she called out as I walked to the kitchen to put the cleaning supplies away.

"Well, he has to be something! And unless you want to meet him in *that,* I suggest you go get ready, too." I looked pointedly at her fuzzy socks and holey sweats, and reminded her, "It's summer."

"Don't knock the outfit because you're not as comfortable as I am."

"You don't look comfortable, you look hot."

Taylor lifted an eyebrow suggestively. "Why, thank you."

I couldn't stop the soft laugh that bubbled up from my chest. "You know that's not what I meant." Turning away from her, I walked toward the bedroom I was sharing with Declan. "Get ready, Taylor."

"I'm going home!"

"No, you aren't. He'll be great, I'm sure!" *I hope. For the sake of this weekend, I really hope.*

If I was about to spend the weekend with Declan's mom, then I didn't need Taylor blaming me if Jentry ended up being anything less than amazing.

Jentry

Declan rolled the passenger window down as he rolled to a stop where I stood on the sidewalk waiting for him, and called out in a high-pitched voice, "Hey, Marine, wanna go for a ride?"

My chest shook with silent laughter. "God, I don't know why I'm friends with you."

He held a hand dramatically to his chest and gave me an offended look as I slid into the passenger seat of his truck. "That hurts."

"I'm sure you'll be fine," I mumbled, and knocked his shoulder with my fist. "Thanks for coming to get me, man. I need this weekend."

"Of course. It's been too long, and it was too good an opportunity to pass up." He glanced at me with a mocking grin. "Really, though, how many girls pulled up and asked you that before I got here?"

My mouth curved up, because even though Declan had sounded ridiculous when he pulled up, he *had* sounded like one of the many overly confident girls who scoured the base, looking for any lonely guy. "Let's just say it was more than one."

He laughed, then grimaced. "Aren't you afraid you'll catch something . . . or meet their husbands?"

"Which is why I don't go near them," I said honestly. "Not worth it; I'd rather find someone who didn't want me for a uniform."

He sucked in a breath through his teeth. "Yeah, about that. Taylor—Rorie's friend that you're meeting tonight—she heard the word *Marine* and about died. So she's probably not your best option, either."

A huff shot from my chest. I hadn't even been in the truck for three minutes, and Declan was already mentioning his girlfriend. That might have been a new record for him.

"Thanks for the heads-up. I'll be sure to stay away." Not that I'd needed his warning to want to. It would be impossible to find another girl I wanted to give even half an hour of my time to. It had been impossible for over ten months now. I reached over and swatted at Declan's tie and said, "Maybe I'll just steal Rorie, since she prefers contractors in ties."

He shot me a weak glare and loosened the tie to slip it over his head. "Touch my girl, see how long it takes me to kill you."

A wicked smile crossed my face as I taunted him. "But it would be such a fun challenge."

"Okay." He shrugged and nodded. "I guess I'm killing you now."

A sharp laugh burst from my chest. "No, you know I'm happy for you. I don't want your girl. I want . . ." I trailed off and blew out a slow breath before mumbling softly, "I want something I can't have."

"What do you—wait, you met someone and didn't tell me about it? Who is she?"

She's a violet-eyed siren who probably isn't even real. Flashes from a night—or maybe a dream—all those months ago hit me hard, and I welcomed every one of them.

"Is she married?" Declan asked suddenly.

My head snapped to the left to look at his curious expression, and it took me a few seconds to remember what he'd been asking. "Married? No. She's just—I'm pretty sure she doesn't exist."

The curiosity on his face vanished. "Man, how many drugs are you on?"

"Yeah, none," I said with a laugh. "Forget I said anything."

When Dec's cell phone chimed he grabbed it from where it sat in the cup holder and glanced at the screen for a second before setting it back down. As he did, an uncomfortable tension suddenly filled the small space. Before I could question it, he cleared his throat and said, "Hey . . . speaking of drugs, there's something I think you should know."

My brow furrowed as I waited for him to elaborate. "You already warned me about Taylor; you don't need to continue adding reasons for me to stay away." I tried to say it jokingly, but my voice came out strained.

There weren't many reasons Declan would bring up drugs around me, and even though I hoped I was wrong, I had a feeling I knew where this conversation was about to go. The simple thought of it—of her—set me on edge.

"Jessica found me," he finally said with a rush.

I hissed out a curse when his rapid confession confirmed my worries, then sighed through my nose as I tried to figure a way out of this conversation. But I still found myself gesturing to his phone and asking, "Was that her?"

"No. Dad."

I nodded, and after a moment, admitted, "Yeah, she found me, too. I don't know how. We've talked a few times since I got back."

Each time had been worse than the time before it, and much worse than the previous time she'd found me. My hands slowly clenched into fists as I thought about her words and her taunts and her desperate pleas.

Declan looked quickly between the road and me. "I didn't tell her how to find you, Jent, I swear. I haven't been responding to her."

"I know you wouldn't have," I responded numbly. "When have you ever? She just has her ways." After all, psychotic people are usually brilliant. "How long ago did she find you?"

"Just after you got back from this last tour; right before I graduated. She was in my room at the frat house one day when I got back from my classes, and I know I'd locked my door before I'd left."

A sound between a laugh and a sneer left me. "And how did that reunion go? Did you need to tell Rorie about it?"

Declan knew what I was implying and referring to. It had been the only time Dec and I had fought. One of the only times I had ever truly scared myself . . .

He rubbed a hand over his face, and kept it over his mouth when he mumbled, "I didn't know, dude."

"I know."

"And there was nothing to tell Rorie. I made Jessica leave. . . . I had to give her money, but I made her leave." When I just nodded absentmindedly, Declan said, "So you've talked to her?"

I paused for a second before saying, "A few times, for as long as I can handle her."

"About—"

"I don't want to do this," I said roughly. "Not now. Maybe not ever if she can't figure her shit out."

"Well, that's not a possibility."

My brows lifted in agreement though I knew he couldn't see. Clearing my throat, I attempted to put all thoughts of Jessica out of mind by switching the conversation to Declan's favorite topic these days. "So what else has been going on since graduation? I know you moved in with your girl. What is she doing now that you're back working for Dad?"

Dec gave me a look that said he wouldn't forget this conversation, but thankfully let it go for now. "She's been neurotically cleaning our apartment. Actually, she just heard back from an elementary school on a kindergarten position, so she's excited about that."

Declan dated pageant queens and girls that—well . . . that looked like whores. None of them had the *teacher* look or were obsessive cleaners. Knowing Dec had been continuously cheated on by one of those girls not long before he met Rorie,

I was wondering if he went for the first girl he found who was the exact opposite, and now all I could picture was our third-grade teacher, Miss Haggerty.

She had been the very definition of a lonely cat woman and had smelled like she never showered or washed her clothes though she was constantly cleaning the classroom. She also dressed like she was homeless.

Declan glanced at me and laughed at my expression. "What?"

"So she's a teacher *and* a neurotic cleaner." I blew out a slow breath and tilted my head to the side. "She sounds fun, Dec."

He was shaking his head before I'd finished talking. "No, it's not like that. The cleaning . . . Rorie just started it, and I'm positive it's only because she's trying to impress Mom. She's not usually like that. And what's wrong with being a teacher?"

"Nothing. I just know the kind of girls you've been with in the past, and suddenly you're with an OCD girl who wants to be an elementary school teacher. It's the complete opposite of what you usually go for, so I'm picturing a really boring girl who looks like Miss Haggerty."

"Again, what's wrong with that?" he asked innocently, and barked out a laugh when he saw the disgust that flashed across my face.

"I'm joking. Rorie . . . she's . . . God, I don't even know where to start with her, or how to explain her other than what I've told you. She's quiet at first, yeah, but give her a bit and she'll open up. There's just something about her that draws you in. I don't know what it is or how to explain it. You'll see when you meet her. But boring?" He grinned impishly and let that hang in the air for a few seconds. "Fuck . . . the last thing you could say about that girl is that she's boring."

His tone hinted at everything he wasn't saying, and made his attraction to a girl I was still picturing as Miss Haggerty make sense. "Really?"

He raised a brow and looked over at me for a second before looking back at the road. "Best of my life."

"Come on, Dec. . . ."

"I'm not kidding. It's like someone unleashes her, she becomes a totally different person." He stopped talking abruptly, and I knew in the way he was clenching his jaw that he was done talking about that part of their relationship.

Before, we would share stories about every girl—but I understood his want to keep Rorie to himself. I had one of those, too.

"Damn you for finding the girl every guy wants," I mumbled, but couldn't stop the genuine smile that crossed my face. He deserved Rorie after his last relationship. "You better marry her before your dumb ass messes up."

Aurora

An hour and a half later, I was showered and shaved, my hair was falling down to my waist in large, loose curls, and my makeup had never cooperated so well. If everything else failed this weekend, at least I would have tonight.

"Are you re— Whoa, Rorie!" Taylor skidded to a stop just inside the closet. Her eyes were wide when she found me. "Just which one of us is meeting someone new tonight?"

I rolled my eyes but didn't respond as I started dressing.

"Since when did you start wearing sexy lingerie?"

"Since I started sleeping with a boyfriend who *really* likes finding out what I'm wearing underneath." I gave her a knowing look as I fought a grin.

She patted her covered chest for a second, and her tone dropped. "I feel like I should go change."

"It's not like anyone is going to see it until later," I said through my laughter. "Besides, I've seen what you wear underneath your clothes, and it puts mine to shame."

Taylor narrowed her eyes and opened her mouth to argue, but then nodded. "True."

My phone chimed repeatedly from where it sat on the bathroom counter, and I finished pulling my shirt on as I went to check who the texts were from.

Dec: Got the package.
Dec: Meet me at the restaurant.
Dec: Bring the money.
Haha. Be there in a minute.

"One guess who that's from." Taylor's face pinched like she'd eaten something sour when I looked up at her with confusion after I sent my reply. "You're all smiley and whatever."

"He was being funny."

She lifted an eyebrow to show she didn't agree that *that* would be my reason for smiling. "Uh-huh. You know that you two are so cute it's nauseating."

"Oh, is someone jealous?" I teased, and bumped into her as I walked out of the bathroom. Taylor thought relationships were pointless and always made fun of mine, so I knew *jealous* was the last thing she was. "Anyway, they're at the restaurant. Are you ready?"

Her eyes widened like she'd just remembered the reason we had been getting ready. After a handful of seconds, she finally nodded. "Yeah, sure. Jentry time. Blind date and Jentry time. Oh God. No. No, wait, I can do this. He'll be great."

"Yes, exactly. Now let's go."

Thankfully the restaurant was only a few minutes from the house, so I didn't have to listen to another one of Taylor's meltdowns over Jentry for long. I was so ready for this dinner to start so I could have my overly confident friend back that I practically shoved her toward the entrance of the restaurant when she started hesitating again.

"Average in every way!" I reminded her, and wondered if this was how she felt when she had to give me pep talks.

If so, I felt sorry for the years that Taylor had tried to bring me out of my shell.

I breathed a silent sigh of relief as I followed her into the restaurant, and after a second of talking to the seating hostess, we were taken back to the table where the guys were waiting for us.

My eyes were on Declan as he talked to a guy next to

him, so I saw when he caught sight of us. Within seconds, he and Jentry were standing. My smile widened as my eyes shifted over to get my first glimpse of this best friend, and then promptly fell. I blinked quickly and shook my head, and wasn't sure if I was still following the seating hostess and Taylor, or if I was rooted in place.

But I knew with one hundred percent certainty that I couldn't take my eyes off the person next to Declan. The guy who was supposed to be Jentry. The guy who was supposed to be Declan's adopted brother that I'd heard countless stories of. Instead, it was the guy who had spent an entire night worshipping my body nearly a year before. The mysterious guy, who'd said his name was *Jay*. The same *Jay* I'd gone back to find when I'd ended up meeting Declan instead. *Jay*, who could have my skin covered in goose bumps with just the thought of his lips against my skin. *Jay*, who had somehow managed to touch my soul within the span of a few hours. *Jay*, who was now standing next to the guy I loved.

4

One Month Ago

Aurora

Feelings I couldn't begin to describe rushed through my body the moment his eyes met mine. This had to be some cruel joke.

Jay—no . . . *Jentry's* dark eyes widened a fraction before narrowing as they traveled the length of my body. His gaze seared everywhere it touched, and my cheeks heated in embarrassment when I shivered from his knowing stare alone.

"Gorgeous," a deep voice muttered into my ear as familiar arms wrapped around my waist.

I turned to look into crystal-clear green eyes an instant before Declan's lips brushed against mine.

Keeping an arm wrapped possessively around me, Declan held out his other arm toward the tall, intimidating-looking man Taylor had just finished introducing herself to. "Rorie, I want you to meet my brother, Jentry. Jentry . . . this is her," he said with pride and a wide smile.

"Her," Jentry teased as he stepped closer, his tone and the curl of his lip almost making the word a sneer. Just having him this close had another shiver ripping through my body; had our night flooding to the surface.

That night had stayed etched into my soul, hidden from everyone else ever since I'd met Declan. Now that the man who had helped me write that nearly indescribable night was so close, it was as if our story were crawling over my skin for everyone to see. As if that part of my soul was reaching for him.

I wondered if Declan noticed any of the guilt, devastation, or betrayal that were currently pulsing from me, but I was pulled from him before I could judge his reaction.

I inhaled sharply when Jentry drew me into his arms for a hug that lasted entirely too long. That intoxicating smell teased my senses—just as I'd remembered. Something sweet, but warm and spicy that I couldn't put my finger on. When he released me, he stayed close enough that I had to take a step toward Declan, and watched as Jentry smiled slowly in response.

"Declan talks about you so much that I feel like I already know you."

"Likewise," I forced out, then cleared my throat. "It's great to finally meet you." A weighted silence passed between the four of us, so I glanced at the table and asked, "Should we sit?"

Taylor waited until we were sitting and the guys were going

to their side to turn toward me with an "Oh my God!" look while dramatically fanning at her face. By the time the boys were sitting, she appeared calm and collected.

I understood her previous look all too well. I knew the kind of effect Jentry could have on a girl just by looking at her. I also knew other kind of effects—*stop it, Rorie!* I took a deep breath in and held it for a moment before releasing it, and tried to mimic Taylor's posture and expression. But I doubted I looked half as calm as she did. I was freaking out and doing everything to keep my eyes away from Jentry.

A foot connected with my shin, and I grunted, but managed to bite back a curse as I looked up at Declan.

"You okay?" he mouthed.

I just raised my eyebrows, hoping to go for innocence and confusion.

"So . . ." Taylor drew out the word and shot me an awkward look, then focused her attention on Jentry. "Marine Corps, huh?"

He nodded slowly, and I glanced over in time to see his dark eyes slide away from me. "Yeah."

When he didn't elaborate, Taylor glanced uneasily at me, then back to him. "Um, Rorie said you planned on getting out soon. What will you do when you're back in Wake Forest?"

Jentry shrugged and leaned back in his chair as he folded his arms across his chest. He looked relaxed and amused, like he couldn't wait to see how the rest of the night was going to play out—let alone the weekend. His dark eyes flickered toward me again, and the corner of his mouth twitched up.

It was a challenge—there was no other way to describe it—but I would not be stepping up to it.

"Not sure yet, but I'd rather know more about the two of you. You're from . . ." He trailed off, and kept his eyes on Taylor for only a second before looking at me questioningly.

I kept my mouth tightly closed.

"We're from Raleigh," Taylor answered easily, either ignoring or not noticing the way his eyes kept lingering on my face. "We've been best friends since high school, roomed together in college."

"And you went to Duke, too?" he assumed. My pulse pounded when he obviously directed the question at me.

Thankfully Taylor still hadn't noticed, and Declan was talking quietly to a waiter and slipping him a credit card for later.

"No, we went to NC State."

"Rorie."

I looked slowly over to where my name had been called from, and tried to keep my breathing steady. "Hmm?"

"Taylor was just saying that the two of you went to NC State. I was wondering how you *happened* to meet Declan up at Duke."

Taylor's laughter broke through the tension that had crept between Jentry and me, and while her laugh would have normally had me smiling, at the very least, I was now worried that I was going to hyperventilate. Or have a panic attack.

Taylor nudged me and snickered. "Oh, that's a good story. Rorie here had dragged me to a party up at Duke—"

"You volunteered," I added breathlessly, and was suddenly wishing for the insecure Taylor to come back, as long as it would shut her up.

"—because she was dying to find this guy she'd met the weekend before."

My eyes fluttered shut at the same moment Declan said, "Wait, what?"

"Shit," I mouthed, and tried to swallow. I couldn't tell if my mouth had suddenly gone dry, or if my rapid breathing was getting in the way of me swallowing. I opened my eyes and reached for the water in front of me anyway, and shook my head once at Declan.

"You never told him?" Taylor whispered quickly, but loud enough that both guys heard.

"No, she didn't," Declan answered for me. "You were there looking for another guy?"

It took all of my energy to keep my eyes from going back to Jentry as I silently pleaded for Declan to understand. I tried to keep my voice from shaking and my tone nonchalant. "It was nothing, really. I'd just talked with him the week before—"

Taylor snorted.

"And when was this?" Jentry asked.

"Beginning of September," Declan answered without taking his eyes from me.

"So about the time I was there," Jentry said with a guessing tone.

I wanted nothing more than to shoot a glare in his direction.

Declan finally looked at Jentry as he thought for a second,

then shrugged. "Yeah, I think I met Rorie a week or two after you visited me at Duke."

"Huh." Jentry sent me another challenging smirk. "Guess I'd just missed meeting you back then."

"Guess so," I bit out with a smile. At that same instant, Taylor's hand slapped down on my thigh and squeezed.

Declan looked back at me, his brows pulled low over his eyes. "If it wasn't a big deal, why didn't you tell me why you'd been there? I thought you'd been there for Taylor."

"Well, hey!" Taylor interjected—her hand was squeezing my leg so tightly, I didn't know if I would have feeling when she let go. "If we hadn't gone back to find him, she never would've met you. Right? Right. Moving on."

I glanced quickly at Taylor as she told the story in a rush, and saw in a brief, shared look that we were going to have a long talk later.

"So I'd just given Rorie a huge Jolly Rancher, and this massive naked guy ran into her and she started choking. I thought he was going to kill her with the way he was trying to do the Heimlich maneuver on her. Anyway, while he was helping her, her shoes flew off, and both hit Declan in the head. He came over after and called her Cinderella, and it was super-romantic . . . and the end! Love at first sight and all that." Taylor was breathing hard, and I was pretty sure my breaths matched each one of hers.

"That's awesome, man," Jentry said after a beat of silence, and bumped Declan's shoulder. "I'm happy for you. Cinderellas losing their shoes, love at first sight, happy ever after. It's what you deserve." Gone were the taunting tones, the challenging smirks, and heated stares. His focus was solely on Declan, and he seemed genuinely happy for Declan . . . for us. Hard and soft, just as I remembered.

Declan's confused expression melted, and he rolled his eyes at the sappy words coming from Jentry, but then those clear green eyes settled on me and warmed. "I got lucky."

My lips had been pulling up into a smile but froze halfway when Jentry called my name. I looked in his direction but wouldn't make eye contact. "You take care of my brother."

My eyes shot to his, and a foreign feeling slid through my veins and gripped at my chest. It was like being hot and cold at the same time. Being able to look into the eyes of a man I had fallen for, and who I knew without a doubt loved me . . . only to turn and look into the eyes of a man who had consumed my mind and fantasies for more than ten months. My chest hurt as my heart stumbled over differently paced beats. Hard pounding connected with a pair of dark, sinful eyes—light fluttering with pale green. As my heartbeat settled into a familiar flutter, I whispered, "I will."

"YOU CAN'T BE serious!" Taylor yelled as soon as we were in my car and driving out of the parking lot an hour later.

The air whooshed out of my lungs, and my hands tightened on the steering wheel as my entire body began trembling. I was sucking in air so fast that I was afraid I was going to make myself pass out, and was worried that possibility was a little too close when the street in front of us went blurry.

"No, no, don't cry," Taylor said quickly, and placed a hand on my shaking arm.

I blinked quickly, forcing the built-up tears to stream down my cheeks, and took the smallest bit of comfort in the fact that I was crying rather than about to lose consciousness. "This isn't happening."

"It really is him, isn't it? The guy we went back for. I mean . . . the way he looked at—"

"Maybe he doesn't remember me!" I said in vain, and a sharp laugh burst from Taylor.

"Oh no, he definitely remembers. There was no way not to know what had happened between the two of you."

"Damn it." I muttered, and tried to focus on the road in front of me. "This isn't happening."

"You need to tell Decl—"

"Are you insane?" I yelled, and whipped my head to the side to look at Taylor. "You saw how hurt he was just finding out that I'd been looking for another guy before I met him. There is no way that I can tell him I slept with his *brother, Taylor*!"

Her hands flew out to the side, and she made an exasperated noise. "Declan isn't stupid, Rorie. He's going to find out! The tension between you and Jentry alone is a dead giveaway, but then Jentry kept giving you looks, and you were being rude to him and ignoring him in the most *obvious* ways tonight. Declan isn't going to remain in this oblivious, I'm-just-so-happy-to-be-with-my-brother phase for long."

I exhaled heavily and gripped the steering wheel over and

over again. When I spoke, my voice was barely above a whisper. "I also won't be caught off guard again. Declan can't know."

"Ro—"

"It would ruin our relationship, Taylor, and possibly his friendship with Jentry. If it didn't, it wouldn't be the same, at least. I can't—I can't do that to him. I love Declan, and it was just a night with Jentry." There was no denying my love for my boyfriend, but Taylor and I both knew my encounter with Jentry hadn't just been a night. That night . . . it had been everything.

"If you'd just gotten his real name—"

"Well, I didn't. And I don't know what it would've changed other than having prepared me for seeing him. It would still be a night Declan couldn't know about."

"Wasn't he wearing dog tags? Couldn't you have looked at those?"

I looked at Taylor's exasperated expression and made a face. "I would have probably had a clue that he didn't go to Duke if he'd been wearing any! We probably wouldn't have even attempted to go back looking for him if I had thought he was in the military."

"And if I disappeared tomorrow?"

My eyes shot open to find his dark ones staring intently at me, and my head shook once. "As long as you don't disappear tonight."

"Oh my God. He told me he was leaving. He told me, but I had figured it was a line he was feeding me." *Somewhat*, I mentally added.

I'd heard enough from Declan to know that Jentry went through girls like they were nothing. It was why Declan had told Taylor not to get her hopes up for any kind of commitment, because Jentry would be with a girl only for a night. I felt so stupid for ever hoping that there could have been something between Jentry and me beyond that first night.

"What?"

I glanced over to see Taylor's confused expression, and wondered how long I'd been thinking about that night. When I looked back at the road, I told her what Jentry had asked that night at Duke all those months ago. "I should've known he wouldn't have been there when we went back the next weekend."

Taylor's face pinched. "Seriously? A guy used something as douchey as that, and you obsessed over him that much?"

My face fell. "I didn't obsess."

"Whatever, it was enough that we went back to look for him. But back to my point: he used *that* line on you, and you didn't immediately walk away from him?"

I wanted to defend that night. I wanted to try to explain that Jentry's words had rung with a sadness and truth. But I knew in trying to get her to understand, I was just showing her the opposite of what I needed her to believe. That it had only been a night—a night I never thought of anymore, and a night that I'd rather forget.

Instead, I shrugged. "I don't know. It was my one attempt at being rebellious, and it obviously ended with bad decisions."

"Clearly," she huffed. "Incredibly hot decisions, but still. I can't believe you always left that douche part out." She mumbled the last sentence to herself. "And I still can't believe the one night you decided to be all crazy was the night I had a family dinner I couldn't get out of. What kind of friend are you?"

"The best?" I said uneasily, and gave her a wary look.

Her eyes slid over to meet mine, and a few seconds after I went back to looking at the street, she asked, "So you really aren't telling Declan?"

"I can't," I said weakly. "I can't risk losing him. Not over a night that was a mistake before I'd even met him." I forced my breathing to remain steady, and hated that the words felt wrong as they fell from my lips—like every part of my body knew I couldn't label that night as a mistake.

"Mistake?" she asked skeptically. "You better be sure about that, Aurora Wilde, be—"

"Don't call me that."

Taylor huffed in annoyance. "Well, it's a serious conversation. And serious conversations call for your full name! Anyway, if there is even a part of you that isn't over that night with Jentry, then this could only get worse from here."

My brow furrowed, and I turned slowly to study her. "Well, I already had to deal with you being insecure. Don't start being vague for the first time in your life now, too! What exactly are you getting at?"

After a moment of hesitation, she said, "This weekend is just the start. Once he gets out of the Marine Corps he'll be in your life even more. He'd Declan's best friend. He's his *brother.*

Do you realize how often you'll see him? Do you realize the kind of temptation that will be in your life? You'll be playing with fire."

I already have. I'd lain in the flames that we created, welcoming them as they burned brighter. "There won't be any temptation." *Lie. Lie, lie, lie.*

From Taylor's expression, she didn't believe my words, either. "You need to tell Declan, and you need to do it soon. Because if your relationship with him continues and he finds out about your past with Jentry sometime down the road, it is going to be a lot worse for you when Declan thinks about all the time you and Jentry spent together."

My stomach twisted nervously, and guilt spread through me slowly, mockingly. "I can't do this," I said when I parked next to Declan's truck in the driveway of the rental house. "I can't—I have to tell him. He'll understand, right?"

Taylor's eyes widened slowly. Her lips pursed and her tone was suddenly hesitant. "So, about that. Yes, you have to tell him. No, he isn't going to understand."

A rush of air left my body, sounding like a whimper of pain. It didn't make sense. The night with Jentry had been before Declan had entered my life, but the guilt I felt over it was consuming me.

Grabbing a fistful of my hair, he wrenched me up off the bed until my back was flush with his chest. My surprised gasp faded into a soft whimper when he bit down on my shoulder, then placed a soft kiss in the same spot.

Hard, soft, hard, soft. The contradicting combination never ended, and I didn't want it to. I wanted more.

My breath caught, and I knew in that brief flash of a memory why . . .

Why this was wrecking my heart just thinking of telling Declan. Why I felt the guilt of an adulteress. Why I'd wanted to crawl under the table at dinner and die.

Because after all this time, I hadn't forgotten Jentry, or the way it felt to give myself to him. After all this time, my skin still tingled with the remembrance of his lips and fingers on me. After all this time, he was who I saw when I closed my eyes during every passionate time with Declan. And after all this time . . . I wanted to experience it again.

5

Present Day

Aurora

This was what it felt like to breathe.

I couldn't remember the last time I'd just breathed. Not this fully, anyway. Without worry or stress pressing down on my chest, always a reminder that I was in a constant state of unknown. That there was something missing from my life. That I wasn't happy.

But this, being in my new classroom that was somehow chaotic and organized all at once, was giving me a strange sense of peace. Now that it was decorated and ready for school to begin in four days, I felt more at home than I did in the apartment I shared with Declan. That place was beginning to feel like a prison. A spotless prison.

I reveled in the feel of another deep breath, then slowly

looked over to my phone and let the ache and uncertainty come flooding back.

My fingers stretched toward it as if they had a mind of their own. Before I could stop myself, I had the phone pressed to my ear and was holding my breath as I waited. . . .

And waited . . .

And waited.

My eyes shut and tears slipped down my cheeks when Declan's voice mail picked up.

"Where are you, Dec?" I asked softly, speaking over his voice.

I hung up without leaving a message, and tried to find the peace that I'd had just moments before. But I wasn't seeing my classroom, I was seeing dozens of other things that made that peace impossible to grasp, and was thankful when my phone chimed.

Taylor: Got coffee for you. Be at your place soon.

I tapped out a response, then gathered up my things and left before I could ruin this place with regrets.

"I NEED TO get to work," Taylor said a couple of hours later, but didn't make an attempt to move from where she was lying next to me on the floor of my living room.

I hadn't made it to my couch once I'd finally gotten back to the apartment. I don't know if it was exhaustion, or if messing up the vacuum lines in the carpet seemed like a better idea than messing up the perfectly puffed up pillows, but I hadn't moved since. Thankfully Taylor hadn't questioned my placement when she'd shown up; she had just joined me and handed my coffee over.

I loved her.

"You could always ditch and stay here."

She scoffed at the offer even though it was something she did often lately. "Nah. What are you doing tonight?"

"I think I'm hanging out with Declan." My voice was hesitant, as it was so often recently.

"Watch out now, Linda might get mad that you're trying to steal her time."

I huffed in annoyance and rubbed at my eyes. "She makes my life miserable no matter what I do. I can't win with her."

"I don't know, I think she's a pretty pleasant person." Taylor sent me a teasing grin, but her mouth fell, as did my stomach when we heard a key in the lock.

We scrambled over so we could have a clear view of the entryway, and I found myself holding my breath as I waited for the front door to open.

All the air rushed from my lungs, and I forced a smile on my face even though I felt defeated just at the sight of her.

"Well speak of the freaking devil . . ." Taylor said on a breath, her already soft voice trailed off until it was inaudible. "Definitely not staying now."

"Hi, Linda!"

There were no fake smiles from her now since there was

no family around, just a calculating eye as her lips pursed with her disapproval. "Rorie, go make me a sweet tea. I'm just parched, it's so hot outside."

"No 'hello' then," I mumbled toward the floor as I pushed myself up.

"This place is absurd," Linda said as I passed her.

The fake smile that had been plastered on my face from the moment Linda had walked into the apartment fell as soon as I hit the kitchen and heard her words.

I opened the fridge and grabbed the pitcher of sweet tea I'd made that morning—as I did every morning specifically for this type of unannounced event—and walked to the cupboard for a glass. My body tensed when I heard a *tsk* behind me, but I didn't turn around.

"It's just devastating for you, I'm sure."

I glanced to the side when Linda leaned against the counter I was at. "What do you mean?"

"Well, honey, if I wouldn't have been the one who sent you off to the kitchen, I would've been sure there was a little boy standing in here with a wig on! A woman needs curves, and you just don't have them."

I laughed uneasily and ignored Taylor's furious expression from where she now stood at the bar that separated the kitchen and living room. This wasn't new with Linda, and Taylor knew it; I got this most often. "Well, maybe one day."

Linda just looked away. "I came to check on your décor. I would have thought you'd change the couches at—"

I shoved the glass in her direction and cut her off. "Here

you go, Linda." Once she took the glass, I snuck a quick, annoyed look at Taylor before fixing my expression again. We all knew Linda wasn't here to check the décor; she just wanted to be mad for a few minutes.

"Oh dear." Linda's words were distorted, and one hand waved frantically in the air for a second before she took off for the sink.

I watched in stunned silence as she spit out a mouthful of sweet tea. She looked at the remaining tea before dumping the contents of the glass down the drain.

"Oh, Rorie. First you can't bake, and now this? Your tea is getting worse every time I try it. You need to learn how to make sweet tea; that tasted like somethin' awful. How old is it?"

I ground my jaw and bit out, "I just made it this morning."

Linda tsked again, and studied the glass before setting it down and going to the cupboard to pull down another glass. "Bless your heart, didn't you ever listen to your mama? You need to wash dishware between uses. These are filthy. Who knows what kind of dust mites and old foods I just ingested."

My eyes widened and I bit my tongue as I took careful steps toward her. Taking the unused glass from her, I searched it but found nothing. "I always wash—"

"Look at that," she interrupted. "Look how filthy. My poor son." With a glance around the kitchen and another analyzing look at me, she made a face and asked herself, "Well, what do you expect, Linda? She's not Madeline."

"Yeah, so I'm gonna go," Taylor said slowly, her eyes were wide with shock from the past few minutes.

I set the glass down on the counter and backed up toward Taylor to walk her out. "And I actually need to head out soon, too, Linda."

Linda held up a bare wrist, then glanced over to look at the time on the stove. "Weren't you planning on spending time with Declan tonight?"

I looked from Linda's disapproving face to Taylor's confused one, then back again. "Uh, yes . . ."

"Not dressed like that you aren't."

Taylor's startled laugh stopped as abruptly as it started, and I had the strongest urge to echo it.

Linda's tone suggested that I looked like I was homeless. I didn't mention that I had planned on getting into something a little comfier, or that Declan had seen me at my worst and my best, and this outfit was very much in the middle . . . because I couldn't get past the fact that it would matter to Linda what I wore around Declan at all.

"Best get to changing. You look filthy in more ways than one," Linda sneered as she passed me on her way to the front door.

My eyes slid shut and hands clenched as I tried to calm my breathing.

"And, Rorie?"

I placed another smile on my face as I turned to look at her, and raised my eyebrows in question.

"Declan was a good boy before he met you, and one day soon he'll realize what a mistake he made in you. Don't think you can trap him in a marriage because you 'accidentally' got pregnant." She pointed at my stomach as she took a step closer. "And if I find out *that* is the reason you are getting a little too pudgy in your midsection, believe me, little girl, you will find out what a southern woman's wrath looks like if you don't get rid of that problem before it's too late."

A sharp, incredulous laugh burst from my chest, and my nails dug into my palms until it became painful.

"Wow." Taylor drew out the word when the front door slammed shut. "She is a real peach, that one." She waited until I looked at her to add, "And by 'peach,' I mean 'psychotic.'"

My body felt drained and oddly on edge—as was usual after a visit from Linda. It was impossible not to feel beat down from her verbal assault, but it always left me with so much anger that I was shaking as well. It was a confusing combination that left me even more exhausted once I finally got over it.

"She hates you," Taylor whispered, as if her statement were news. It most definitely was not.

"I know."

With a sigh, Taylor wrapped me in a hug. "I have to go. Are you going to be okay?"

No. I couldn't remember the last time I was okay. "Yeah, of course. Talk to you later."

I knew in the look she gave me that she didn't believe me, but she didn't push it. As she wouldn't. Because she knew me too well to try to. "Love you, Rorie."

"Back."

Once Taylor was gone as well, I went to my room to

change, yanking at my clothes as I did. Each movement was rough from the anger that pounded through my veins. As I walked through the bathroom to the closet, I jerked to a halt and looked at my profile in the mirror.

I let my eyes fall to my flat stomach, and ran my hands gently over it. I knew I wasn't pregnant. I'd been on birth control since I met Declan, and was obsessive about taking it. I'd also never thought of myself as even the slightest bit overweight until about three minutes ago, and now I was worrying over every part of my body.

"She's hateful. She's just being hateful," I whispered to my reflection. "She's trying to do *this* to you. She wants to drive you crazy."

And I realized that Linda had succeeded when I was still thinking of nothing but her words hours later.

I JOLTED AWAY from the offensive sound later that night, and blinked up to find Linda holding the book I had been reading in both of her hands, as if she'd slammed it shut.

One of her eyebrows was already raised to match the curl of her lip as she studied me.

"Linda. Hi." Surprise laced my rough words, and I cleared my throat.

"Is this your idea of cleaning up?" Before I could respond, she scoffed. "I shouldn't be surprised. Sit up, you look like a slouch."

My body ached as I straightened in the large chair, and I wondered how long I had been in that position reading . . .

and sleeping. "Um, I wasn't expecting you." *Again,* I added silently.

"If it will cause you to dress better than this, then you should always expect me, Rorie."

"No, that isn't what I—never mind. What time—"

She tossed the book at me and walked a few feet away as she began talking over me. "Well, I was hoping you wouldn't be here, but I guess it's for the best that you are so we can get everything taken care of all at once."

A breath of a laugh left my lips, and though I tried to control my expression, I knew I was looking at the woman as if she'd lost her mind. "You were hoping *I* wouldn't be *here*? Why wouldn't I be?"

"Because you do not belong, child. You never will. This should be family time, and you will never be part of my family." Before I could ask about the supposed family time, she suddenly straightened and a sweet-as-sugar smile lit up her face. "And now aren't you just the sweetest thing for offering?" she drawled loudly.

"Uh . . ." I was still too disoriented from being woken the way I had in order to follow her bipolar mood swing.

"I know he'd love to stay with y'all. After all, it's not like I have any room anymore. I mean, the girls' room was turned into my crafts room. Declan's was turned into Kurt's gym. And Jentry's is the guest room now, and he just won't be comfortable there now that it isn't his space anymore. Besides, my mama's coming into town, and I can't put her in a hotel."

Hearing Jentry's name sent a thrill through my body that

I tried to ignore, and failed. Just the thought—*wait.* "Wait. Someone stay at the apartment?" My mind raced as I frantically put together her words. I knew what she was doing, I knew. But she didn't. There was no way she could understand what she would be putting us through.

"I always knew I could count on you, darling girl!"

No, no, n—

My head snapped to the left when two tall figures stepped into the room. My heart skipped a beat before it took off excruciatingly fast.

Dark, sinful eyes locked with mine before dropping to the floor, but it had been clear in that one look that he hadn't expected me to be here. He hadn't known what he was walking in on. And so much had passed between us in that brief look.

Need, regret, control, pain, indecision. Hard and soft. Hard and soft. But wasn't that how it always was with us? One look and my soul opened to his, begging for what it couldn't have.

"What did we count on Rorie for?" Kurt's voice pulled me back into the room and away from the past. I looked up to see him smile adoringly at his wife, then me.

"She offered their guest room for Jentry to stay in now that he's moved home. Isn't that sweet?"

Kurt was saying something, but I didn't hear it. All I could focus on were the intense eyes that were back on me.

Jentry's jaw was locked tight as he looked at me, as if he were pleading with me for something. But then his eyes drifted to my left and shut to hide the flash of pain.

His pain matched my own, and while I wanted to comfort

him and to let him comfort me, a small part of me hated him. Hated him for not being there before now. For leaving me to deal with this.

"Maybe he would be happier somewhere else." I sounded out of breath and terrified, and hated that my tone laid bare everything I was trying to hide.

Linda sounded as appalled as she looked. "Rorie Wilde. You already offered the guest room, and would you really have him sleep on a couch or the floor after he just finished serving our country?" She didn't give me or anyone else the time to respond, just immediately turned to Jentry and said, "Now, let's plan a welcome home party."

"Mom, no." Jentry looked from her to me, his eyes lingering a second too long before he shook his head and glanced away. "A party? No."

"You are finally home. We will be throwing you a party and that is the end of the discussion." When Jentry started to speak, Linda just talked over him as she ushered Kurt to the door. "Honey, why don't we let the kids have time to catch up?"

Kurt looked at us, then down at his watch. "You want to leave already?"

As much as I loathed being in Linda's presence, I would have begged her to stay so they could be some sort of buffer, but I was too confused by her sudden rush to leave. It didn't matter where we were; if it was any kind of family time she tried to make me leave first.

"Yes, I need to start planning the party. Now let's get."

My confusion faded, and a mixture of panic, guilt, need, hatred, and warmth moved through me when they left, and Jentry shut the door behind them.

Memories slammed into me as he turned and walked slowly toward the chair I was still sitting in. My breaths deepened and that need grew for a few seconds before his eyes drifted to the side and pain filled their dark depths. And then my need was nothing but hatred on top of more hatred.

My jaw trembled and arms shook with rage as he came closer. When his eyes became glassy with unshed tears, I snapped.

I let my book fall to the floor as I stood and swung at him, but Jentry grasped my wrist before my palm could connect with his face. I shoved my free hand into his chest, but he barely rocked backward, and that pissed me off even more. I wanted him to hurt. I didn't care about the pain I saw in his eyes. I wanted to make him *hurt*.

"Where have you been?" I gritted out, my voice cracked on the last word. I hit his chest over and over again, but he never made an attempt to stop it. "Where have you been? It has been weeks, Jentry!" A sob burst from my chest. "*Weeks!* Do you have any idea what I have been going through?"

Throughout my hitting and demanding, he just kept repeating, "I know," over and over again, the words so soft they were hard to hear over the anger that pounded through me. "I got here as fast as I could."

"It wasn't fast enough!"

"I know." He released my hand and curled his arms around

me when another sob forced its way through me. "It's gonna be okay."

My head shook back and forth, because he couldn't know that. "I'm sorry. I'm so sorry."

"Don't," he ordered gently. "Don't do that."

"If I—"

"Don't."

He continued to stand there holding me as minutes passed. Like that morning, I suddenly realized that I could breathe again with him there. I didn't want to ever move from his arms, but knew that just being near him was dangerous. Because I knew that soon the energy in the room would shift and swirl with something that always accompanied Jentry and me, and I wouldn't know how to leave him. Jentry was a weakness. An addiction. One my body and soul would never be able to get enough of, but one I would have to fight against in the coming weeks and months . . . who knew how long. Because no matter how much we needed each other, needed *this*, there were other things far more important than us that needed to be addressed and cared for first.

"What took you so long?" I asked minutes later, my voice rough from crying.

Jentry hesitated for a moment. "It's complicated."

"Uncomplicate it," I begged.

"Now isn't the right time." With a reluctant sigh, Jentry slowly released me enough to be able to look at me. And just like that, that energy started swirling when his dark eyes found mine. "Just know that I got here as fast as I could."

"It wasn't fast enough," I unnecessarily reminded him.

"I know, but I couldn't leave."

"You should have."

His mouth twitched up in a sad smile. "I thought about it a thousand times a day." One of his hands came up to cradle my face, and his thumb brushed along my cheek. "Aurora . . ."

That energy shifted and spun faster and faster. That name from his lips . . .

I knew he felt it by the way his chest's movements became more exaggerated. But he suddenly released me when that pain filled his eyes again. "I guess I should talk to Dec."

A shuddering breath left me as my eyes blurred. Agony pierced my chest over and over, but it didn't stop me from noticing the deep sense of loss that resonated through my soul when I pulled away from Jentry.

PART II

That Night . . .

W HAT?" I ASKED breathlessly.

One hand dropped from the door to grip my waist and pull my body closer, and his mouth made a line of slow, burning kisses down my neck. "Tell me what you want before I make a mistake in showing you what I want."

Oh my God.

My knees shook and heat flooded my veins, but somehow I admitted, "I want a night where I'm not me."

There was a pause before he nodded slowly, but he didn't seem to be acknowledging my words; it was as if I'd just confirmed something he'd already known. His kisses resumed across my shoulder, and he removed his other hand from the door to pull the sleeve of my shirt down. Despite the heat that swirled around us, goose bumps covered my skin.

"And I'm a bastard for considering it," he whispered.

He brought his face back in front of mine, and my heart pounded in my chest when his dark eyes met mine. "I can only promise you a night."

"That's all I want," I responded quickly, but from the look in his eyes, he didn't believe me.

He leaned forward to kiss my collarbone, and murmured, "If you like it gentle, we're going to have a problem."

My eyes fluttered shut, and I steadied myself against the door when it felt like my knees would give out. "Don't assume to know what I do and do not like." My voice shook through my false bravado, and I prayed the sound was lost in the music that filtered into the room.

I felt his lips curl up against my skin. "I'm not the kind of guy you want to get hung up on," he assured me in a husky tone as his nose made a soft line up the side of my neck. Even as his words gave me yet another chance to stop this, his large hand gripped me closer while the other slowly pushed my shirt up.

I arched away from the door, trying to get closer to his touch as he roughly palmed my breast, and said, "And I'm not looking for someone to meet my parents."

His lips pressed against mine softly, teasingly, but when I leaned forward for more, his teeth bit down and tugged on my bottom lip. Every touch from him contradicted the previous . . . hard to soft, and vice versa.

I wanted more.

"And if I disappeared tomorrow?"

My eyes shot open to find his dark ones staring intently at

me. For as much as that line had to have been used by guys just looking for their next lay, it rang with a truth that I didn't understand when coming from the guy holding me.

My head shook. "As long as you don't disappear tonight."

A smile played at his lips before they crashed down onto mine. His hands went to the button on my shorts, and I pulled at his shirt until he tore it off for me. We were a mess of frantic hands and discarding clothes as he backed me up into the room, but he suddenly stopped when my legs hit the bed. It felt as if time slowed. His eyes studied me as he pulled off my bra and ran his large hands up my bare body.

"Perfect," he whispered so low I barely heard the word.

6

One Month Ago

Aurora

The lights were on and there were muted sounds coming from inside the rental home, but the guys weren't in the living room. I didn't hear the talking or laughing I'd expected, and I worried my bottom lip as I crept silently toward the bedroom I was sharing with Declan. Thoughts of what the silence could mean sent the guilt tearing through my stomach again, and my hands began shaking as I prepared to admit to everything.

But Declan didn't start yelling accusations as soon as I saw him. He didn't demand to know why I hadn't told him of my night with Jentry—even though I hadn't known before tonight who my night had been with. He just gave me a confused look, then focused on changing into something more comfortable, as if it took every ounce of his concentration.

"Why didn't you tell me?" he finally asked.

Declan's eyes were still locked on the floor, and I was thankful for it when mine immediately filled with tears. Again, it felt like the air had been knocked out of me, and I struggled to suck in shallow breaths. I didn't know what to say or how to explain myself. . . .

Again, I didn't even know Jentry's real name before tonight.

"Dec—"

He laughed, but it sounded off. When he looked up, he didn't meet my eyes right away. He looked around the room slowly, then back to me. "I don't know why this is pissing me off so much. It was before I met you, but knowing that you were looking for some other guy the night we met is tearing me up. All I keep thinking about is . . ." He trailed off, and I blinked quickly in an attempt to dry my eyes.

Declan didn't know about Jentry.

"I just keep thinking that if I hadn't talked to you, that if I had just given your shoes back and left you alone, then you would've ended up with someone else." Another mocking laugh blew past his lips. "That night . . . that's the kind of night that I thought we would tell our kids about one day. The way I met you, it wasn't how I pictured meeting the girl I would end up falling in love with, but it was perfect for us. Now all I can think is that it was supposed to be someone else. That our entire relationship was supposed to be yours with someone else."

"No, Declan, no. It wasn't."

He shook his head slowly and shrugged. "It's ridiculous,

but it's going through my mind on repeat." Declan huffed, and ran a hand agitatedly through his hair. "For Christ's sake, I'm unreasonably jealous of some guy, and I don't even know who he is, Rorie!"

"How did you expect me to tell you?" I asked, and hated that there were tears streaming down my face. I was positive that if it hadn't involved a guy somewhere in that house, I wouldn't have been crying. "That isn't something you tell your boyfriend!"

"Maybe not right away, but . . ." Declan hesitated, and I watched his shoulders sag. "I don't know, Rorie. I don't know. Honestly, I don't even want to know. If it's driving me this crazy to know that I only met you because you went back to find another guy, then I don't want to know the rest." He walked past me, headed toward the door leading to the hall, but stopped before he left the room. "I had a life before I met you, and I know you would never hold it against me. But to find out from Taylor the way I did, to see the look on both her face and yours—like you'd been keeping something from me . . ." He rolled his eyes. "Now I have so much unfounded rage for something that happened before I even knew you, and it's killing me. And at the same time I have no idea why I'm even upset." With a sad smile, he left the room, shutting the door behind him.

I hadn't been able to decide between telling Declan the truth or not, but I knew from the ache I'd heard in his voice and the pain I'd seen on his face that I couldn't. If just the idea of me with someone else had this effect on him, then knowing who it was would surely destroy him.

Jentry

My hands fisted over and over again on top of the kitchen table late that night, and it seemed like the more I tried to relax, the harder my jaw clenched. I shut my eyes and blew out a harsh breath, but all I could hear were her pleasured cries and pleas . . . and they'd stopped a couple of minutes ago.

Each one had fueled my anger, and I'd felt myself spiraling down into this person I'd fought so hard not to be. Each one had sent a memory of her crying out underneath me through my mind—all of them so vivid it was like I could feel her. And each one made me want to tear my own heart out. Because out of all the shit I'd done in my life, nothing had felt like this. This agonizing mixture of guilt, hatred, and jealousy I currently felt for one of the only people I'd ever truly considered family was driving me insane.

I'd heard of her, of Declan's Rorie. How could I not? It was all he wanted to talk about ever since I'd come back from my last deployment. But I'd been so focused on just getting adjusted to life back in the States that I hadn't absorbed the specifics he'd told me. I hadn't asked for the right details about her. I hadn't had a fucking clue what I was walking into tonight. That I would finally come face-to-face with my Aurora again only to find out she was also Declan's Rorie.

I'd waited for it . . . for the moment Declan put it together. Because he would eventually put it together. And with his frustration and Aurora's inability to speak or look at me when we'd first gotten back to the house, I'd put money on it happening sooner rather than later.

But as the night had dragged on, Dec had remained oblivious as the four of us hung out and I'd acted as though I weren't being assaulted by memories of a night with his girl. His frustration eventually cooled and Aurora loosened up, and soon they were curled up with each other while I forced myself not to pull her away from Dec and claim that she should have been mine.

Should have. Because I'd had her first and let her go. Something I'd regretted every day since. Every time those dark blue eyes of hers found mine, my mind and body went wild as I fought to control that same mixture of emotions that was flooding me now, and just savored the fact that she was real and she was here.

I had convinced myself that I would never see her again . . . and now I would give anything to just be able to touch her again.

Instead I'd had to listen to my best friend, my brother, fuck the only good I would ever dare touch.

There were girls who stayed with you for different reasons. Body, face, lay . . . whatever it may be, good or bad. Then there were girls who destroyed you for anyone else after that, because they were so far from your world that having them again consumed you.

Aurora had destroyed me, and I'd welcomed every minute of it.

She's perfect, I thought to myself again when I came back to stand in front of her, and took in her naked body lying on the bed, waiting for me. I gripped the still-wrapped condom in my hand as I forced myself to warn her one last time, "Last chance."

Her eyes were such a dark blue that they looked violet in this light, and they were now studying me while unknown questions swam through them. She didn't look real, and I wondered if I would wake up tomorrow just to find that all of this had been a dream.

Her gaze briefly ran over my body, and when she finished she held my stare. "Should I be scared of you?"

If anyone else had asked that, it might have triggered something: a fear in myself that I was doing something I'd spent my life burying and running from, or flashbacks from a lifetime ago. Some distant part of me thought it was funny that this girl who didn't know me knew the exact question not to ask. But at the same time, coming from her, I didn't care.

Because anyone could see just by looking at this girl that she was good down to her soul, and the guy I'd spent years becoming would protect this kind of good—not harm it. That didn't mean I should be allowed to have it.

I shook my head once as I crawled onto the bed and hovered over her. Again, I wanted to beg her to consider leaving when she looked at me with complete trust, but the words that came out instead shocked me and embarrassed her. "No, but a guy like me shouldn't be allowed to stain your good."

"I'm not a vir—"

"That's not what I meant, but good to know," I said quickly, cutting her off and enjoying the way she blushed too much. Placing a hand on her chest, I watched her closely as I clarified, "This."

Her eyes widened and full lips opened slightly as she realized the weight of what I was saying. She nodded absentmindedly and whispered, "Let me worry about my heart tomorrow, and stop trying to give me reasons to leave."

I stopped. Then gave both of us every reason to want to stay even though I knew I wouldn't.

Allowing myself to darken the good that burst from her had been inevitable. I gave her every chance to run from me because I hadn't been able to leave her. She was like my own personal siren—calling to me, pulling me closer with those hypnotic eyes and that *good*. It was like a drug that I couldn't refuse, and one I'd never forget even though I knew I could never taste it again.

My eyes lifted slowly when I heard her soft footfalls, and my hands clenched again at the sight of her messy blond hair as she walked through the darkened house. She was so lost in her own mind that she never looked up or saw me sitting there when she entered the kitchen and started rummaging through cupboards.

"Aurora."

She sucked in a startled gasp and tripped over herself as she turned to face me. Through the single light in the kitchen, I watched as heat filled her cheeks. "Jentry." My name was a breath as her hands went up to clasp the top of her robe together—not that anything had been showing before—and I had the sudden urge to open it.

The thin, satin material ended at the tops of her thighs and was tied together at her tiny waist with a thick belt that fell slightly longer than the rest of the robe did. I blinked away thoughts of taking the tiny piece of material off her when she started stumbling over her words.

"You—we—I thought—why aren't . . ." Her eyes were wide, and a dozen emotions flashed through them as they darted over my still form. "I thought you were asleep."

I lifted my hands just barely off the table as if to prove I wasn't, then let them fall. "I don't sleep much."

"Did you . . ." She trailed off, then shut her eyes. "I have to go."

I stood slowly from the table and walked toward her. My lips tilted up when she met each of my steps with one of her own, taking her deeper into the kitchen instead of out of it, until she'd backed up against the counter.

Placing my hands on the counter on either side of her, I pressed close and my smirk grew when she inhaled softly.

"Jentry . . ."

My name from that mouth with her body pressed to mine after so long had my blood heating. I wanted to hear it again as I slowly opened the top of her robe and studied parts of her that I already knew so well. I wanted to place her on the counter and remind her what we were like together. I wanted to go back to that night and refuse to let her go. I wanted so many things that also made me want to die.

She belongs to Declan, I reminded myself.

The parts of me that wanted to push her away and pull her closer fought as I splayed my hand across the small of her back and pressed her harder against me. I felt the shiver that moved through her body like it was my own, and it took every ounce of self-control to say words I knew would piss off my little siren instead of ones I had wanted to say for so long.

"Tell me," I began, and bent to whisper in her ear. "Are you always that loud with him, or was that performance for me?"

Her body stilled against mine. "Excuse me?"

"If you were trying to remind me what it's like to be with you—"

"You asshole," she said through gritted teeth as I continued speaking.

"—I can assure you, Aurora, I never forgot."

Her chest rose with a sharp breath. Seconds passed before she placed a hand on my chest and pushed. The movement only caused her to arch back. Regret and longing danced throughout the anger and embarrassment in her darkened eyes when they met mine.

I brought my free hand up to trace the tips of my fingers over her soft skin. I told myself to stop, but watched in fascination as they continued down until I was cradling her slender neck in my hand.

She whispered something too soft for me to hear a second before another shiver moved through her body. When my eyes found hers again, all that was left in those depths were the longing and regret.

"I thought you were asleep." Her voice was still soft, whether out of fear of being caught, or that anything above that felt wrong right now. I didn't know. I didn't care. She was fucking *here*.

"I wish I hadn't been here at all."

She loosed a ragged breath at my honest response, and her head shook. "I need—I need you to let go of me."

"Aurora . . ." I trailed off, unable to settle on one thing to follow. Ask if she remembered that night—if she thought about it? Tell her that I hated every piece of myself for wanting her, and for hating Declan because he had her? Beg her to let me keep holding her—this *good* I never should've had and had thought was lost forever?

I released her and took a step back, but she didn't move, and that just made me want to pull her back into my arms.

"You told me to call you Jay."

I lifted a brow at the accusation in her tone. "First letter of my name, not really that much of a reach. And you don't have a lot of room to talk when I've been dreaming about a god-damn fairy-tale character for over ten months."

"You—" Her eyes widened before dropping to the floor. I watched as she swallowed roughly, and her head tilted to the side like she wanted to push my words from her mind. "That's my real name, but no one calls me that. I never let anyone call me that."

"And yet—"

"You *can't* call me that," she said firmly, cutting me off. "I've never once let him or anyone get away with calling me that. If Declan heard you . . . you just can't."

She was insane if she thought I would stop.

"I haven't been punched yet, so I'm going to guess you haven't told him."

When she looked back up at me, those eyes that edged on violet were full of panic. "I can't. He would—he would . . ."

"I know." She didn't have to tell me how he would react, because it was the same way I would.

It wouldn't matter to him that it'd been before they met; it would soon be all he thought about—because it was all I had thought about since Dec had pulled her into his arms at the restaurant tonight. That's all it had taken for a jealousy unlike anything I'd ever known to surge through me. And I only had a *memory* of her . . . Declan *had* her.

"The night you met Declan, why did you go back?"

Her expression fell at the reminder, but she didn't look away. After a second, her brows pinched together. "You know why," she mouthed, like she was afraid to admit it too loudly.

"I told you I could only give you a night, Aurora. I meant that."

"Literally. You *literally* meant that. I didn't think you were flying halfway across the world. I thought it was just a line you used on girls. And I didn't care! I told myself all I wanted was a night, but you . . . you consume my mind!" Her confession sounded like an accusation, and she hurried to correct herself. "Consumed."

"Well, it definitely didn't take you long to move on."

Hurt flashed through her eyes. I hated that I was the reason for it, but knew it was for the best. Hurting her meant she'd want to stay away from me. Like that first night, I needed her to be the one to leave, because I didn't know how to.

"It's not like I went there to meet Declan, and what did you expect? It was a *night* with you."

My eyebrows pulled down low over my eyes as the pain I had just seen on her face tore through me. "A night?" I asked calmly. I wrapped my arm around her waist again and held her stare as I pulled her close. My memories of her were always vivid, like I was back at that night again. But with our chests now brushing against each other's with each breath, and with her body pressed against mine, those memories seemed like hazy pictures.

The softest whimper escaped Aurora's lips when I dipped my head to slowly trail the bridge of my nose along her jaw. Her hands fisted against my shirt, weakening my already frail resolve, and my entire body shook with the need to taste her again. She trembled when I stopped with my mouth hovering over hers, just a breath away, but I forced myself not to move closer to her. Not to take what I had thought was gone.

Leave, Aurora. Leave because I can't.

As soon as her eyes slowly blinked open again, I curled my lip and released her. "Yeah . . . a night sounds about right."

Her breath came out in a hard rush as she seemed to deflate on herself. She took a hesitant step to the side, away from me, and then another. With one last look, she dropped her head and hurried from the kitchen.

7
One Month Ago

Aurora

Taylor and I were cleaning our dishes from our late lunch the next day when the back door of the beach house opened and the boys' voices filled the house.

"Dec?" I called out, and waited until he came into view of the kitchen.

He was shirtless from his and Jentry's run on the beach, and instead of appreciating the view in front of me, I tensed in preparation of seeing Jentry the same.

Declan's green eyes brightened when he saw me, then searched the kitchen quickly. "What are you doing?"

My brow pinched. "Doing dishes . . ." I said, letting it sound like a question since it was obvious and he seemed confused by it.

"Did you eat?"

Taylor suddenly stopped cleaning the plate she was holding, and set it in the sink as she waited for me to answer. Her eyes bounced between Dec and me, then dropped to the floor. "So I'm pretty sure I have somewhere to be."

"No, you don't," I argued.

"You ate? I thought we were going out to dinner." Jentry's voice met us before he entered the kitchen, and my relief was minimal seeing him shrug into a shirt. Having him near at all was too much for me to handle.

"Didn't your mom say anything when you passed her on the back porch?" I laughed awkwardly when their silence gave me my answer, and hissed a curse at Taylor as she backed out of the kitchen with an apologetic expression. "Uh, it was kind of suggested that she wanted this to be a family weekend. A few times. Maybe more than that." I turned to set my drying towel down, and kept my eyes from Declan's when I said, "*Family* dinner was emphasized enough times for us to understand that your mom didn't want us to go. Not a big deal."

Declan's face had fallen by the time I turned back around. When he finally spoke, his voice was a hard mixture of irritation and disbelief. "Are you fucking kidding me?"

His frustration surprised me, causing me to jerk back subtly. "Dec . . ."

"Did you remind her that you're my girlfriend, and that this had originally been *our* weekend, not a family weekend?"

"It's not a big deal. They want to have dinner with the two of you. Taylor and I will be fine."

He ran a hand through his hair, his movements jerky from his agitation. "You should have told her to get over it."

I blinked slowly as I tried to understand where this was all coming from, and reminded him, "Declan, she's your mom!"

"Yeah, and I don't know why you try so damn hard to make her comfortable. The decorating, the cleaning . . . *this*. She'll be fine if something isn't exactly how she wants it just once, Rorie. She acts like this because you let her and never try to give her any resistance. Lately she acts like you aren't fucking there because you're always so embarrassed around her now. She'd get over what happened if you'd just act normal around her."

"Dec."

My shocked gaze darted to Jentry at his small warning in time to see him shake his head once at Declan.

Declan looked like he was going to argue his point again, but closed his mouth tightly and turned to leave. "I'm going to take a shower."

I didn't try to stop him. I was too embarrassed and stunned to. We hadn't brought up the way Linda hardly acknowledged my presence ever since that day she'd walked in and heard me moaning and screaming Declan's name. I'd figured it was because her reaction was understandable, all things considering. I hadn't known that Declan thought I was causing it. And he'd never mentioned the cleaning or the decorating. He'd never even shown a hint of annoyance over it until then.

My body sagged when I heard the bedroom door slam shut.

"Want to clue me in?" Jentry asked.

I glanced at him but didn't respond as I turned to walk back to the sink.

It was the first time he'd spoken directly to me since our run-in late last night, and no matter how much my body ached in protest that I was walking the wrong way—that I needed to go toward him—I didn't want to face him.

Not after the things he'd said to me the night before. Not after being humiliated in front of him by Declan. Besides, I didn't even know the answer to his question.

I'd just reached for the plate Taylor had put in the sink when I heard the same bedroom door fling open, and seconds later Declan came storming through the house and out onto the back porch.

Where his parents still were.

"Oh no," I breathed. My stomach fell and I rushed through the kitchen to stop him, but Jentry wrapped his arms around me to stop me. "No, let go!"

Jentry's voice was calm and sure. "Let him do this."

"But it's nothing. It's just dinner!"

"Declan doesn't get mad. I don't know what's been going on between you and Mom, but if it's gotten to this point, then he needs to do this."

"Nothing. There's *nothing* going on." I pushed against Jentry's chest but quickly gave up as the short burst of adrena-line left me. "I don't want this," I said softly.

"What?"

I looked into Jentry's dark eyes, and for a second I was in a dark room again. I wanted it—I wanted that room, I wanted that night. The way my breaths deepened and my fingers curled against his chest in that one second proved that I would never be able to get away from that night or this wanting.

Declan. My hands flattened against his chest, and I shoved. "What do you mean, what?"

"You said you don't want this," he reminded me, but his dark eyes were still piercing mine, and though I was shouting Declan's name in my head, the small space between Jentry and me came alive, and slowly got smaller.

"I don't," I agreed, the words sounding like a lie.

Jentry's brows pinched together for a few moments before relaxing as his eyes dipped to my mouth. "What are we talking about, Aurora?"

I wasn't sure anymore. All I knew was this, this energy that flowed between us, and the memories of us together—the ones that begged to be repeated—that couldn't. I shook my head slowly. "I can't do this. I can't be near you. I'm with him, Jentry."

One arm released me, only for his fingers to trail from my jaw to my throat in a slow, torturous dance across my skin.

I trembled beneath his touch and exhaled breathily, a plea for more from him—anything—on my lips. One touch and I was already quickly losing all control to him, and God I wanted to.

"You were mine first," he murmured gravelly. His head dropped toward mine as he tilted mine back with his hand twisted in my hair almost painfully.

Hard and soft, everything I'd been cravi—*Declan, Declan, Declan!* "I was never yours," I whispered just before his lips could touch mine.

Jentry's features hardened, and this time when I pushed, he didn't try to keep me there. He ran his hands over his face and took a few steps away from me until he bumped into a wall. When he dropped his hands and opened his eyes, the indecision I felt coursing through my own body was playing out on his face.

Guilt for what we'd done and what I still felt. Love for the man outside. And a soul-deep longing for the one in front of me.

"A night?" I asked, bringing up our conversation from last night.

His dark eyes flashed. "You and I both know it wasn't just a night, Aurora. We knew it then, too. And that one night with you will never be enough."

Never . . . "But it has to be," I whispered, and turned to escape his stare though my soul screamed for more of his touch.

I jerked farther away from Jentry when the back door opened, and looked up to watch Declan walk in. I focused on him and the way my heart fell into a familiar flutter when I looked at him, and tried to rein in everything that was pouring from me, and everything that I knew I couldn't feel anymore.

Shouldn't.

Because it wasn't for the man I was staring at, and although I shied from the realization, I knew I was incapable of ever feeling something as strong as *this* for anyone else. And no matter how hard I'd tried, the emotions that were spiraling through me could never be forced to fit my relationship with Declan. Not when they'd been created from another man's touch.

"What exactly did Mom say?" Declan asked as he closed the distance between us. He stopped on the other side of the counter and folded his arms over his chest, exhaustion etched in the set of his face and his stance.

My shoulders sank. "I don't want to go over—"

His eyes slid shut and he mumbled, "Please, Rorie, don't do this right now. I need to know exactly how she said it in that conversation."

I was shaking my head and kicking myself for ever saying anything in the first place. "Decl—"

"Rorie," he pleaded again.

I chewed on my bottom lip, and finally told him: "She just kept saying that family time was so important, and that *some people* should understand that. That it was for *family,* and *family dinners,* and that *some people* should consider that some families have been separated for a while and haven't been able to have family dinners. It wasn't one conversation; she just kept dropping hints."

"Mom said—" Declan began, then stopped and shook his head, like he wasn't sure if he should continue or not. "Mom admitted to saying something close to that, and said that it was in response to you saying you didn't think Jentry should go to the family dinner tonight."

"What? No!" I dared a glance to Jentry's unreadable expression before looking back at Declan. "I wouldn't . . . why would I even say something like that? I didn't even think of it as a family dinner until your mom kept saying it! And why would I think Taylor and I would be allowed to one, but not your *brother*?"

"I don't know, Rorie. Did you ever say anything about Jentry when you were talking to her?"

I thought for a few seconds as my head shook. "No!"

Jentry folded his arms over his chest as he watched Declan for more to his explanation, but Declan just sighed. His body looked weighed down.

After a few moments, Declan asked, "Is it possible that you both thought the other was talking about something else?"

My heart sank when I realized that he didn't believe me. The small distance he'd put between us in this conversation suddenly felt immense and significant. As much as I wanted to defend myself, I didn't know how to anymore. I'd felt humiliated before, but this was worse.

"Yeah," I said quietly. "Of course. I was, um, I was also talking to Taylor, so I was distracted. I probably just heard her wrong."

Declan only nodded in acknowledgment as I took a step. And another. And then another. Each step steadier than the last until I was walking from the kitchen toward the room Taylor was staying in. But when I heard her talking behind the closed door of her room, I turned back around and walked to the front door, and slipped out of the house.

Jentry

S hit." Declan groaned and dragged his hands through his hair when the front door shut.

"Wow," I said with a huff.

"Don't," he warned as he dropped his face into his hand. "Rorie will do anything as long as it makes Mom happy, and one of these days it's gonna make me lose my damn mind. And then Mom walked in on us the day we moved in together, and now half the time she pretends Rorie isn't even there."

I kept my face blank though jealousy and my irritation with him were making it hard to remain calm. "Do you believe Mom?"

He exhaled heavily and let the hand covering his face drop. "I don't know, man. Mom seemed really surprised and upset when I confronted her."

I nodded in understanding. Mom was a horrible liar. But what Mom had said didn't make sense, and there was no mistaking the shock or hurt that radiated from Aurora when she realized that Declan didn't believe her. My tone dropped dangerously low when I said, "So you think Rorie would say that shit about me."

"No, did you not hear me? If she tries so damn hard to get Mom's approval, she wouldn't do anything to piss her off. Besides, she's too nice to say something like that."

I gave him a few seconds to see if he would continue. When he didn't, I asked, "*I* heard you, but did *you* hear you? You more or less told your girl that whatever is going on between her and Mom is her fault." *My girl.* My *girl.*

He tensed, and for a second I wondered if I'd said that out loud until Declan shook his head. "No, I didn't."

"And fuck whatever's happening between her and Mom," I continued. "*You* were rude as shit to Rorie, and that was long before you let her know that you were taking Mom's word over hers."

He threw his arms out to the side and yelled, "What the hell are you talking about? I never said anything about believing Mom over her!"

My chest moved with a silent laugh, and my eyebrows rose. "You implied it. The entire time you sounded like you were accusing Rorie of something, and then came up with the bullshit of their miscommunicating. And you and I both know what Mom's saying happened doesn't make sense." I pushed away from the wall I was up against and paused after taking a step away. "You can't stop talking about how much you love her, but you sure as shit don't treat her like it." My hands clenched into fists, but I forced myself to walk away. I knew if I stayed I would let him know exactly why he didn't deserve her.

Aurora

R orie . . ."
My heart took off in a familiar fluttering pattern at the sound of my name, but my hurt and embarrassment kept

me from turning to look at him, and kept me on my path. I didn't know where I was going. I just needed to walk.

"Rorie, wait," Declan begged, his voice closer now. After another second, his hand clasped around my arm and pulled me around so I was facing him.

"What, Declan?" I tried to snap at him, but my voice came out as a plea. "What else do you want to tell me that you've been keeping from me?"

His face flashed with regret. "Rorie . . ."

"I don't want to do this," I said immediately.

He hesitated, and a harsh breath left him as his expression drained.

"I don't want to be constantly trying to get your mom to notice me or approve of the way our apartment looks or the way we live. And now to know how you feel about it, and to find out *like that*!" I cried, and gestured toward the beach house.

"What I said came out wrong," he said. "Came out so wrong. I'm still a little pissed over what I found out last night, and I'm frustrated with my mom and was trying to figure out what actually happened, and I let it all get to me. I'm sorry I hurt you, I'm sorry I yelled at you, and I'm sorry if it seemed like I was siding with my mom over you. Rorie, you have to know that I would choose you every time."

"But I don't want that," I nearly yelled. "I would never want you to have to choose one of us over the other! I don't want you to ever fight with your family because of me."

"I know you don't," he said calmly, and wove one of his

hands into my hair. "And I don't want to fight with you. I'm sorry for what I said. I'm sorry I let what annoyed me build up until I was an asshole to you. Babe, clean all day. Decorate over and over again until you think you have it right, I don't care. Just as long as you're cleaning and decorating *our* place. And no matter what I might say or fights we might get in, know that I love you."

My breath caught as his mouth crashed down onto mine.

I tried to throw myself into that kiss.

I tried to feel Declan's hair beneath my fingers.

I tried to know who I was kissing.

I tried to force my heart into a familiar cadence.

While everything in me called to a guy waiting in the house just feet from where we stood, those things felt impossible.

8

Present Day

Aurora

I drummed my fingers on the side of my mug the morning after Jentry had moved back to Wake Forest, and into mine and Declan's apartment, and narrowed my eyes at the mountain of things just outside the hallway leading to my guestroom. *Linda,* I thought for the hundredth time this morning with a frustrated sigh.

I'd been sitting at the kitchen table trying to read for a while before I went into work, but my book had long been forgotten as the pile of things continued to capture my attention, and my anger had built. And I had no doubt where the stuff had come from. Placed neatly on top of where I'd found the catastrophic pile had been a picture of Jentry and Declan—one I'd asked for months ago. I'd been cursing Linda ever since.

It bothered me more than I cared to admit that she was

coming over to our place when we weren't there. I wondered briefly what all she'd snooped through, and a grin tugged at my mouth at the thought of having a drawer full of sex toys for her to find. Maybe I'd have to invest in some, if only to shock her.

My head snapped up as soon as I heard the guest room door open, and I quickly moved back into the kitchen so it wouldn't look like I'd been waiting for Jentry to wake. Because I hadn't . . . not really. I hadn't been able to sleep knowing he was there, and had been up and ready for the day for hours. And while I was ready to get the pile of crap into his room, I wasn't ready to see him.

"Building a shrine?"

I automatically glanced up from where I was now sitting at the kitchen table, and all thoughts of his question fled my mind when I found him walking toward me, shirtless.

Despite how hard I tried to look away, my eyes continued to dance over his half-naked body of their own accord. Memories warmed me as I looked over a body I had learned so well over the course of only a few hours, and one that had changed since I'd seen it this way.

It was thicker, more muscular. My own body ached to feel his arms wrapped possessively around me again—as if I'd been missing a crucial piece of me all this time—as my eyes lingered on the corded muscles in his arms before traveling back to his broad chest and down his muscled stomach. Jentry was tall and had a lean, almost sleek look to his body. Like he could destroy you, but was still light on his feet. A fighter's body, with the calm, calculating mind of a sniper—as I knew Jentry had been in the Marine Corps.

Strength, trouble, hard, and soft. Everything I remembered of him from our first night and that weekend at the coast, and now he was so close after only haunting my mind for all this time. It made something inside me stir, and my fingers twitched with the need to touch him.

Unable to stop myself, I looked into his dark eyes and found them locked on mine. So many of the same emotions from last night were there. Pain, need, sorrow, passion . . .

Words didn't need to be spoken between us to know what the other felt, what the other needed. They never had. Our silence said more than our words ever could.

"Gift from Linda," I mumbled, and reached for my mug again. I froze with it halfway to my mouth when I saw Jentry's expression fall as he looked back at the pile.

If I hadn't been watching him so intently, I would've missed it. Before I could ask what was wrong, his mouth curved up in a withdrawn smile.

"Funny. This is something I'd bet she would have done if I'd refused to move back home, but she seemed fine with me being here last night."

I huffed and mumbled, "That might be an understatement," into my mug, then took a sip. When Jentry gave me a confused look, I just shook my head.

"What is?" he asked, not willing to drop it that easily.

"Nothing. Really." I pushed the chair out and stood, but didn't move away from the table yet. "I know there isn't a lot of space in the guest room, but just put everything in there for now, and we'll figure out what to do with all of it later."

Jentry laughed and gave me a sarcastic look. "You mean between all the boxes of books?"

It took a second for his words to register, but when they did, my body stiffened. "The what?"

"All the boxes that were piled on the bed." He said each word slowly, drawing them out so it sounded like a question. "They were overflowing with books."

I clumsily set the mug down and was rushing from the kitchen toward the guest room before he'd finished speaking, ignoring my name on his lips as I ran past him. I flung open the door and was immediately hit with Jentry's intoxicating scent—but just as soon as I registered the warm spice that I'd thought of and missed, my stomach dropped as the rest of the room came into focus.

The week after Declan and I had moved in, I'd used my credit card for more than I cared to admit to in order to decorate each room in our apartment in a way that I'd hoped would impress Linda.

Since that was during the time she was mostly ignoring me, I wasn't sure that it had.

Not that that mattered now. Because there was no bedding or pillows on the bed, or anywhere to be seen. No curtains. No lamp on the nightstand. Everything was gone. An olive green duffle bag was in the corner of the room. And boxes upon boxes crammed full of books that hadn't been there just yesterday afternoon. My boxes. My books. All had been put away that same week I'd spent charging up my card and decorating.

Linda, I thought, and forced down the large lump in my throat. "You have got to be kidding me," I gritted out.

I quickly blinked back the tears that gathered in my eyes when I heard footsteps coming down the hall, and hurried to pick up one of my boxes.

"Aurora?" Jentry's voice was soft, hesitant.

I knew in that one word that he knew there was more to this than me simply forgetting about some boxes, but I didn't want to get into this with him. Not now. Not when he'd just gotten back and there was already so much else going on.

Before he could say anything else, I forced out a dry laugh and started walking out of the room with my box, refusing to meet his confused stare. "I'll, uh, I'll fix your room up today after work."

I didn't give him a chance to respond. I walked as fast as I could to Declan's and my bedroom, and choked out a sob when I dropped the box in the back corner of the closet floor—where the boxes had been for months, and where there were still indentations on the carpet from them.

Pressing one hand to my mouth and the other to my burning chest, I willed a mixture of angry and pained tears away as I thought about Linda's hateful words and actions. Maybe if this had all started long ago, it would be easier to deal with. Or at the very least, it wouldn't hurt so much. Because then I wouldn't be reminded of why she was doing or saying the things she was, and I wouldn't remember that I couldn't even fault her for it . . .

I jumped when I heard my name and turned to see Jentry standing there with two boxes in his hands.

His dark eyes studied my face for a few moments before finally asking, "Where do you want these?"

All I wanted was to drop my head, but I knew he'd already seen too much and that would just make it worse. Instead, I forced a look of indifference on my face and pointed to where the other box sat. "Just put them next to it. The other two will go on top."

He quickly set the boxes down, and as he stepped away from the far corner toward me, his gaze lingered on the boxes—his brow pulled tight as he studied them.

I knew he had seen the indentations on the carpet, and was seeing how perfectly those three boxes fit in that space, as if the other things on the closet floor had been molded around them.

His eyes were full of confusion and frustration when he looked at me again. "What's going on?" When I just shook my head and backed up to get out of the closet, his voice dropped and his tone got harder. "Aurora."

"I'm just going to get another—"

"Not that. What is going on with the boxes and the room? Why do you look like you're about to cry?"

"I'm not," I said quickly, and fumbled for something to say as I continued through my bedroom with him behind me. Because what was there to say? My things were gone, but I didn't actually have proof it was Linda. "No, I just . . . I'm just embarrassed that you had to sleep in that room."

Jentry wasn't convinced. Worry and disappointment mixed with the confusion in his eyes. "I've slept on dirt. But you—"

"I'm fine," I tried to assure him. "I'm fine. I just need to finish this so I can leave for work."

He grasped my arm and turned me around, but I backed away from him as though he'd burned me. His mouth had been open to say something, but closed slowly as his dejected eyes studied my arm. After a moment they faded to indifference. "I'll take care of it. Go to work."

"Are—" I cut off when there was a knock at the door, then glanced over to the kitchen to see what time it was before going to answer it. My steps faltered when a key sounded in the lock and the door opened, and my stomach dropped when I heard an all-too-familiar voice mumbling nonsense.

Linda's eyes skipped right over me until she found Jentry, and her excited smile fell. "Oh! Well, looks like you lost something, son," Linda said disapprovingly. "We're gonna have to find a shirt for you to put on. Help me with these, will you?" She stepped into the entryway, then turned to pick up a bunch of large, reusable bags at her feet.

I stopped breathing and prayed that she wasn't about to do what I thought she was.

"Now let's—oh, good morning, Rorie."

I planted a smile on my face and forced myself to close the distance between us. "Good morning. What's all—"

"I have some dishes in the car. If you would be a dear and go get those, it would be such a help."

"Of course," I mumbled, and clenched my hands into fists as I passed her and caught a glimpse of curtains in one of the bags. Curtains that looked eerily similar to ones I'd had hanging in the guest room.

By the time I got back in the apartment with Linda's homemade breakfasts, I could hear Jentry and Linda talking in the guest room, and walked slowly in that direction. My scowl deepened as I did and Linda's rambling continued.

". . . last night, but no one was here. So I thought I would leave your things in the room, only to find that the room was practically bare save for some junk. I just couldn't stand to think of this room looking so miserable—not after everything Rorie's done to get this apartment to look so . . . so unique!"

Jentry didn't respond to her. And though his eyes found me as soon as I turned the corner into the room, I couldn't tear my eyes from Linda and the bags. Anger built and flowed faster and faster through me until my entire body was shaking as I watched her pull out item after item that had been in the room already. As if he wouldn't think it was odd that they weren't in packages. As if he wouldn't wonder why they didn't have tags.

"Where'd you get all this?" Jentry asked Linda, his voice dark and low as he continued to study my every breath.

"Well, I'd bought it when I redecorated your old room, but it just didn't look right in there."

Of course she had an answer ready for that. I wasn't able to hold back the scoff, and tried to disguise it as clearing my throat instead when Linda turned to look at me. "Wow, Linda, what is this?" I asked a little too brightly.

"All this? I just thought I'd help you out since Jentry came home so suddenly. Do you love it?"

I raised my eyebrows, unable to respond to that question without lashing out at her. "Ah. Um, the food is in the kitchen."

"Oh yes!" Linda flashed an adoring smile at Jentry before going back to my décor. "Go eat before all my cookin' gets cold. Let us girls have some time to decorate."

Jentry didn't move. He was now staring at a spot on the wall above the window with a curious look.

I went to follow his line of sight, but his eyes slowly drifted to the adjacent wall and stopped again for long seconds before sliding to the décor piled on the mattress. His brow was furrowed, like he was looking for something, and suddenly he took a few steps toward the bed and just stared. If I didn't know any better, I would just think he was looking at everything with an absurd amount of interest. But I did. I knew nothing got past Jentry. Ever.

He was a sniper. He took in and studied his surroundings. And he was studying this room and the decorations.

"Well, now, get," Linda ordered, and swatted at him with a pillowcase.

A muscle in Jentry's jaw popped when he turned around.

His dark, knowing eyes held mine as he approached me. There was a question hidden in the frustration there, but I stood still and tried to ignore the excruciatingly fast pounding of my heart the closer he got.

My eyes widened when he stepped close enough that his body brushed against mine, though he could have easily slipped out of the door without touching me, and I sucked in a soft gasp when the tips of his fingers teased high up on my waist.

"We're talking later." His voice was soft enough that Linda wouldn't hear him, but his tone left no room for questioning.

No sooner had Jentry started making noise in the kitchen than Linda tsked at me. "Is that the way you dress when there's company over?"

I looked down at my outfit, then up at the back of her head as she made the bed. I didn't move to help her. "I didn't know you were coming over." I also didn't know what was wrong with what I was wearing. It was nicer than what she'd seen me in the day before.

"I meant my other son," she snapped.

Again, I looked at what I was wearing, and tried to think about what Linda was seeing. The jeans were dark and torn, but had been made that way and were expensive. The top was loose-fitting and was probably too nice to wear for a kinder-garten teacher. But school didn't start until next week and we only had meetings today. Besides, I was behind on laundry, so it was really all I had. "Um, I—"

"Just because you look like a boy doesn't mean you should

dress like a prostitute to prove you aren't one—especially in front of my sons. If I'm going to allow Jentry to stay here then you better cover yourself up."

I ground my jaw, but refused to respond to her insults. Instead, I bent to pick the curtains up off the floor. I tried to make my tone thoughtful though I spoke through gritted teeth as I examined them. "These are nice. Exactly what I would've picked."

Linda glanced over at me from where she was putting pillows on the bed, and smiled sweetly with a tilt of her head. "Don't sass me, Rorie. It's not flattering; you just look stupid."

I held the curtains up and stepped close to her. "I bought these."

"Whatever do you mean?" she asked innocently, and gestured to the door. "As Jentry heard, I'd bought all this for *my* guest room but it just didn't fit. I brought it as a favor to you since you can't get it together." She straightened her back and tilted her head up in an attempt to stare me down as she spoke her next words, the warning in them was clear. "Despite this *living arrangement* you have now where you still get to stay here, it will not last. None of this will. Soon you will be gone, and I will only be too happy to pack your things and send you on your way. But for now, you will make yourself scarce and give me time with my boys. After everything you've tried to ruin, it's the least you could do. You do not belong in this family, so get used to being gone by *being gone*. Finish the room."

I didn't say a word as she walked past me and out the room.

I stood still and straight with my jaw locked tight and eyes burning as I held back tears.

When her sweet drawl filled the front of the apartment, I broke. I hurried from the room and avoided their eyes as I collected my purse and left the apartment.

I didn't get more than five feet from the door before I crumbled.

I stumbled to the side and started falling; my hand shot out to the wall to help me slide down to the ground. My chest heaved with a muted sob and my head dropped to hang between my knees. My fingers gripped at my head as if I could force Linda's cruel words from my mind.

That hadn't been the worst, not by far. But after nearly a year of trying to prove myself to that woman, and after weeks of insult on top of insult from her, I was bound to break. I'd tried to be strong. For Declan, for me . . . I'd tried. Finding inner strength when you've come to hate yourself proves to be impossible.

I moved numbly as I pulled my phone from my pocket and tapped on the screen, but I paused before I tapped on DECLAN.

My finger hovered over the contact for long seconds as I stared at his name, before I dropped my phone into my purse and let out a heavy breath.

There was no point in calling. He wouldn't answer my call . . . he never did anymore. I wouldn't know what to say the day he finally did. Because he was lost and I was weak, and I hated myself for more things than he would ever know.

9

Present Day

Aurora

"We need to talk."

Jentry's sudden appearance in my closet that evening should have scared me considering he hadn't been in the apartment when I'd come home, and I hadn't heard the front door open or shut, but it hadn't.

I'd felt him long before I heard him.

As odd as that was, I had *felt* him. My entire body had come alive, making it feel as though I were lying in the coolest of flames for long, confusing seconds before he'd spoken.

Hot and cold. Hard and soft. All Jentry—*always* Jentry.

I refused to think about how often Declan scared me just by rounding a corner or entering a room when I wasn't expecting him. And for Declan's sake, I wanted to ignore the pulling I felt deep within me. The reaching for the man behind me.

What an impossibility.

I finished pulling on my shirt and pretended not to notice the way my skin covered in goose bumps, knowing his eyes were on me. "I'm leaving to go hang out with Declan."

"We can talk here or there. Your choice."

I paused from slipping into my sandals. I hadn't known Jentry had planned on coming. I hadn't known when I would see him again at all. "I thought you were gone."

"I went to help out my dad at work. They've gotten behind on some things in the office and on one of the locations."

I finally turned to look at him, and my chest filled with air I hadn't known I'd needed just seeing him standing there: arms folded over his chest as he leaned against the door frame like he was completely at ease even though his expression showed he was anything but. "No. I thought you were *gone*."

I'd come home to find the guest room set up almost exactly how I'd had it before Linda had taken and brought back everything, and all traces of Jentry had been removed.

His eyebrows lifted slowly. "Why would you think that?"

"Your bag was gone."

He uncrossed one of his arms to gesture to the wall behind me. "Mom said your washing machine was broken. I took my stuff to their house this morning to wash my clothes since I already had to go there to pick up my car."

I let out a huff but wondered why what he said surprised me. Before I could tell him that the washer and dryer were working just fine the last time I had used them, Jentry's confusion transformed to frustration.

"You really think I would just leave you?" His voice was soft, but the dark tone spoke volumes.

"Why wouldn't I? It's what you do."

"Leave? You think that's what I do?" He laughed edgily and rubbed at his jaw. "I had a fucking job, Aurora."

Tears burned my eyes, and I hated that they were there for this man when there were so many other things to cry for right now. I hated that he could see my pain for him at all. "Yes, you had a job. You still *left*. You left me after that night even though you knew you had already wrecked my heart. Then you left me to deal with the devastation of seeing you after that weekend. And when I needed you the most during these last weeks, you weren't there!"

"I couldn't leave, Aurora! I couldn't fucking leave without risking being arrested for it!"

His admission made me pause for a second before I was able to continue. "That doesn't matter. You still could've been there without physically being here!"

Jentry pushed from the wall and stepped closer. The intensity that rolled off him as he approached me made it feel as though he were already gripping me though there were still feet between us. "I smashed my goddamn phone after that call from you—the *only* call I've ever gotten from you. Your number was obviously gone when I got a new phone, and I didn't hear from you after that. I had no way to get a hold of you."

"Why would I have contacted you after that? I thought for

sure you hated me like everyone else did, and when I didn't hear from you again for nearly three weeks, it kind of confirmed it!"

His brow pinched. "Hate you? Why would— This wasn't your fault."

A short laugh burst from my chest, but it sounded more like a cry. He had no idea just how much it had been. "If I had just—"

"*Don't,*" he said suddenly. "You can't think like that."

He reached for me, but I shot my hand out in a silent plea for him not to. I was already shaking from keeping myself from him. I didn't want to think about what I would do if he touched me now.

The past was standing right in front of me, begging to be seen. As if I had ever stopped seeing him. As if I had ever pulled myself from the embers of that night. That night was a dance of flames that had no ending, only respites. One touch from him and those embers would roar to life again, burning hotter and higher.

I wanted it.

I couldn't allow it. Not now, not with everything going on.

I dropped my head and took quick steps to leave the closet, but Jentry's arm shot out to stop me, his hand curled against my waist possessively.

"Aurora—"

"Don't. Please don't."

He ignored me and pulled me against him so my side was

pressed to his chest. My body trembled as those flames got higher. But with the flames that guilt grew and grew, threatening to cripple me.

"You hurt, I hurt," he reminded me. "And, Aurora, seeing you like this and not being able to fix it is killing me. I'm sorry for what happened. I'm so damn sorry, and I'm sorry I wasn't here sooner." Each word was laced with pain, echoing the aches in my heart and my soul. "But you are out of your mind if you think it was easy for me not being here. I have regretted letting you go, every minute of every fucking day. If I could do that first night all over again I would, and I would've been there for you. I would have been *here*."

The tears that had filled my eyes finally slipped free at his words and the memory of that night. "But you did let me go, and no matter how much we beg time to reverse, it won't."

His body deflated against mine as regret leaked from him. "No, it won't. But I'm here now. I'm here, and we're going to get through this."

So much indecision and confusion wove through me. Wants and needs at war with one another as they had already been for an agonizing amount of time.

My heart had bled out through each battle until I'd made a life-changing decision, a decision that Declan and I didn't speak of, and one that Jentry still didn't know. Now any move I could make from here on out would be the wrong one. I was sitting in a minefield, waiting.

Just waiting.

"I tried to forget that night," I whispered before I could

stop myself. "I tried to forget you, but somehow you embedded yourself so deeply into my soul in just one night, that forgetting you—forgetting that night—was impossible. I don't need a lifetime with you to know that no one and nothing will ever compare to what's between us. But it's too late for anything involving *us* even if it's just *us* getting through this, because that night and you are now some of my biggest regrets."

He released me as if I had burned him, and didn't try to follow me as I walked out of the closet and left the apartment.

10

One Month Ago

Jentry

I stepped onto the back porch of the beach house that night and walked toward the far end as I placed the cigarette between my lips to light it. I took one quick drag, then a longer pull, holding it in and savoring the way this simple act calmed me, before I let the smoke curl from my lips as I exhaled slowly.

I'd been pacing in the bedroom ever since Declan and Rorie had gone to theirs an hour before. Each pass through the room left me more agitated as I thought about him touching her again.

I'm a sniper. I don't pace . . . ever. But this weekend and that girl had pushed me to start.

I turned on instinct, letting my eyes drift over the other houses and the darkened beach that came all the way up to the porch, and stilled.

It was too dark to make her out from this far, but I didn't need light or the distance to disappear to know that the figure I could see sitting on the beach was her.

There's no mistaking the girl who destroyed your entire being.

I'd thought she called to me that first night. I'd thought she was a drug that was too pure to resist . . . and that was before I'd ever touched her. The way she had called to me that night was nothing compared to now.

She was light and I was dark.

She was bliss and I was a man dying.

Need was too weak a word to describe what was coursing through me.

Because I had left a part of myself with her that night, and I knew I would never be whole again until I had her. It was as if she'd forced a piece of her soul into me, and taken mine in return.

She could keep it. I didn't want it without her.

I was walking down the beach toward her before I ever realized that I'd left the porch. With how our last couple of conversations had gone, I knew I should turn around and go inside.

For Declan, I knew I *needed* to.

Because no matter how much I tried to push her away, it was impossible to stop myself from saying things I'd thought of for ten months now.

I saw her stiffen before I even got to her, and I wondered if she could feel it, too. This awareness that I was closing in on where I'd left my soul.

She looked over her shoulder as I got closer, and the expectant look in her violet eyes made me think that she could.

At the last second before I sat next to her, she recoiled. "What are you doing?"

I finished settling in next to her and gave her an amused look, though I had no idea why her question sounded so horrified. I removed the cigarette from between my lips and huffed. "Sitting. But I thought that would have been obvious."

Her eyes stayed locked on my mouth as I spoke, then slowly traveled to where my hands were resting on my knees. The disgust on her face made sense seconds before she blurted out, "You smoke?"

I didn't move or respond as I watched emotion after emotion pass over her face. Disgust, realization, shock, denial, disgust again, confusion . . .

"I would have thought that was also obvious. Before tonight."

"Why?"

I pulled in one last drag, then gestured behind us before pinching off the cherry. "Considering I don't hide the fact and go outside a lot, I thought it was known."

She shook her head quickly. "No. Why do you smoke?"

A sharp laugh burst from my chest. "Uh, I don't know. No one's ever asked me that."

"That's what I smell . . ." Her voice trailed off, lost in the sound of the crashing waves. A soft, humorless laugh fell from her lips. "I feel so stupid."

I placed the cigarette in my pocket, then resumed my

original position. Holding my hands out for a brief second for her, I waited until she was looking up at me again to say, "Gone. Care to elaborate why you feel stupid? Because if it's the fact that you slept with someone who does something that clearly disgusts you, let me remind you that we didn't play twenty questions first."

Her eyes widened, and even in the dark I could see the way her cheeks darkened before she dropped her head. "No, that's not . . . no. I just—I've thought it was cologne all this time."

My chest vibrated with a silent laugh. "Good or bad?"

She didn't respond, but her expression and the look in her eyes when they flashed to mine told me all I needed to know. "How long?"

"Since the first tour. A few of the guys smoked these, and sitting near them and just breathing it in used to calm me. Eventually . . ." I trailed off and lifted a shoulder. "They have cloves in them. That's what you're smelling."

The corner of her mouth lifted, then fell into a frown. Like she wasn't happy that I'd just explained why she liked the smell. "And you just came home from your . . ."

"Fourth."

Those eyes of hers darted up to mine, and it was clear that she hadn't expected my answer. I just didn't know what about it she hadn't expected. "Will you have to go again before you get out?"

"No, I'm just waiting to be released now."

She exhaled quickly, nodding absentmindedly as she did. "Declan says you're a sniper." I held her thoughtful stare until she broke away to let her eyes travel over my body. "Ever since I walked into the restaurant yesterday, I've wondered how I didn't know that first night. The way you hold yourself, the way you silently study everything . . ." Her lips twitched with amusement, but she didn't continue.

"Hold myself," I said dully. All I could think of were the Marines who walked around with their dog tags out, and like they were too ripped to put their arms down at their sides.

"Like you're so sure of yourself, but withdrawn. Like you're dangerous, and calm."

"Dangerous? And you didn't run screaming?" I challenged darkly.

She'd been looking down at the sand as she spoke, her fingers trailing through the grains, but her hand abruptly stopped and she glanced up from underneath her eyelashes at my question. Her full lips parted, and the rise and fall of her chest deepened as my question hung in the air.

She didn't need to answer. Not with that look. Not with what I already knew of that night. The energy that was stretching between us pulled tight, begging for me to take her into my arms, to hold her again, to kiss her, to get a taste of that *good*.

"I should get back," she whispered, and sat back suddenly, making me realize that we'd been leaning closer and closer during the conversation.

"Why are you out here in the first place?"

I didn't think she was going to answer when long seconds slipped by and she rolled to her knees. "Declan wants to talk to Linda about how she's been ignoring me, and I don't. We started to argue about it, and I didn't want to argue, so I figured it would be best if we just took a minute away from each other to calm down."

I nodded slowly. Declan had somehow convinced Aurora and Taylor to come to dinner with us tonight, and Mom hadn't once looked at Aurora or even acknowledged that she was there. I had witnessed it, but I still didn't understand it. "My mom has to be the most caring and loving woman I've ever met, so I can't imagine what happened between the two of you if she reacts to you that way."

Aurora hesitated for a few moments, then admitted softly, "She walked in on—"

"I don't want to know," I said quickly, and ground my teeth at the reminder of what I'd tried so hard to forget. The anger and jealousy I'd felt earlier when Declan mentioned it flared back to life.

Aurora's eyes met mine again when she said, "I don't like this person I'm turning into because of her. I feel like I'm in a constant state of worry that she's going to show up and see something that makes her say, 'Oh sweet girl, bless your heart.' I hate cleaning . . . I hate it. I'm the kind of person who likes things cluttered to the point where it looks homey, and I know where everything is. Now everything is stored up in our apartment closets and I freak out if I see a smudge on the wall. I've never been the kind of person to try to make someone like me, and I hate that I go to these lengths just to get approval from her because I want her to." She blew out a long breath and her shoulders sagged, like she'd just voiced things she'd been keeping inside for too long. "And now I know it's wearing on Dec, too, but I can't stop. I don't know why. I just know I'm not this person."

"I know you aren't," I mumbled softly as I remembered the way Aurora had seemed tense all throughout dinner. Her expression had bordered on nervous, and her words came faster and faster with the slightest tremble in her voice whenever she'd attempted to talk to my mom.

Her eyes rolled. "You say that with such assertion, and yet you hardly know me."

I reached out slowly and pressed my hand to her chest, and waited until she was looking up at me. "I see you," I whispered gruffly, and searched her conflicted expression. "I knew who you were that first night, Aurora. I didn't need to know your name, or your friends, or what your favorite color was to know you. I still see the girl I met that night."

I knew I needed to move my hand away from her, but the way her heart was pounding beneath my palm was mesmerizing. Her chest's movements deepened and matched my own, and with each breath, a flash from our night together assaulted me.

Her body beneath mine. My mouth and hands claiming her. Moving together in a way that was too perfect for strangers. Knowing that it would never be enough.

Her eyes dipped to my mouth, and she suddenly said, "Purple."

"What?"

She moved away until I dropped my hand, and I tried to

ignore the pull between us, but it was impossible. It was still there—in the background—as it always was. A slow burn that couldn't be suffocated or satisfied.

"Purple. That's my favorite color."

A relaxed grin spread across my face, and I nodded. "Of course it is."

Her eyebrows pinched together. "Why do you say that?"

My body moved on impulse, and I pressed two fingers under her chin to lift her head higher so I could study her eyes. "Your eyes look violet when it's dark. That's how I always remembered you: the violet-eyed siren. The *good* I got to hold for a night."

Awe lit up those eyes of hers before confusion and sadness touched her face and her expression fell. "You mean you had time to think of me between all of your other girls?" Now it was my turn to be confused, but before I could ask, she spoke again. "I heard a lot of stories about you before I ever realized who you were."

"So because you heard stories from Declan, you think you have me figured out?" A harsh, irritated-sounding laugh burst from my chest, and I released her face to rub at my jaw.

"It fits with our night, doesn't it?" Her voice was detached, but there was a hint of her hurt on her face again. "Best friend, brother, sniper, player . . . I've heard those things about you more times than I could count. The latter most of all."

I stood to walk a few feet away, only to turn back toward her. Each movement was fueled by my sudden frustration. I hadn't thought about, looked at, or touched another girl since

Aurora. For her to say that when this entire time she'd been with my brother pissed me off more than I could begin to describe.

I told myself this was where I should leave her for the night, on a bad note, like we had left our last conversations . . . but when had I ever been able to leave her?

I dropped down in front of her to look directly into her eyes so she could see the honesty that poured through every aggravated word. "What other girls, Aurora? There have been no other girls since you, because I couldn't get past you. You are the only girl I have refused to tell anyone about because I never wanted to share even the thought of you. I would have given anything to make that night continue—*anything* to come back to the States and have *you* there waiting for me. Now that you're in front of me again, I want nothing more than to remind you over and over again what that night was like. I want to make you forget every other guy, because the thought of you with anyone else has a rage burning inside me that I hate more than you'll ever understand. It is a constant struggle not to pull you into my arms and *keep* you. But despite all of that, I owe Declan my life. I hate myself for wanting what is his, and I would never forgive myself if he ever looked at me with the betrayal that goes with the guilt I already feel."

Her mouth slowly parted as the weight of my words crashed down on her. Confusion, awe, and denial lingered in her eyes.

"I told you I see you, so I see what you're doing. You're spouting off bullshit to protect yourself. I get it, because I'm doing it, too. Like before, I've been trying to give you every reason to walk away from me before I take you and never let you go. That guilt that you're feeling just being near me, I feel it. That pain of being so close and keeping yourself from what you need, I feel that, too. If you hurt, then I hurt. And this *hurts,* because it feels like I need you to fucking breathe, and you're just out of my reach."

A shaky breath tumbled from her mouth as indecision settled on her face. Want, need, guilt . . .

Everything I felt, played out for me to see.

"Damn it, Aurora, I see it. I can see everything you're fighting, but just say it. Fucking *say* it so I don't feel like I'm the only one losing my goddamn mind trying to keep myself from you."

"The only one?" a sharp, disbelieving laugh burst from her. "But like you just said, Jentry, you love him. I love him. This is so much more complicated than finally finding you again! I thought you were gone. I thought I would never see you again. I don't know how to navigate this now that you're right here! And like before, you're constantly pushing me away and confusing me more than ever."

"Because like I told you that first night, a guy like me shouldn't be able to stain your kind of good. But that night— fuck, Aurora, you destroyed me. I have never been the same after it. And now I don't know what to do because you're with Declan when you should have been mine!"

"Then stop challenging me like all I am is a game to you!"

"A game?" I cupped her slender neck in one of my hands and brushed my thumb across her bottom lip as I leaned closer.

"This is not a game. It's not about wanting what I can't have. It's about wanting the girl who makes me feel like I'm touching heaven. It's about wanting the girl who makes it easier to breathe because she looks at me like I'm something more than I am. It's about needing the only girl who has made me believe that I deserve something as beautiful as her even though I know I can only ruin her."

"Will you stop?" she begged, forcing her words over mine. "Why are you so hard on yourself? Why do you always say things like that? From that first night it has torn at me that you think so little of yourself. If you could only see what I see!"

"I do," I responded quickly. "When I'm with you."

Her shuddering breath washed over my thumb, and I made another sweep across her lip.

My body was vibrating from keeping myself from her, from keeping myself from what was mine. "Should've been mine," I whispered, reminding us both that she belonged to someone else. "Letting you leave that night was the biggest mistake of my life, but not letting you leave now would be the second. So leave before I start fighting for you in a battle I can't win."

Uncertainty swept over her face again, and her head shook slightly. "Stop pushing me away," she said, her tone pleading as she leaned closer.

"Aurora . . ."

I was so focused on the girl I'd thought I lost that I didn't hear the footsteps in the sand, quickly getting closer and closer until someone else was right next to us.

"Oh, hell no!"

I stood and stepped in front of Aurora in a move so fast that Taylor stumbled backward.

"Kiss my best friend, and you will no longer have the necessary organs needed to reproduce," she hissed at me. Her eyes dropped to where Aurora was now scrambling up beside me, and she pointed to the house behind her. "I could hear you two perfectly from my room. If I could hear you, then Linda's gonna hear you if she wakes up and Kurt stops snoring for five seconds! And Declan was coming out of your room looking for you when I was headed out here to warn you."

Aurora mumbled a worried curse, and Taylor glared at her.

"We are going to have the longest talk when we drive home. As for you." Taylor shoved her hand against my chest, then pointed toward the water when I didn't move. "Declan's putting a shirt on, but if you don't want him to know that you were out here with *his girlfriend* then you better disappear, like five seconds ago."

My nostrils flared with my rough breaths. Turning to look at Aurora's worried face, I held her stare and spoke softly. "You know you have to be the one to leave."

Everything in me begged her not to go. To give me a reason to fight for her even though I knew it would kill me to do it.

Now that I was on alert, my attention snapped to the house just as the back door shut to see Declan walking across the porch.

None of us spoke as he walked down the beach toward us, but I finally looked back to find Aurora staring at me with the most heartbroken expression. Her eyes broke away just as Declan got close.

"Didn't know we were having a party out here," he said warily.

I laughed quietly and slipped my hand in my pocket to pull out the cigarette when neither Aurora nor Taylor said anything. I held it up briefly and said, "If your girl giving me a verbal beating for smoking is what you consider a party, then welcome to it. Came out to smoke and found her; apparently I didn't know what I was walking up on."

He laughed, and the suspicion instantly left his face. "Ah. Yeah, I think I forgot to warn you, Jent."

I felt like a bastard for deceiving him so easily.

11

One Month Ago

Aurora

Once I had water heating up in the kettle the next morning, I turned to grab a mug out of the cupboard. My movements slowed as awareness pricked at my skin. I didn't have to turn to know he was there, but that didn't mean I was capable of keeping my eyes away from him.

Jentry glanced at the book I'd set on the counter for a few seconds as he walked into the beach house's kitchen, then let his eyes drag over to me. "You're up early." His already husky voice was even raspier this early in the morning. I wanted to hear it again.

"Morning person." I lifted a shoulder in a weak shrug. "I like reading and watching the sun rise."

I glanced over my shoulder to follow him when he walked to the fridge, and fought with words I'd been thinking since we'd all come in from the beach the night before. Jentry and I had left so many things unsaid, and now I didn't know how to approach them.

Talking to him in the dark had been easy, effortless. But with the sky lightening outside, and the kitchen lights on, it all seemed different. I felt exposed.

The door to the fridge shut and he began walking out of the kitchen with a bottle of water in his hand, and I was afraid that if I didn't say something now, I wouldn't get another chance. There would always be someone else with us until we left.

Dropping my eyes to the floor, I asked, "What happens now?"

I listened as his footsteps paused, then he hesitantly came closer. "What do you mean?"

"What happens when you leave? With us," I clarified, and glanced up in time to see his eyebrows rise.

"With us?"

The way he asked made me feel like I'd gotten everything wrong from the night before, but I only had a second to regret bringing it up before he huffed, "Didn't you make your decision last night?"

"What?"

He took another step closer and dropped his voice so it wouldn't carry throughout the house. "When Taylor and Dec showed. You looked terrified that Declan would know what we'd been doing, and you didn't say anything to him or Taylor."

I stared at him blankly for a few seconds. What had he expected me to say? "You had just shaken up everything I thought I knew, Jentry. I had just been on a roller coaster with you, and suddenly my boyfriend was coming out to look for me. Everything happened so fast and I froze. And don't forget that you tried to get me to leave *again*."

"Because no matter how much I want this, it is eating at me to even think about it. I told you, it would be entering a fight I can't win. None of us will win. Not when Declan and I are as close as we are. We may not be blood, but he *is* my brother."

"You think I haven't already thought of that? Haven't thought about what would happen to the two of you? But we will still lose, Jentry. When this weekend ends, you and I still know things that change *everything*. Do you know that I've felt like I was betraying him our entire relationship because of you? Because you're—" I cut off with a rough exhale.

Jentry's dark eyes filled with want and need. His voice dropped when he demanded, "I'm what?"

Heat rushed to my cheeks, and I wished I could take those words back.

He took the last step between us and pulled me close to him. "I'm what, Aurora?" His mouth went to my ear, and regardless of the way my mind shouted at me that someone could walk in, my head rolled to the side. Goose bumps covered my body when his lips brushed against my skin. His tone was low and seductive when he asked, "When you scream, whose name is on the tip of your tongue?"

A shiver raced down my spine and I gripped his shirt in my hand.

His fingers dug into my back possessively, but his lips ghosted along my neck.

Hard and soft.

"When you beg for more, are you wishing it was me instead?"

My voice was as soft as a breath, as though my mind knew I shouldn't respond, and my soul rebelled against it. "What do you want me to admit that you don't already know?"

"Fuck, Aurora," he growled, and leaned back enough to look into my eyes for long seconds. "Tell me you don't think of that night, so I'll stop."

"You know I can't."

He nodded, then shook his head as it dipped closer so the bridge of his nose faintly brushed against my jaw. "Tell me that night meant nothing," he begged, but his tone didn't fit the way he was gripping me tighter, like he was afraid I would.

It meant nothing. Three words that could have stopped this—stopped everything. Three words that would have meant a future I had been so sure of before Jentry stepped back into my life. Three words that would always be a lie with this man, and that I couldn't force myself to say with his touch searing my skin—branding me again.

Jentry whispered my name against my lips, another plea. He kept his face close to mine and held my stare as he gave me one last chance. "Tell me you don't want me . . . tell me to walk away, and I will."

My chest ached at the barely concealed fear in his eyes. "I can't."

It was as if I'd been sleeping through the past ten months. The moment his mouth met mine every nerve ending came alive. An exhilarated tremor rolled through my soul now that we'd stopped fighting and had embraced the connection we had both been longing for.

He cradled my neck in one of his hands and pressed me impossibly closer as his mouth coaxed mine open. His tongue slid against mine, teasing me with the slightest taste of him, and a pained whimper sounded in the back of my throat when he bit down on my bottom lip. Just as fast, he pressed the faintest kiss in the same place before claiming my mouth again.

Hard and soft.

My body melted against his, silently begging for more.

"Because it feels like I need you to fucking breathe, and you're just out of my reach."

I understood his words from the night before all too well.

Kissing Jentry was exactly like breathing—each brush of his lips against mine was like a rush of oxygen to my lungs that I'd been deprived of all this time.

As he pressed me back against the counter and leaned into me, deepening the kiss and sending a cool shiver through my body, I wondered what *time* I had just been thinking of. Because as the kiss progressed, it felt as if there had been no time lost with Jentry. Not really.

There hadn't been a day where my mind hadn't been consumed by his memory. Where the blood flowing through my veins hadn't felt like fire burning me from the inside out as I craved him—craved this. And now that all-too-familiar fire was there, building and building, engulfing us in its wild flames until nothing but us existed.

Our kiss broke for the briefest of seconds when his large hands gripped at my waist and lifted me onto the counter. His dark eyes flashed to mine, need raging through them, a need I felt too well.

I cradled his face in my hands and brought us together again before he'd even finished setting me down, and moaned into his mouth when he pulled me to the very edge of the counter and stepped between my legs. I had ached to feel him again, and he was so close.

His fingers gripped my hair and pulled back roughly, and his mouth made a soft, teasing descent down the front of my neck.

Hard and soft, I thought. My soul soared.

My fingers trailed back to his buzzed hair, and for once, I wasn't transported back to that night. I was there—right there with him.

My eyes fluttered open, and I just barely had time to slap one of my hands over my mouth to mute the shocked cry that tore from my throat. Jentry whirled around, his head snapped up to take in our company as his body seemed to expand, as if he was protecting me, just like he had the night before.

Our fire instantly diminished as icy dread filled my veins. I couldn't speak; I couldn't remember how to breathe. I just stared at her.

PART III

That Night . . .

H IS EYES MET mine again, and with a slowness that made me think this night was going to go a certain way, he laid me back on the bed. After searching through the night-stand and pulling out a couple of condoms, he left one on top of the nightstand, but kept the other in his hand as he came to stand in front of me again. "Last chance."

I didn't understand his tone, but for a brief moment, I wondered if he was giving me all these chances to leave for a reason. I looked at his beautifully sculpted body and face, and my heart raced. Trouble and strength, just like I'd thought all night, but there was something in his eyes. Something I didn't understand, just like his voice. "Should I be scared of you?"

He shook his head once, then crawled onto the bed and hovered over me.

With complete sincerity, he said, "No, but a guy like me shouldn't be allowed to stain your good."

I blinked quickly and heat rushed to my cheeks. All of this was new: the party, the night with a complete stranger . . . but that didn't mean I was new to what was about to happen. "I'm not a vir—"

"That's not what I meant, but good to know." Again, a smile briefly danced across his face before it left. He placed one hand on my chest, just above my heart, and studied me intently. "This."

His honesty overwhelmed me as I finally understood his meaning, but I still wanted this. I wanted this night where I abandoned my morals and I knew without a doubt that I wanted it with this contradiction of a man, even if he thought he was going to stain me. "Let me worry about my heart tomorrow, and stop trying to give me reasons to leave."

Gone was the charmer who had been tripping up my heart; in his place was the trouble my body had been drawn to before. A wicked smile covered his face before he dipped his head to kiss me, then moved down my body, leaving a trail of slow kisses as he did.

A sharp huff burst from my chest, and I arched away from the bed when his mouth covered where I was already aching for him. His fingers flexed against my hips, and his soft, teasing licks stopped for a brief second before resuming. And even though I didn't know him, I knew without a doubt that that mischievous smirk I had seen hints of was playing on his face in that moment.

I dropped my head back against the bed and ran my hands over his buzzed hair, silently pleading with him not to stop as something inside me tightened, and my legs began trembling.

Long fingers encircled my wrists, and with a hard yank, he forced my hands down to the bed; pinning them there with his own. A whimper filled the room when he sucked my clit into his mouth, and I struggled against his strong hold and fought to get closer to him. I was so close; just a little—

His hands released mine the same instant his mouth disappeared.

My eyes flew open and my mouth fell wider. Before I could protest the loss of his mouth on me, his body was hovering over mine, and his head was dipping so he could pull my nipple into his mouth as he hurried to put a condom on.

Within seconds his fingers had replaced his tongue, and a greedy moan slid up my throat—and abruptly ended with a shocked cry when he bit down on my nipple and pinched my clit. The pain immediately transformed into body-numbing pleasure as the orgasm that had been evading me tore through me and he pressed his long length inside me.

It felt as if those few seconds had been spent suspended in air, experiencing a high no guy had ever been able to give me . . . until he began moving inside me.

His movements were rough, but not uncoordinated; hard, but oh, so welcomed. It had never been like this before, and I wondered how I would ever be okay with anything less again. Because this was like being consumed by fire. His mouth, his touch, all of it was building the fire higher and higher until the flames were all I knew.

His mouth met mine gently, teasingly, not matching the way his body screamed power or the fierce way he was moving, but somehow just matching him. One of his arms curled under my back, pulling me closer to him and forming a protective cage around me—I just wasn't sure if he was protecting me from things outside this room, or from himself.

My fingernails dug into his back as I tried desperately to hold on to him when his pace quickened, and a hiss escaped his mouth before his lips spread into that smile again.

"Please."

"What do you want?" his husky voice whispered in my ear.

"More," I begged.

I felt more than heard his laugh. "What was that?"

"Oh God, more . . ." I said with a moan as he gave me exactly what I asked for.

12

Present Day

Aurora

"This is bullshit," Jentry mumbled under his breath the next afternoon as we pulled up to the Veils' large home.

Cars lined the front of their property and the ones surrounding it.

I shook my head even though I agreed with him.

Jentry had shown up to spend time with Declan an hour after I'd left him standing in my closet the night before. The uncomfortable tension that had passed between us during those first couple of hours had been nearly unbearable because all I had wanted was to take back my cruel words, but he wouldn't even look at me.

The words had been a lie. I'd known it when I'd said them even though I wanted them to be true.

Because I wanted to regret him. I wanted to regret that

night. They had caused so much pain and confusion for me, but how do you regret the night you met the man who can touch your soul? How do you regret him?

I'd kept my mouth shut. This was what Jentry and I did. We said things to hurt each other in order to protect ourselves. He'd called us both out on it weeks and weeks ago, and it was still just as true. But it was better this way. It *had* to be better this way.

The only reason we'd spoken was because Linda had called to let him know that she'd forgotten to tell him she'd already set a date for his welcome-home party: the next afternoon.

Today.

And since two of my tires happened to have all the air leaked out of them when I'd woken up this morning, something I had no doubt was a warning to stay away from this party, I was getting a ride from Jentry.

He was withdrawn and hardly spoke; frustration radiated from every part of his body.

This strain between us was slowly killing me.

"I can't believe I'm about to say this," I whispered when we pulled into an opening. "Linda's right. You fought for our country; you deserve so many things for that. This party is the only thing anyone can give you. You deserve to be celebrated."

He hooked his arm over the steering wheel and turned his furrowed brow on me. "I didn't do anything so I would be celebrated, Aurora. I don't want this. And I know you don't, either."

"No. I don't." He was right: this party was ridiculous, and the woman planning it was being even worse, all things considered.

It was the most we had said to each other since our talk in my closet, and I would have given anything to just make him keep talking, but those dark eyes and his voice were full of frustration, and I couldn't stand to look at him when I'd been the one who put it there.

I opened the door and stepped out of his car, but didn't look at him while I waited for him.

We fell into step easily. That tension mixed with something that always occupied us, making it hard to stay an appropriate distance from him and to keep my thoughts quiet.

Just before we reached the front door, Jentry gripped my wrist to pull me to a stop.

My heart stuttered and soul ached. One touch and I was ready to crumble under the pain of these last weeks. I knew he'd let it happen and not judge me, because that one touch and the look in his eyes said everything that he wouldn't.

It was tender and full of sorrow. It was possessive and caring.

"If it gets to be too much, we'll go."

"Jentry, it's—"

"If it gets to be too much, we'll go," he repeated, talking over me. "Say the word, Aurora, and we're gone. I swear."

I nodded when his eyes begged for a response, and tried to remember how to catch my breath when he released me.

There were a few people in the entryway who stopped

Jentry as soon as we walked in, so I quietly maneuvered away from them and walked toward the living room.

I didn't get there.

Linda hurried from the kitchen when she heard Jentry's name, and slowed when she found me. "Oh, Rorie!" she said loudly with a sweet, fake smile plastered on her face. "Wow, what a surprise. I didn't think you would show today."

I forced my smile to match hers, but it felt like I was grimacing. "Oh, I'm sure you didn't. Someone let the air out of my tires, so I almost didn't come." Letting my voice drop so it wouldn't carry, I said, "It was a valiant effort, but Jentry's car fits five people."

Linda's face fell into a sneer for all of two seconds before that smile was back, bigger than before. "I'm sure I have no idea what you mean, darling girl." She turned suddenly and clapped her hands together. "Oh, but here she is!"

I started to turn to see who it was Linda was talking about, but froze when she spoke again.

"Madeline, let me introduce you to Rorie."

My face fell as I looked back at Linda's smug grin.

That woman had beaten me down too many times to count, but I hadn't expected that. Hadn't dreamed that she would have a plan B in place for this day if the tires didn't stop me.

I looked up when a tall, leggy brunette walked past me and took her place beside Linda, and fought to control my features. Because there she was. Declan's ex, who broke his heart six months before we met, and Miss North Carolina herself—she was even wearing the tiara. The same girl I'd heard about at every recent family dinner, because Linda refused to tell a story about Declan without somehow bringing Madeline into it.

"Oh, Rorie, I've heard so much about you." Madeline made a face like I was an adorable little child, and talked to me the same. "It's so nice to finally meet you, sweetie."

"Nice to meet you, too," I mumbled automatically. It wasn't.

"Did you get it, dear?" Linda asked, and reached for the large frame in Madeline's grip.

My eyes slowly shut and I forced myself to take even breaths, because even though the back of the frame was facing me, I had no doubt what I was about to see when they turned it.

"Ah, yes! One of my favorites of you two."

My eyes opened against my will and narrowed on the picture in front of me. It hadn't been the one I was expecting, the picture from one of Madeline's pageants that Linda liked to show me. This one I'd never seen before, and I probably could've done without it.

Madeline was on Declan's back, his face turned so he could kiss her. It was innocent, and a sweet picture . . . really. You know, if it wasn't my boyfriend with another girl, and if they didn't look so happy.

But I couldn't take my eyes from it. It was like trying to look away from a horrible car wreck when you knew you didn't want to see the specifics of the scene. No matter how hard you tried to turn away from it, your gaze just kept sliding back.

Or maybe it was because the jealousy that should have been in my stomach was absent as I stared at them, and I hoped that if I kept looking, it would appear. But all I felt was the same defeat and anger directed at Declan's mother instead.

"I just hate that it sits back in the hall where hardly anyone ever sees it. It should be out here with the rest of the family pictures. Don't they look great together, Rorie?" Linda asked wistfully.

My hard stare flashed up to her, but I didn't answer.

"Madeline's just so beautiful," she continued. "Their children would be perfect."

"I don't know, have you seen the girl standing right in front of you?" a rough voice asked from beside us.

Though my skin tingled, I didn't look at him. I knew if I did, Jentry would see my frustration and defeat, and I stubbornly wanted to keep both from him. Because he would see too much in my emotions—he always did—and I wanted to keep what Linda did and said from him. Linda's hatred and cruelty was my cross to bear.

"Jentry!" Linda called out as she turned to see him. "Welcome home, son!"

People throughout the house echoed her sentiment, but Jentry didn't acknowledge them. He just asked Linda in a low tone, "What is she doing here?"

Madeline squeaked and spread her arms wide as she strutted toward Jentry. "I've heard so much about you over the years! I've been dying to meet you!"

Before she could get too close, Jentry pinned her with a

dark stare. "Unfortunately I can't say the same. I usually stay away from whores."

Madeline stopped suddenly. Her mouth fell open in a way that made her look unattractive for probably the first time in her life, and it felt like Linda's gasp sucked all the air out of the room.

"Jentry Michaels! I raised you better than that. You do not speak to women that way. Apologize to her. Now."

Jentry nodded absentmindedly. "Yeah, probably a little harsh to call her out in front of everyone."

My eyes widened in amazement, and I finally turned to look at him. His dark eyes bored into mine; his jaw was clenched tight and his arms were vibrating from his anger.

"If you apologize to Rorie and Madeline apologizes to Dec . . . then I'll apologize to her," he continued through gritted teeth.

Linda looked shocked. She placed a hand over her chest and whispered, "Apologize for what? I have done nothing!"

"Then I have nothing to say." He grabbed my arm and pulled me from the group.

"What are you doing?" I hissed when he towed me down the hallway that led to the bedrooms. "Jentry, stop!"

Panic flooded me when I thought of what Linda could be piecing together about the two of us going down there. But I knew it was just my guilt over my feelings for the man holding on to me that fueled the panic. Because we were still in plain sight of everyone, and he released me as soon as we were far enough away to talk without being heard.

"We never talked last night, so we're talking now. What is going on with you and my mom?"

"Nothing."

"Aurora—"

"*Nothing,* Jentry." I looked up the hall to try to gauge Linda's reaction, but there were only a few people I didn't know standing near the entrance.

"Tell me what happened yesterday with the guest room." His tone was hard and unforgiving, but I knew the majority of his frustrations weren't with me anymore. When I just shook my head, he bent closer to hold my stare. "Don't forget that I know how you two react to each other. What I saw at the beach was nothing compared to what I've seen since I've been home, and she's not ignoring you anymore. Now tell me what's going on."

My shoulders sagged, and that all-too-familiar ache in my chest flared. "This is not the time."

He grabbed my arm when I started walking away, and pulled me back. "Damn it, talk to me! I know you're hurting, Aurora, I *know.* But seeing you look like you've just gone three rounds with my mom whenever you're near her, seeing you look so fucking broken each time she talks to you, that isn't you. It isn't even the version of you who tried so damn hard to get my mom to like her." His other hand gripped my free arm until it felt like he was pleading with me in his touch alone. "Tell me what is happening."

Seconds of silence passed between us. Tears pricked at my eyes, but didn't fall. "You know what's happening. Don't pretend not to, or act like you don't know why. The last thing I need now is another person *pretending*. Pretending like everything's fine, like nothing's wrong, like your entire family doesn't hate me."

His brow pinched and his eyes searched mine. "How could I when I don't have a damn clue what's even happening with you because *you're* pretending like nothing is?"

"I'm not," I said numbly. "I just don't want to pull you or anyone else into it when I know it's deserved."

"Deserved." His hands tightened on my arms when realization hit him. I'd thought he was angry before, but this—this was different.

When he started to speak, I talked over him. "We're at a party for you, Jentry, and right now we're standing in a darkened hallway. You're holding me, but everyone knows I'm Declan's girlfriend, so nothing about how we are right now is okay."

He released me slowly, and though he didn't try to stop me when I started walking backward, his eyes were pleading with me to stay and talk to him.

"Even though it seems like the worst time to celebrate, your family needs this, and they need you to be *here*," I said softly. "So be here, and let what's happening between Linda and me stay that way."

13
Present Day

Aurora

The next two hours of Jentry's party consisted of people I didn't know, or people who stared at me like they didn't know what to say to me. Conversations flowed on around me about everything and nothing, but there was something that was always avoided. Or rather, some*one*. The conversations that began heading in that direction came to a sudden halt when the people taking part would search the room until they found me.

It was as if even speaking Declan's name was a sin, and not allowed. But those rules didn't apply if Linda was the one talking, and then it was as if Declan were by my side. Or Madeline's.

Where are you, Declan?

With each unsure look or conversation that ended abruptly,

and with each casual mention of his name, my pain and guilt and frustration grew until it became too much.

I practically ran for the front door, and stumbled onto the porch.

My chest felt heavy and tight—too tight. I pressed a hand down on it, thinking that would somehow ease some of the tension, and kept the other firmly pressed to my mouth.

I felt trapped in this space, claustrophobic though I was outside and had never had a problem with small places. I couldn't breathe.

That could've had something to do with the fact that I was vainly attempting to keep sobs from creeping out of my chest, but I felt like I needed air. I felt like I needed to get free. I felt like I needed to run.

I looked wildly at the large field that backed up against the Veils' home, and without another thought, I took off for it.

There were a dozen things I could've done to make today easier for myself: Taken the warning of the tires more seriously and not come. Grabbed Jentry's keys and left since I absolutely hated running. Or just tried to breathe . . . to name a few.

Instead, I ran until my legs threatened to give out, and ignored the pain in my lower legs where I'd been nicked by the rough grass. I swayed slightly. My body wanted nothing more than to fall to the ground; my mind wanted nothing more than to scream. Scream for what Linda was doing. Scream for how everyone was acting. Scream for the guilt and pain I couldn't escape from. Scream for Declan.

But no sound came. No whimper, no cry, no scream. I just stood there as the wind whipped the knee-high grass against my legs and blew my hair in a tangled mess of blond waves across my face . . . and I breathed.

"Aurora . . ."

No . . . no, why is he here?

I turned, and tears blurred my vision when I saw Jentry standing there. His chest was heaving with heavy breaths, arms slightly bent with his palms facing me, as if he didn't know whether to approach me or reach for me from where he stood, a dozen feet away.

"Please go back."

"Not when you're running from something I can't see. You hurt, I hurt," he reminded me. "You run, I'll chase you."

My heart pounded as he came closer. I shook my head quickly and tried to step away but couldn't move my legs. "I can't handle it—any of it."

He paused and his face morphed into grief and understanding.

"I can't take the pretending, and the way no one talks about what happened! No one could even say his name in there except for Linda!" I yelled, and threw my hand out in the direction of the house.

"I know," Jentry said gently, and took another step toward me.

"I can't take the way Linda acts like he's right *here*. Like he's okay when he's not. Declan's gone. He's *lost*, Jentry, and it's my fault! Everyone keeps going on with their life acting like he'll show up at any moment when he *can't*. I don't know if he's ever going to wake up, and it's my—" A sob burst from my chest, and the pain that had been threatening to cripple me finally succeeded.

I fell to my knees as hard sobs racked my body, and tried to push against Jentry when he knelt next to me and pulled me into his arms.

"It's my fault. He needs to wake up, Jentry!"

"It's not your fault. It's not. It was an accident—"

"You don't understand!" I cried, and looked up at him. "He—he left because of me. He was driving to get away from *me* and what I said! He would've never been in his car or gotten into that accident if it weren't for me!"

"I told you, you can't think like that," he said roughly, and cradled my face in his large hands. "It was an *accident*, Aurora! Thinking about the ifs and trying to take the blame for something you had no control over will only make you hate yourself."

"Stop saying that! Can't you see that I already do?"

It felt like that guilt had consumed me, swallowed me whole. Because Jentry was gripping me, and tears were slipping down his cheeks. And he was holding on to me like he needed me . . . like I hadn't destroyed everything.

"I told Declan," I choked out. "I told him about us."

Jentry's face fell, but he didn't speak or move away from me.

"I know you asked me to wait, but I just couldn't do it anymore. I couldn't keep living a life with him when I knew I would never feel for him a fraction of what I was capable of.

I understand why you asked me to wait, but you have no idea what you actually asked of me! Every day felt impossible to get through and was darker than the one before it. I hated myself long before the accident, Jentry, and it was because all I could think of with every passing day, and with every touch, was how I was going to break his heart! The night I was going to leave, he proposed. Everything about you and us just started spilling out, and I couldn't stop, and he *left*."

Jentry's eyes slid shut like he was in pain, and his head dropped.

"Do you understand why I can hardly live with myself? Do you understand why I want to regret you and push away from you forever? I finally allowed myself to want you, and that decision caused so much pain! Linda can say and do whatever she wants. I told you, it's deserved!" I shouted between sobs. "Declan had told them that he was going to propose that night. All they know is that instead of the phone call they'd been expecting from him, they got one from the police that he was being airlifted to the hospital. They know we fought and that that's why he'd left, but they don't know why we were fighting. They don't know that I was leaving him for *you*!"

Jentry let out a low curse toward the ground. "He called me the night of the accident. He called me twice, but I didn't have my phone on me. He didn't leave messages, so I hadn't known—I didn't realize. When I called him back, it went straight to voice mail. It had already happened. . . ."

"I'm sorry. I'm so sorry."

He lifted his head and ran his thumbs over my cheeks, trying in vain to wipe away tears that were falling too fast. "We're gonna get through this. I swear we will. And when Dec wakes up, we'll figure everything else out."

"I told you, there can never be an *us*. Not after how I've destroyed everything!"

"Aurora, it'll always be *us*."

"How can you say that after what I've done?"

Jentry leaned close and pressed his forehead to mine. "Because I fell in love with you the night you took my soul."

Before I could respond, his mouth crashed down onto mine and my world went up in flames.

Jentry

The tall grass whipped around us as I pressed her closer, deepening the kiss when my name passed from her lips to mine. My blood pounded through my veins when our tongues met in a slow dance we knew well.

Every brush of her lips against mine, and every sweep of her tongue, were perfectly in sync with my movements.

It's how it had been from the beginning with us. We'd never moved like strangers, never come together with the unfamiliarity of two people learning each other. I'd known her and she'd known me from that first night.

Her hands slid up my arms and over my shoulders quickly, and slowed as her fingers reached the back of my neck. Her nails lightly grazed the skin there, then dug in when I bit her bottom lip.

She inhaled softly and swayed closer, but steadied herself less than an inch away when my phone started ringing.

Aurora's blue eyes begged unspoken questions as my phone continued to ring. Her chest rose and fell as roughly as it had been when I'd found her in this field.

I reached into my pocket to silence the ringing, then brought my hand back up to sweep her wild hair away from her face. "It'll always be us," I repeated.

Pain sliced across her face as seconds passed. "I don't know how it can be," she finally whispered.

"We'll figure it out."

"You and me . . . it would have already been so difficult without Declan's accident. Telling him, telling the family . . ." Her head shook slightly and her eyes searched mine as if I would have the answers. "They wouldn't have understood. And now I've hurt everyone so much; how is it going to look to them now after everything?"

I opened my mouth to respond, but only a growl of frustration came out when my phone started ringing again. Pulling it out of my pocket, I cursed and ignored the call when I saw Jessica's name on the screen.

Aurora's eyebrows were pinched together when I looked up at her again, but she didn't comment on what I knew she had seen.

"We can figure this out." My words were a promise.

She nodded after a second of hesitation, but it didn't look convincing. "But not right now."

I'd asked her to wait to choose between Declan and me until I'd come home from Camp Lejeune, never once doubting that I would be the one she chose once I did. Granted, neither of us had thought we would all be in this situation when I finally had, but I couldn't let her do what she was trying to. "So, what, you're going to keep pretending to be in a relationship that you couldn't last another three weeks in? For how long?"

Tears filled her eyes, and she dropped her head in an attempt to hide them.

I slid the hand not holding my phone around her slender neck and brushed my thumb along the underside of her jaw until she looked up at me again. "You think you're saving my family more now by not telling them, but they'll find out eventually." I muted the next call that came through as soon as it began, my focus never leaving Aurora, though her eyes darted down at the sound.

"I think you're needed," she whispered.

I ground my teeth, but didn't respond to that. "I'm selfish enough to want you when you belong to someone else, but I'm not selfish enough to make you mine when my family is going through this shit. Right now they need their minds taken off what is going on with Dec, but they don't need to be lied to. How much worse is it going to be when he wakes up and tells everyone what all went down on that night?"

A few tears slipped down her cheeks, and her voice was

rough when she responded. "I don't know how to handle this." She shrugged helplessly. "I care about him, and I'll always love him. I would've never forgiven myself if I hadn't been there for him every day, and I have no doubt that Linda would've tried to stop me from being there if she'd known the truth."

"I wouldn't have let that happen," I assured her.

"You wouldn't have been there to be able to stop it."

My hand clenched around the phone when it began ringing for the fourth time, and Aurora's stare dropped to look at it.

"Looks like this Jessica person really needs you." She stood and took a step away from me, and spoke over me when I tried to stop her. "You and I both know that we can't be together the way we want. Not right now when all of this is going on. And right now . . . right now you're *here* and it's killing me to be close enough to touch you because I *can't* be with you." Her voice broke and her tears came faster when she quickly closed the small distance she'd put between us and placed her hand on my cheek. "Do you see me, Jentry?" she whispered as her dark blue eyes searched mine. Without waiting for my answer, she said, "It has never been a question of who I would choose, and it isn't now. I would have blindly followed you across the world after that first night if you'd asked me to. Don't make this time harder than it already is."

I watched her walk quickly away from me in the direction of my parents' house, and forced myself to stay rather than run after her.

Another low growl built in my chest and rumbled up my throat when my phone started ringing for the fifth time. I didn't need to look at the screen to know who was calling. If she called once, she'd call a dozen times in a row until I finally answered.

"What do you want, Jess?"

She spoke in her low, husky voice, talking about random things and far too fast before I caught one key word: *Declan*.

My body stilled. "Where are you?"

Her wicked laugh filled the phone and ended on a sigh. "He does look pretty rough, doesn't he? Not that it would stop me from getting on my knees again if he woke up."

I bit back a curse as I started walking. Slowly at first, then faster as she continued to talk about Declan more and more.

"How did you get to the hospital, Jessica?"

"I'm sure there are these things called taxis that drop people off, but I can't be sure if I was ever in one of those, or just a car, or if I ever paid the man driving it. I do have my ways of not paying, as I'm sure you know, Jent."

I grimaced, then said in a low voice, "I'm coming to get you, don't move."

"Oh, sounds like someone might be getting angry. I think I'll sit right down here and wait for the show. I wonder what this wire goes to," she murmured to herself before hanging up.

14

One Month Ago

Aurora

Taylor stood on the other side of the rental house's bar, leaning against it with her head propped up on one hand as the fingers of her other hand slowly drummed against the counter. I'd never seen her look so disappointed in all the years I'd known her, and I'd definitely never been on the receiving end of it. "No, by all means, continue," she drawled sarcastically.

Jentry's chest was rising and falling roughly as he stared her down, but he didn't speak, either.

After a few silent moments, Taylor continued. "I thought you would have been, I don't know, more observant or something. You know, since you're supposed to be a sniper, or something like that. Nothing?" she asked when Jentry didn't respond.

"I usually am," he said through gritted teeth.

"Hmm." Taylor's tone and expression showed she didn't believe him, or didn't care. She turned her anger-filled eyes on me. "You . . . I don't even know what to say to you right now. Do you realize that last night and just now, it could have been anyone other than me? You know, like your *boyfriend* or his parents?"

Guilt, fear, and confusion flooded me, but I still didn't speak. I just sat there shaking my head slowly.

Taylor pointed between Jentry and me and whispered, "My best friend wouldn't do this to her boyfriend. Let's go, Rorie."

I lifted my eyebrows, but didn't move from my spot on the counter.

"You and I are going to go talk about this, and we're not about to do it where someone else could easily walk in or hear us. Let's. Go."

Jentry's hand gently grasped my leg, but he didn't try to stop me from slowly sliding off the counter. Only when I passed him did he turn me around and cup the back of my neck in his hand. His dark eyes searched mine as indecision and agony played over his face.

Hundreds of words passed between us in that short time, but none that left our lips. It had been like that with Jentry from the beginning, and having that with him now, after all this time, after months and months of thinking I'd imagined our night, assured me that this was real.

When Taylor cleared her throat pointedly, Jentry reluctantly let me go and took a step back, but his dark stare never left me.

Once I was at Taylor's side, she leveled a glare at Jentry. "You know, Declan talks about you constantly. What a shitty way to treat your brother."

"Taylor," I hissed, but she didn't seem to care. She just turned and grabbed my arm, then dragged me across the living room and out the back door.

We walked in a rush through the sand, away from the house. It wasn't until we got to the shoreline that she slowed to an easier pace, but still we didn't stop, and she didn't speak. The silence left me alone to my own thoughts, thoughts I didn't want to deal with now but knew I had to face at some point.

My chest ached and tears blurred my vision as I thought of Declan sleeping, unaware, in the bed where he'd claimed my body just a couple of nights before. I would never want to hurt him, but I knew I had in the worst way possible. Not just this morning, but for months.

I *had* fallen for him, and I knew I loved him. And while I knew I could have a happy, safe life with him, I would never belong to him. Not completely anyway. Even if Jentry had simply remained a memory as *Jay*, I had a feeling I would have continued my vain attempt of trying to find a fraction of the chemistry and connection that he and I had shared in that one night.

It wasn't fair to Declan; it never had been. But I was selfish enough, and had fallen for him so quickly, that I'd pretended it wasn't happening. And now Jentry was here. Now he was real and completely exceeding the memory of him even when we were trying to make ourselves hate the other.

And I felt like the worst kind of person.

Declan deserved someone so much better than I could ever hope to be.

It wasn't until we were several minutes from the house that Taylor finally spoke again. She didn't yell, but her voice was full of disappointment and accusation. "You really had me believing you in the car the other night. You know, that there was nothing between you and Jentry . . ."

Tears had been streaming down my face as we'd walked, and a sob rose up in my throat at her words. "I'm sorry. I'm sorry, I thought if I said it enough—if I said it out loud to you and to myself, then I would believe it."

She nodded, but didn't speak for another minute as we walked along the shore. "The Rorie I know would never cheat on a boyfriend, especially one like Declan."

"I know. I didn't—I didn't mean for it to happen, but I—" I broke off as another sob tore from me, and wiped furiously at my face. "I don't know, I knew it was going to. I don't know how to explain it. I knew, and I wanted it . . ." I admitted. "But I didn't mean for it to happen like this. And neither did Jentry. He loves Declan. That's what we were yelling about last night when you found us."

"What, how long you should wait to cheat on him?" Taylor asked, sneering.

"No! Taylor!" I looked at her in shock. "No, we both love Declan, but we both—what this is between us, it's the strongest thing I've ever felt in my life. I knew it that first night with him and I've known it every day since. I've tried to re-create that feeling and those emotions with Declan since day one, and I've never been able to. I love Declan, I swear to God I do, Taylor. But . . ." I didn't know how to tell her without sounding cliché, or just sounding like I was trying to excuse what she'd walked in on.

She stopped walking, and grabbed my arm to turn me so I was facing her. "But what?"

My head shook as I stared at my best friend, but I held her stare, willing her to understand. "It felt like Jentry touched my soul last year. It felt like he took part of it with him. The only reason I got on with my life with Declan was because I knew I would never see Jentry again, and because I *do* love Dec. Seeing Jentry this weekend . . . I don't know how to explain it. But from what he said, it was the same for him. He's angry at himself for wanting me because he loves Declan, but this . . ." I trailed off, and clenched at my stomach. "I don't know, Taylor, I don't know."

"Or maybe he's just saying that because he knows what to say to get a girl in bed. His words worked last year, didn't they?"

I took a step away from her as if she'd slapped me. "What? No!"

"Yes, Rorie. You've been—" She broke off and looked around as she searched for the right words. "You've been glorifying this night you had with Jentry. Glorifying *him*. If you hadn't, if you had just let that night slip into the past the way it should have once you decided to enter into a relationship with Declan, then you wouldn't be acting like a whore when that is the last thing you are!"

I gaped at her, but knew I deserved those words. "I'm not—I haven't been. I'm being honest, I have *tried* to forget about him. God, you have no idea how hard I've tried. But he's always there in the background. That night is always there."

"Well, good fucks can be hard to forget!" she yelled. "But that doesn't mean that you imagine them instead of your boyfriend! That doesn't mean that when they enter your life again, you lose who you are and forget about what's right and wrong!"

"It isn't like that!" My voice was hoarse as I screamed back at her. "You don't understand!"

"You're right. I *don't*. I don't understand who you are all of a sudden."

I glanced up at her when the anger trailed from her words, leaving only her disappointment. For long moments, there was only the sound of waves crashing as we watched each other. Taylor, like she was looking at a stranger, and me, pleading for her to understand.

"Why did you start dating Declan in the first place, Rorie?"

My head jerked back. I hadn't expected that question. "What do you mean?"

"I mean, you've never really cared about guys or relationships before Declan. You didn't care about the label, and you never seemed that invested in a guy even if you liked him or hooked up with him. *That's* why I was so on board with going back to find your mystery guy that night, because it was so unlike you to be that caught up in a guy. But then he wasn't there and Declan was, and suddenly it was Declan, Declan, Declan—*everything* was about Declan."

My head shook subtly when she didn't continue. "I don't know what you're asking me."

"Did you start dating Declan just because Jentry ended up not being there, because you were so wrapped up in a guy who wasn't as wrapped up in you?"

My shaking grew more pronounced. "No."

She continued as if I hadn't spoken. "And if everything you're saying is true, then are you forcing yourself to love him?"

"No, Taylor!"

"Well, how else can you explain it? That's all that makes sense to me! How can you love Declan the way you claim to if you are still so obsessed with Jentry?"

I let the *obsessed* part slide as I tried to figure out a way for her to understand—but it was hard when I wasn't even sure I understood.

It felt like there were two parts of me, and each belonged to one of the guys. The part of me that I had willingly given to Jentry had been filled with a soul-deep ache for the better part of a year while the other had grown to love Declan.

When I told Taylor as much, she said, "You can't love two people at once, Rorie."

My brow pinched. "Love? I never said anything about loving Jentry."

"So then you would sabotage your relationship with a guy you *do* love for someone you *don't*?"

"It's not— You can't compare them that way!" Something deep down told me that what Jentry and I had was about so much more than falling for someone over the course of dates and phone conversations.

Taylor nodded slowly. "I think you're making a mistake. I think you saw Jentry and remembered your night, and you wanted it again. I think you'll realize soon that he's good for a night, not for forever like Declan is."

My face fell and, for the first time this morning, my stomach twisted with something other than guilt. I hated that my best friend viewed Jentry that way, but then again, after what she'd seen this weekend and knew from ten months ago, I wasn't sure what other conclusion she could have come to.

I took a deep breath and hoped she understood the depth of my confession. "I haven't felt whole since I walked away from Jentry last year. I do love Declan, and I know he would be good to me—good *for* me. I know how our future would go. I've known how it would play out since we started dating, and it's something that has always made me smile because I've loved the promise of it. It's a safe future, a sure one. It's the house with the white picket fence and the two and a half kids, Taylor. I could be so happy in that future, but I know now I would never be whole, which means he would never get all of me. No one has ever gotten more than a fraction of me, because like you said, I wasn't ever that invested in them.

Never really cared. Giving Jentry all of me was like deciding to wake up. Natural."

From the way Taylor's expression cleared as I spoke, I knew she believed me. But there was still a lingering disappointment in her eyes.

"Thinking of a future with Jentry hurts because it means I've hurt Declan. But thinking of a future with Declan—now that Jentry's back, I don't know how to even see one."

After a while, her head dipped in acknowledgment. The movement contradicted her words. "This isn't okay."

"I know."

"Declan has to know."

"I know," I whispered, my voice filled with guilt and sorrow. "But don't hate Jentry, Taylor. He tried to stop us so many times. He has always tried to give me every chance to stop. I pushed him."

"I doubt you had to push hard," she mumbled, and turned back toward the house.

We walked to the house in silence, and when we got close, Jentry came out to meet us. He was dressed to go running. His arms were folded over his chest and his face was hard. "Can I talk to her?" he asked Taylor.

She matched his stance and stood her ground.

A muscle ticked in his jaw as his dark eyes came back to me. As seconds passed, dread filled me. Because whatever he was about to say was clearly hard for him to get out. "You need to go home with Declan."

My brow pinched. "What?"

Jentry took in a ragged breath and looked away from me. "You need to go home with him and think about what you want."

My heart sank. "Jentry." His name was barely a whisper. "Isn't it obvious?"

He continued as if I hadn't spoken. "Whether you decide to tell him about this weekend and about last year will be your decision, and one I'll stand behind. Just wait until I'm home so I can be there to actually stand behind you—*next* to you."

A few seconds passed before I said, "I think I'm not understanding everything."

"Go home and be with Declan, Aurora," he said through clenched teeth, pain filled his eyes.

"Wait, you want . . . what?"

"Such an asshole," Taylor said. "What a coward's way out of this. Instead of dealing with it, just shove her back to him."

His unforgiving glare snapped to Taylor. "No, if I were a coward, I would let Declan find out, then throw Aurora into the middle of the shit storm that follows while I go hide out on base."

"But why are you doing this?" I demanded. "Why would you tell me how you feel? Why would you say the things you did last night just to tell me to go back to Declan? What do you want me to do with him now? *Pretend* like everything is fine?"

He reached out as if to hold me, but stopped himself. Whether because of Taylor, our proximity to the house, or because he needed to keep a small distance between us to stay firm, I wasn't sure. "I can't let you make a decision that could potentially change your life, only for me not to be there to help you through it. If you made that decision today—*right now*—you and I both know what it would be. I have to go back to base, and you would be left to deal with Dec, Mom, and Dad."

"And me."

He ignored Taylor's interjection, his eyes begging for me to understand what he'd said. "I can't do that to you. And after everything over this weekend, now that I know where you are, now that you know I'll be coming back for you, I want you to have time to really think about this. I don't want you to make a decision right now. It's too much all at once."

My jaw trembled as pain spread through my body. What he was saying made sense, and in the back of my mind, I knew I should thank him for being thoughtful and selfless enough to recommend it. But at that moment, it felt like it had all those months ago. Like I was about to wake up from a dream. As soon as I walked away from him, I would never see him again, because there was no way he could be real. The connection between us, the energy swirling around us . . . all of it was in my mind, and the thought of losing it was making it hard to breathe.

He took a step closer to me, and his husky voice dropped low. "Every day, Aurora . . . every *second,* I regretted letting you walk away from me. You were supposed to be mine. So go home and think, really think, because you know that where Declan is, I'll always be, and vice versa. And if in the end you do choose me, then I'll be there with you to face what's coming. If you choose him, then . . ." He trailed off and swallowed roughly. His gaze darted away to stare at the ocean, but he didn't finish his thought. There wasn't a need to.

"I hear you, but I can't do this," I said. "I can't go home with him and pretend."

Jentry ground his teeth, making the muscles in his jaw twitch. "You love him. I love him." His eyes flicked back to mine. "I told you that this would be entering a battle I couldn't win. No matter what it looks like now, you have to realize how much I hate telling you to do this. But I've already entered. I already fought. I want to continue to, but I know I can't. I owe Declan a lot—I owe him fucking everything—the very least of which is a chance to fight back while you decide."

My eyes burned with unshed tears, and my chest ached at the thought of Declan unknowingly entering into a battle for my heart. I hated what I had done to him—what I was going to do to him.

Jentry cradled my face in his hands, but my tears made it hard to see his expression.

"Don't ask me to do this," I pleaded.

"You hurt, I hurt," he whispered.

"No, I don't—it's because you're—would you stop being selfless and keep fighting!"

There was a brief pause from him when a few tears finally slipped free, and I dropped my stare so I wouldn't have to look at the anguish and indecision on his face. "I see you, Aurora. You need this just as much as Dec does."

My head shook, as if the action alone could force his words away.

His lips pressed against my forehead and stayed there when he spoke. "You know you have to be the one to walk away."

My body deflated, and I wanted nothing more than to beg him to change his mind. I wanted to force myself to believe that I didn't need or want this time with Declan. But Taylor grabbed hold of my hand and slowly pulled me from Jentry, and after a moment's resistance, I stepped away from him and stumbled after her.

I didn't look back at him, and he didn't stop me from leaving.

Déjà vu swept over me, my entire being rebelling at this scenario. That soul-deep ache had just flared back to life, worse than ever.

15
Present Day

Aurora

I hadn't gotten halfway through the field on my way back to the Veils' home when Jentry reached me and turned me around.

I wiped furiously at the tears on my face to see his features hardened with anger, but before I could speak, he said, "I need to go. Can you stay here?"

"Here?" I hadn't been able to make it through the party, and I could barely handle being around Linda, and he wanted me to stay?

"Yes, here, can you stay?"

"Why? What happened? Is it Declan?"

Jentry's head tilted, like he was about to say no, but instead he said, "I don't have time to explain everything right now. Declan's condition is the same as far as I know."

I searched his furious expression and only managed to shake my head when I couldn't figure out where all his anger was coming from.

"Just stay here," he pleaded, then turned and ran across the field toward where he had parked his car.

For the rest of the walk to the house I thought of his insistence on my staying here, and by the time I reached the front door had told myself that I would stay as long as possible for him.

I had barely slid back into the party—most of the guests unaware that Jentry wasn't in the house, let alone gone—when Linda spotted me.

Her eyes had darted around to make sure no one was close enough to hear us before she'd sighed. "Well shit," Linda said disgustedly, but kept her sweet smile firmly in place. "You know what they say about those people who speak too soon? Well, apparently the same goes for those who hope too soon. I'd nearly gone down to the cellar to get some wine because I'd thought you had left my sight for good. A number of things could have happened. You could have been trampled by pigs for all I knew." Another sigh, followed by a pat on my shoulder. "One can only dream of it so many times before it finally comes true, sweet girl."

Only three minutes in, and I'd already hit my limit on staying in that house.

I left and decided to start walking toward a little coffee shop not far from the neighborhood, and texted Taylor on my way, begging her to meet me since she had to be out that way for work that evening anyway. I could have waited for Taylor outside the house, but I didn't want to risk having to talk with anyone since it would take well over half an hour for her to drive there. *Anyone* meaning Linda or Madeline again.

When Taylor found me in the café just a few minutes after I'd arrived, her eyes were wide and greedy, as if she couldn't wait to get the juicy details of everything that had been happening since I'd last seen her two days before.

Only two days, but it felt like weeks . . . lifetimes, even. Being near Jentry and dealing with Linda had been physically and emotionally draining in so many ways.

I already had both of our drinks sitting on the table in front of me, so Taylor bypassed the line and walked right up to our table. As soon as she was in the seat, she said, "So he's back."

I nodded once, and my chin quivered. "Yeah."

The eagerness to hear everything quickly vanished from her expression, and one of her hands shot out to grip mine. "Oh, Rorie . . . no. No, it's okay. It's gonna be okay."

My head shook quickly as I forced the tears back. I was so tired of crying. "I don't know how it can be," I whispered, then hurried to fill her in on all that had happened since Jentry moved in.

Ever since our weekend at the beach, where Taylor had interrupted Jentry and me, I hadn't kept anything from her. On the drive home that weekend, I'd told her everything. Every emotional detail I could try to explain, from that very first night with Jentry to the way I had tried to find that connection with Declan, had tried to force it, even though I had known it would be impossible.

I had explained my feelings for Declan, the way I'd fallen for him. How his charm and humor had been endearing, and his personality was everything that fit the man I wanted to marry someday. On paper, Declan was it. He was exactly what I would have created for myself. Funny, sweet, thoughtful, safe, the perfect man for someone I thought I wanted to be . . .

I had admitted to her how I'd felt like I was cheating on him every time he'd touched me, every time I'd slept with him, but how I'd thought I would never see *Jay* again, and had tried to push him from my mind.

And even then, I had known that while I loved Declan and had had only one night with Jentry, there would never be any comparison.

I'd recalled every single conversation with Jentry over that weekend as best I could, not leaving anything out: whether Jentry and I were being spiteful to each other or pouring out our stored-up feelings, all the way down to when he'd hugged me goodbye.

To Declan, it had probably seemed like nothing since Jentry had hugged Taylor as well seconds after.

But to me . . . to me, that hug had been everything, and not nearly enough.

He'd whispered, "I'm coming back fighting," before releasing me and turning to Taylor.

Taylor had been the only person for me to speak to afterward as I'd struggled with my feelings, and had never judged me or looked at me in disappointment again.

She'd agreed with Jentry that I needed to give Declan a

chance to fight for our relationship—whether he knew he was fighting or not—and that Jentry needed to be there when I did choose him.

She was also the only one who had known the truth about the night of Declan's accident before this afternoon, when I'd broken down talking to Jentry.

Taylor sat there for a while after I finished talking, staring out the window as she absorbed all of my words. Finally, her eyes rested on me. "Okay, so this Jessica chick—"

"There isn't a point in talking about her. I don't know who she is."

Her head dipped. "Okay, then never mind on that." She took a long sip of her iced coffee, and her eyes glazed over as she thought. When she spoke her next words she did it slowly. "He was right, you know. Even if I still hated Jentry, I would agree with him that it would only end up worse for you if that family found out the truth if Declan ever wakes up. They don't have to know everything right now, but at least tell them that you were leaving him. Because what if he doesn't wake up? Are you going to tell them way later, 'Well, hey, just so you know, this is what actually happened that night. Surprise!'?"

I tore my hand out from underneath hers and pressed it against my chest. It suddenly felt too hard to breathe. I wasn't about to play off what was happening with Declan the way his family was, as if he might walk through the door at any moment, or actually answer my next call. But I refused to believe that he might not wake up.

"And then if he doesn't wake up, does that mean that you

just keep pushing Jentry away forever, or how long until you stop being stupid about it?"

"Taylor!" My mouth slowly fell open at her brazen words. "It's not as easy as you're making it seem. You're looking at all of this as if it's black and white, and it's not. Okay, yes, when you and Jentry put it that way, I don't know why I haven't told their family about what happened. But actually telling them . . . well, it seems impossible. And as for Jentry, he understands that right now has to be about his family and Dec. I don't know when that will change, but as for right now, we're both on the same page."

"Are you?" Taylor said with a sarcastic laugh. "So you said it back?"

I lifted an eyebrow in question, and waited.

When I didn't respond, Taylor gave me a look as if I was insane. "Rorie, he told you he was in love with you. That he'd *been* in love with you. Jentry isn't some creepy lovesick stalker. He's intense, and from what you've told me, is the kind of guy who probably shies away from love."

My chest ached because I would have said the same thing about him. I studied her expectant expression for a few seconds before shaking my head slowly.

Her face fell. "Then, no. You're not on the same page. What's happening is you're going to sabotage what could be the greatest love of your life for someone that you don't love."

I let out a humorless laugh and leaned closer to her over the table. "Excuse me?"

"You can't love two people at once."

"You know, I seem to remember you saying something like this to me a month ago, only you were saying all of this in favor of Declan. And in case you have forgotten, I *do* love Declan. And how would you know what someone is capable of feeling? You think letting yourself love someone makes you vulnerable and weak," I sneered.

My anger didn't faze Taylor. She only watched me until I finished speaking, and then she waited to see if I would continue. When I didn't, and nearly a minute had passed, she whispered, "So, are you telling me you don't love Jentry?"

"What? No, I'm not—I never said that. And why does it have to be one or the other?"

"I know what you're doing, Rorie; and from what you told me of your conversation, Jentry saw it, too. There are ways of being with Jentry when the time is right, and still being there for Declan. But you're going to let yourself get so wrapped up in your grief and guilt for what happened to Declan that you won't *ever* let yourself have a life with Jentry, even when that perfect time comes. So if getting you to finally admit how much Jentry actually means to you will stop you from doing that—then that's what I need to do."

"What do you mean?" I asked, exasperated. "I've told you how much he means to me, and what would that change about right now? I told you that Jentry and I were on the same page."

"You've never said what he did."

Her accusation brought me up short. Not only had I not said the words out loud to Jentry, I'd never said them out loud to anyone—or thought them before a certain dark-eyed man entered my life.

It was easy to tell Declan that I loved him. I loved my family; I loved Taylor. . . .

Falling *in* love with someone was a whole different thing. It was life altering. Soul changing. It was invisible ink spilled onto your skin, writing every second of your story from beginning to end.

"I think you're right in a way, but you're also wrong." I had been staring at my still-full coffee when the words tumbled from my mouth, and looked up at Taylor's curious expression. "I think a person can love two people at the same time, to an extent. I think a heart can be *in love* with someone, and *love* another."

When Taylor's face remained the same, I cleared my throat and laid my hands flat on the table so I could focus on them instead.

"I'm not in love with Declan; I never was," I said just above a whisper. "I fell for him, and then grew to love him."

She shook her head slowly. "Just admit it and stop pushing Jentry away. He can help you through this time. *You* can help *him* through this time."

"I'm not pushing him away for the reasons you think I am. I have to keep him away because it's too hard to be close to him. But admitting what he means . . . I can't right now. Admitting it out loud when I can't be with him would be like losing him all over again."

PART IV

That Night . . .

W HAT?" HE GROWLED, and looked toward the door
long minutes later when we were laying in our bed of
embers. Not speaking; just watching each other as he traced
lazy shapes onto my skin with his fingers.

I looked over his shoulder to see the knob twisting, and
then someone started pounding on the door.

Dark eyes met mine. "Don't move." He got off the bed
and covered me with the comforter, then hurried to step into
his jeans, leaving them unbuttoned as he went to open the
door.

The music from the party flooded into the room, but my
mystery guy opened the door only slightly, so the person on
the other side couldn't see in, and I couldn't see them.

"Dude, did you take my—"

"Mind staying gone for a few more hours?" my stranger asked, cutting off the deep voice.

There was a pause from the guy on the other side of the door. "Really?" he asked, laughing. "Yeah, man. Have fun. You deserve it."

"I can leave," I said once the door was shut and my mystery guy was walking back toward the bed.

"Do you want to?" The way he asked reminded me of the way he kept giving me every opportunity to leave before.

I responded with a slow shake of my head.

His sinful eyes somehow darkened, and his mouth curved up into a smirk. "Roll over onto your stomach."

My eyebrows rose in surprise and apprehension, but I still did as he said. Goose bumps rose over my skin when he slowly removed the comforter from me, and my breaths deepened when he gently prodded my legs to open.

I waited for his next touch, but there was nothing as the seconds ticked on. Just the sounds of my ragged breaths, and him removing his jeans and tearing open another condom. My hands clutched at the sheets below me and my heart raced when I felt the bed dip as he knelt between my legs. He curled his arm between my hips and the bed, and slowly lifted while his other hand pressed down between my shoulder blades to keep my chest on the bed as I settled on my knees.

His hand on my back was fire to my skin, as if he were branding me, and for a fleeting moment my mind and heart rebelled against me, and became too invested in this night and this guy as the words "Yes, I'm yours," resonated through my soul.

A shiver moved down my spine when his hands ran up my legs and back, then down the same path. His touch was gentle, but firm enough to remind me of his strength. To remind me of what he hadn't wanted me to see—of what I was ready to beg him for again.

Grabbing a fistful of my hair, he wrenched me up off the bed until my back was flush with his chest. My surprised gasp faded into a soft whimper when he bit down on my shoulder, then placed a soft kiss in the same spot.

Hard, soft, hard, soft.

The contradicting combination never ended, and I didn't want it to. I wanted more.

His breathing was as rough as my own, and I remotely noticed the thin sheen of sweat covering his muscled arm as his fingers gently trailed over my breast, and down my stomach. He teased me with the faintest hint of a touch between my thighs as his lips went to my ear.

My body trembled when he ordered in a low, hoarse tone, "Bend over and place your hands on the wall. Don't make a sound."

16
Three Weeks Ago

Aurora

Ten days.

Ten days since we'd come home from the beach, and I knew I couldn't last another day.

I'd tried to give Declan a fair chance. I'd tried to remember every reason I'd had for wanting to spend my life with him.

But spending my life with Declan meant a life without Jentry. The pain that filled me at that thought had been excruciating, and had told me everything I needed to know. Because a life without Declan hurt.

It just hurt.

I knew what I'd told Jentry, but I couldn't wait for him to come home to do this. I couldn't keep pretending with Declan. Each kiss and each day left me more miserable than the last, and I knew he could sense it.

I could feel him pulling away just as I had been. There was no point to put either of us through this any longer.

A lump formed in my throat, and I forced myself to stand up from the couch when I heard his key in the door.

The surprise of seeing his bright smile, and the roses and takeout food in his hands, made the thought of doing this that much harder, but didn't make me waver in my decision.

"Hey, how was your day?" he asked as he pressed his mouth to mine.

I wondered if I'd been cringing away from his kisses the entire last week and a half. "Uh, it was . . ." I trailed off when he handed me the flowers and hurried past me to put the food on the table. "Declan, can we talk?"

"Can it wait until after dinner?" I wasn't sure if I imagined the frantic edge to his voice. He must have known I was about to protest, because he hurried to add, "Rorie, please."

I swallowed past the tightness in my throat and nodded, then walked into the kitchen to find a vase for the roses as Declan finished getting the food out.

Soon we were sitting down, the air between us thick with silence, as it had been for the better part of the last ten days. I pushed the food around my plate with my fork as I tried to figure out what to say to him, and after a few minutes, noticed that he had taken only a couple of bites.

I set the fork down and straightened my spine as I faced him. "Dec, have you noticed that the last couple of weeks—"

"I know," he said quickly, interrupting me. A short, soft laugh left him, and his mouth curved up. "I know. I don't know why I even try to keep something from you, because I just give myself away."

My brow pinched and my head tilted to the side. "Wait, what?"

"I'm always afraid you'll find out, so I stop talking in order to keep whatever it is from you. But then you end up thinking something is wrong."

My head shook slowly. "No, that's not it. I was talking about both of us."

"This went differently in my head," he said, speaking over me. His smile broadened as he reached into his pants pocket. "I had tonight all planned out. I had what I would say all planned out. But I can't even eat because it's all I can think about."

I don't remember moving. I just know that I'd been sitting, and the next moment I was out of my chair and gripping the edge of the table as I stared in horror at Declan's hand when he rested it on top of the table.

In his hand was a small, opened box. Nestled inside the box was an engagement ring.

"Rorie . . ."

No. The tightness in my throat became uncomfortable, unbearable.

"I love you—"

No. My eyes burned with unshed tears.

"—and I want to spend the rest of my life with you."

No, no, no! My head shook quickly as I tried to make myself believe this wasn't happening. I couldn't do this to him.

"Will you marry me?"

A sob forced its way from my chest, and I hurried to cover my mouth with one of my hands. My head shook faster and faster before I could tear my eyes from the ring and look up at Declan's hopeful, yet terrified, expression.

And it broke something inside me.

The words I'd hidden for so long about my past with Jentry poured from me until Declan knew everything, and was storming from the apartment.

17

Present Day

ℭ~~~

Jentry

About a half hour later I stood in the living room of Declan and Aurora's apartment with my arms crossed over my chest and stared Jessica down.

I'd found her casually lying on Declan's hospital bed, as if it were a common thing for her to be in that room. As if it were her place to be beside him. Her wicked, knowing smirk had covered her face as soon as I'd stepped inside.

All it had taken was a twenty-dollar bill to get her out of that room, but I knew it would take a lot more to get her to leave here.

"So intense," she said mockingly, and rolled her eyes. "So I guess I'll just give myself the grand tour of your new *fancy* place." She smiled wickedly as she dropped her purse on the floor and started walking toward the kitchen. The purse and her clothes looked expensive, and knowing Jessica the way I did, I was wondering how she'd come to get them.

I shot my arm out in front of her to stop her, and ignored her annoyed-sounding sigh as she stumbled back a few steps until we were facing each other again. "Tell me why you're here, Jessica."

"If I remember correctly, *you* drove *me* here."

"Why are you calling? Why were you in that room?"

"What? Don't you miss me?" she asked teasingly.

One of my eyebrows lifted in response, but she was never the kind of person to be offended easily.

She shrugged one of her thin shoulders. "I told you on the way over. I need a place to stay for the night . . . and maybe tomorrow night."

"Which means you need a place for a week, and obviously I can't help you with that since you know that this place isn't even mine."

Her wicked grin fell as her eyes darted around the apartment at the reminder that I was a guest here. "I want to get my eyes on this little bitch *Rorie*." She sneered her name.

I clenched my jaw and focused on breathing for a few seconds. "Not here and won't be back for a long time."

"So serious and so protective over things that aren't yours," she said in a tone that dripped with curiosity. "Nothing has changed, Jent. Are you sure you haven't missed me?" She barely had the question out before a giggle flew past her lips. "Okay, that may be a reach. But I sure have missed you!" She skipped forward and leaned up on her toes to kiss my cheek, then danced into the kitchen. "I'm hungry. Do you have anything to eat?"

"I'd rather know the real reason why you're here first, and how you knew where Declan was, and what our numbers were."

She glanced at me from over her shoulder and shrugged. "Not hard to find you, Jent. Never has been. All I have to do is find Declan, and then I've found you. Of course, he was always so much harder to find once he started dating this little bitch, and then he had to go and try to smash his head through a tree," she mumbled offhandedly as she continued into the kitchen.

My hands fisted and my body tensed as adrenaline coursed through me, but I bit back my response. "How did you find him in the first place?"

Again, that mischievous grin as she turned to face me. "Now why would I tell you that?"

"Jessica, just—"

"You wondering if I was still sleeping with your 'brother'?'"

I scoffed. "Declan wouldn't touch you after what went down last time. I just want to know why you keep showing up, and why you won't leave him alone."

Her grin turned into a taunting smile. "You gettin' mad, Jent?"

My eyebrows pulled low over my eyes. "No."

"You wanna punch Declan again? He wouldn't even be able to put up a fight this time."

"N—"

"Your hands are clenched," Jessica observed, her tone practically giddy, and looked pointedly at where my hands were still curled into fists from what she'd said about both Aurora and Declan.

I forced them to relax and tried to calm myself, but the realization that I still had adrenaline flowing through my body, and the fact that it took force to keep my hands straightened were making it harder to calm down.

"Look at the way your body is shaking," she added in awe. "You feel it? That anger? How mad are you?" she goaded.

"Shut up, Jess."

"You wanna hit something?" she asked. "Do you want to hit me?"

"Jessica," I said in warning, and took a step away from her.

Her eyes were bright with excitement. "What does it feel like? Is it scary or thrill—"

"I said shut up!"

Jessica jumped at the sudden boom of my voice, but quickly broke into soft, melodic laughter—as if I were a child and she thought I was being amusing. She swayed side to side a few times, then turned in a slow, graceful circle. "God, you're too easy. You want something to eat?"

I shut my eyes when she turned to look in the pantry, and took calming breaths. Through clenched teeth, I said, "You have an hour before you have to be out of here. Get some food in you, and then get out. You know when you can come back."

She giggled again, but it ended in a disappointed sound

when I began walking toward the patio to go smoke. "Aw, there goes Jentry. Running away again."

I faltered, and my eyes darted to hers. "I'm not the one who ran, and continues to," I reminded her coldly.

"You can't run from *you*!" she called out. "It's inside you!"

The last thing I heard before I slammed the door shut was her giggling.

Aurora

I blew out a slow breath as I made my way back to the apartment after finishing up coffee with Taylor. She had taken me to pick up my car at the shop, and as soon as I changed into something more comfortable and grabbed one of my books, I planned on going to hang out with Declan.

I looked curiously at Jentry's car in the parking lot one last time before deciding that I didn't care anymore.

Whatever the reason he had wanted me to stay at the Veils' house, he couldn't have actually expected me to, and I had stayed out long enough anyway.

Besides, it was my apartment.

I shifted my keys in my hands until I found the right one as I neared the door, but when I was still about six feet away it opened suddenly.

I took in a steadying breath, trying to prepare myself for seeing him again, but the breath got caught in my throat, my eyes widened and steps slowed when a tall brunette walked out of my apartment instead.

"Try not to miss me too much!" she called over her shoulder into the apartment just before she pulled the door shut behind her, a teasing smile playing on her mouth for the briefest of moments.

She dripped sex; there was no other way to describe her, from her full lips, to her dark, seductive eyes, to the clothes that accentuated her tiny waist and curves I would die for.

For the first time in years, I suddenly felt inadequate. Linda's words were all I could hear. *I looked like a boy, I was gaining weight, I wasn't pretty, I would never be enough.* Right now I felt like every one of those things.

Because of this stranger. Because of a girl who looked too beautiful to be real. Because I'd allowed Jentry to tell me what I now assumed were heady lies when he was with girls like this moments after.

Jealousy flared in my stomach and quickly spread through my body at the thought of this girl having a glimpse of the Jentry who haunted me in everything I did. Flashes from our kiss just a couple of hours before, and from our night together a year earlier, assaulted me, and the jealousy grew stronger and stronger.

The girl glanced up and caught me staring, and I had the oddest feeling that she expected to see me. One perfectly groomed eyebrow rose, and her mouth pulled up into a knowing smirk as she came closer.

Her lips twisted as she whispered, "One girl leaves, another one enters, and all the while, poor little Declan lies alone in his bed. What will the neighbors think?"

Her eyes never left mine as she shouldered past me.

I stood still for a few moments before I could gather myself enough to move again. Jealousy and confusion and self-doubt weighed down each step as I forced myself to the door and shoved it open. When my phone rang, I considered letting it go but habit took over and I had my phone at my ear just as Jentry appeared at the entrance of the hall.

My chest felt heavy and pained as I turned to avoid his hopeful stare.

"Yeah?" I spoke into the phone through clenched teeth, then froze when Kurt's frantic voice filled the other end.

"He's moving! He's moving, Rorie! We need to get—his fingers! He's moving them!"

My head snapped up and I turned to face Jentry. His hopeful expression had drained as he absorbed the tension radiating from me.

"He isn't awake, but he's moving. We'll meet you at the hospital."

"W-we'll be right there," I whispered to Kurt, and then hung up the phone. The brunette and Jentry's betrayal faded from my mind as I relayed the message. My tone was soft and hesitant as shock and disbelief filled me. "He hasn't woken up yet, but he's moving his fingers."

Jentry didn't hesitate. Within seconds, he was sweeping me out of the apartment and putting me in his car.

We didn't say a word to each other as he sped through the streets. The air in the car was too heavy with a nervous excitement and pressure of the unknown to do so. All thoughts were now on Declan, and what would happen now.

Before this, doctors hadn't been giving us much hope—not that Linda had ever listened to a word they'd said. But just moving his fingers was a huge improvement.

Now if only he would wake up.

Jentry and I were yelled at as we ran through the halls of the hospital on the way to Declan's room, and found the room much like we usually did. One of the nurses was sitting by his bed talking slowly to him; she smiled up at us when we came in, then resumed her work.

"Declan, can you move your fingers again? Any of your fingers?" she asked him.

After a few seconds of staring at them, she turned to face us. "I've been asking for specific ones, but he doesn't seem to be responding to that just yet."

I was frozen in place, still staring at Declan's seemingly lifeless hand, willing it to move.

"Has he been moving in response to you?" Jentry asked when I didn't say anything.

The nurse shook her head. "I don't think so, but this is a great improvement."

I inhaled quickly and reached out to grab Jentry's arm when Declan's fingers slowly curled and then straightened again. "Declan?" I asked shakily.

The nurse stood and excused herself, but I wasn't paying

attention to her. As I took hesitant steps closer to the bed, my eyes were darting all over Declan's body to see if he was moving anything else.

"Dec?" I whispered when I took her seat. "Declan, can you hear me?"

I slipped my hand underneath his and squeezed gently, and waited without breathing to see if there would be any kind of response.

Jentry walked around to the other side of the bed and studied Declan's face intently. "Dec, can you move something?" He waited a while, then said softly, "I bet hearing my voice makes you want to wake up and beat the shit out of me, huh?"

Despite everything, I laughed.

When minutes passed without anything from Declan, I ran the fingers of my free hand along his forehead and whispered, "Where are you, Dec?"

A strained sob tore from my throat, and tears instantly fell from my eyes when two of Declan's fingers curled against mine.

I leaned forward to rest my head against his shoulder, and let my tears bleed into the hospital gown. "I'm sorry. I'm so sorry," I whispered over and over again. "I'm sorry for everything, just come back. Find your way back," I pleaded, and squeezed his hand again.

Jentry and I took turns trying to talk to Declan over the next few minutes, but he didn't move again.

"Where are you?" I asked softly, and looked up into Declan's pale face. "Where did you go, and how can we get you back? We all need you back."

I glanced up at Jentry when the room suddenly felt thick with tension, and noticed his rigid stance, as if he were preparing himself for a fight. But before I could turn to look at whatever he was staring at behind me, I heard multiple people shuffling into the room, and a fake, startled gasp.

I straightened in my chair and turned in time to see Linda clutching her chest, looking at me in horror. Declan's dad, sisters, and their husbands were spreading into the room—as was Madeline.

"Sweet girl," Linda drawled, "it is not appropriate to be that close to my son when he can't even tell you what time of day it is; and it is definitely not appropriate to act in such a way in front of company."

Kurt ignored his wife's absurd comment and stepped closer to get an update from Jentry on what had happened since we'd arrived.

"What took you so long to get here, and why is Madeline here?" Jentry demanded in a low tone.

Kurt gave him a helpless look and shrugged. "Your mother invited her, and we had all those people in our house; we had to wait for them to leave before we could."

I would have left without another thought, exactly the way Jentry and I had, even if people had been in my apartment. It didn't matter that Declan hadn't woken up yet. There had been a response from him after nothing for three weeks, and that knowledge had made the short drive to the hospital feel like it took ages.

When the only change from their son before today had been a very slow, subtle decline, I was disappointed in Declan's family—but Kurt especially—that they would allow something like people and a party hinder them from getting to Declan.

A quick glimpse at Jentry's face confirmed he shared my frustration with them.

"Okay now, it's polite to give up your seat," Linda said pointedly as she stepped closer to where I was seated next to Declan.

I stood up and moved aside without hesitation, thinking she would sit down, and knowing that she should have that time with Declan even though just being near her again set me on edge. . . .

I hadn't expected her to hold out the chair and turn to Madeline.

"Honey, I'm sure he wants to hear your voice." Linda held out her hand toward Madeline, who strode across the room. "I wouldn't be surprised if he even opened his eyes just so he could see you." Even though her last words were clearly meant to be a whisper, she hadn't tried hard enough to make sure that the rest of us wouldn't hear her.

Holly dropped her head into one of her hands, Lara—Declan's other sister—was pinching the bridge of her nose, and both of their husbands were giving each other looks as if they wanted to bolt for the door before it could get any worse.

I knew how they felt.

"I'm not staying here for this," I mumbled when Madeline began talking to Declan in a childish tone. "I'll be back tonight." I didn't say it to anyone in particular. I just spoke to the room as I grabbed my purse from where I'd dropped it earlier, and walked out of the room before I could start yelling at Linda.

The last thing I needed was for her to call security on me—since I knew she was itching to find a way to keep me from Declan's room.

I hadn't gotten halfway down the first hallway before I felt a familiar warmth slide across my skin.

I had been wrong. The last thing I needed was all the eyes of Declan's family on me, seeing things they shouldn't. Like that it didn't actually bother me to watch Madeline hold Declan's hand and talk to him—the whole idea behind it, and Linda's intent, had been what bothered me most. Or that the person I was most upset with, and still needed more than anything, wasn't the man lying in the bed.

"You should stay," I whispered when Jentry caught up with me.

"I drove you here."

"I can find a way home."

"Aurora." My name rumbled from deep in his chest, a question and demand all at once, and very clearly the end of the conversation.

I pressed my lips tightly together and nodded once, but didn't look back at him, just continued to walk.

Because even though Declan's sudden movements had pushed the girl who had been in my apartment aside, I hadn't forgotten about her, and being alone with Jentry right now sounded like pure agony.

18

Present Day

Aurora

My body sagged with an odd mixture of relief and exhaustion when we got back to the apartment and Jentry still hadn't tried to talk to me again. I knew I would feel even more relieved if I could just go lie down, but my bed felt so far away.

"Are we not going to talk about this?" Jentry asked.

I let out a huff that sounded more like a scoff, and kept walking in the direction of my room.

"Aurora." He grabbed for my arm, but I jerked it away. "Aurora, stop!"

I whirled around when he finally grasped my hand, but managed to yank it away again when my apparent anger shocked him. "What exactly do you want to talk about?" I asked.

"The fuck, Aurora?"

"Do you want to talk about the fact that Declan's moving? Or maybe about who the hell you had in my apartment this afternoon?"

Jentry's expression fell, his body stilled. "You saw her?"

I laughed, but there was no humor behind it.

"Another one of your girls?" I asked, bringing up our conversation from the beach all those weeks ago, and hated that my voice shook. "But it's not a game though, right?"

"No, Aurora—"

"Who was that?" I demanded.

He took a step toward me, but I backed away and put my hands up, as if I could ever stop him.

"Wait, no. Let me guess. Jessica?"

Jentry no longer looked sick that I'd found out; he looked terrifying. "What did she say to you?" His voice was deep and severe, and matched his expression.

"What does it matter? You've been lying to me!" I yelled, ignoring the chill that crept through my body from his voice. "You made me believe—you told me—it doesn't even *matter*!" I pointed at him, and then myself as I continued to yell, "We are not together, and thank God for that after what I saw earlier. Screw whoever you want, Jentry, but don't tell me to stay somewhere so you can bring some girl back to *my* apartment. Find your own place if that's what you want."

"*Screw* her? That's not—fucking listen to me!" he begged when I turned and hurried to my room.

"Auror—"

"I don't want to talk right now." I gasped in surprise when he gripped my hand in his and yanked me back to where he was.

"I do," he countered huskily. In two long steps, he had the backs of my legs pressed up against my bed and was pushing me down. My arms covered in goose bumps and my body vibrated in anticipation for something I refused to allow happen. "This afternoon—"

"That kiss was a mistake," I said, cutting him off again as he hovered over me.

His dark eyes flared, and he blew out a heavy breath through his nose. "Never. We could never be a mistake. But I meant Jessica. She's not who you think she is. She's my sister," he said, his words rushed.

Right. I laughed miserably, and wondered if he really thought I was so stupid to believe that. "You tried to keep me away while you brought *your sister* here."

"Yes, and I'd do the same thing in a heartbeat because I didn't have a lot of time to think of another option. But just so you know, I'll probably see her again in the future."

I blinked slowly as I waited for him to give me something else, for him to realize that I didn't believe him. When Jentry didn't offer anything else up, I pressed my hands against his chest and pushed. "Right. Okay, please get off me."

He didn't move. "What'd she say to you?" he demanded suddenly.

"Who ever said that she spoke to me?"

His dark eyes looked into mine and the corner of his mouth

lifted in a sad smile. "I saw your expression when you walked in here. Knowing Jessica and knowing that you saw her tells me that you talked. Tell me what she said to you."

When I only responded by continuing to shove at his chest, he blew out a harsh breath.

"Fine. Just promise me something: if you ever see her again, stay away from her. She's insane; she is literally crazy."

"Oh good. So you sleep with psychotic girls now."

Jentry recoiled and his face pinched with disgust. "Sleep with—no. Did you not hear me? Aurora, stop pushing me away and just talk to me!"

I didn't stop. I gritted my teeth and said, "I don't want to talk to you. I don't want to know about what or who you do. I just need you to leave!"

Jentry grabbed my wrists and slammed them down on the bed, his face now directly above mine. Pain unlike anything I'd ever seen from him flared in his eyes, and his jaw clenched as seconds passed.

When he finally spoke, his words seemed to drain him of his energy. "She's my twin. I don't know how to get you to believe me without her here, but I'll never want you that close to her again." There was no mistaking the honesty that wove through each word, or the way it seemed as if he was admitting a dark secret.

I lay there, stunned. A denial was on the tip of my tongue, but it wouldn't leave my lips the way it had before. "What? No, because she . . ." I trailed off and gasped softly when I remembered her dark eyes and wicked smile. One that could have matched Jentry's so perfectly if it hadn't been so hateful. "But you . . . you grew up with Declan. You were adopted by . . ." Each word came out sounding confused. My head shook slowly at first, then faster. "She's really your sister?"

Jentry nodded. "It's a long story, one I'm not ready to tell you yet. I only saw Jess a handful of times growing up. She calls when—she only called today because she needed a place to stay. I try to avoid her. I haven't seen her in over a year, because like I said, she's insane. But she always seems to know too much. She already knew I was back in Wake Forest and staying here, and when she kept calling me over and over again when we were in the field today, she was sitting in Declan's hospital room."

My eyebrows shot up in surprise and confusion, but Jentry continued before I could question that.

"Again, I can't explain it right now, but I need you to know that her calls weren't what you thought. Her being here wasn't what you thought. I didn't want you to see her because I don't want her crazy near you. Understand?" Putting all of his weight onto one of our joined hands, he slowly slid the fingers of his free hand from my jaw to my cheekbone, then cradled my face. "The way you looked at me . . ." He trailed off and shook his head. "How can you not understand by now that I only see you?" he asked softly, and dipped his head until his lips were just above my own. His breath mixed with mine, and my eyes slipped closed when that intoxicating scent overwhelmed me, as it always did.

"Jentry," I breathed, but didn't continue.

The hand on my cheek moved slowly down until the tips of his fingers were nothing but the faintest brush against the soft skin of my throat.

His mouth curved up in a sad smile, but he didn't respond. His eyes dipped to where his hand slowly continued down my throat to my chest, then back up again. The touch was soft as a feather, and contradicted the way his other hand seemed to claim me as his in the tight way it gripped my hand.

Hard and soft.

He dipped his head lower to trail his nose along my jaw before he placed two deceptively soft kisses there that caused my heart to stutter before it took off again in the pounding beat that was so familiar with the man above me.

"Every second, Aurora. Every second I regret that I let our night end without telling you that I wasn't ever letting you go."

The pain in his voice didn't fit our current positions, or the promise of more that lingered between us; but it made sense when he suddenly shifted to get off the bed. And for the first time, Jentry Michaels walked away from me.

WHEN I WOKE, I was curled up on top of the comforter on my bed, still in my clothes from the day. My body felt stiff, but oddly relaxed, and my mind felt clearer than it had in weeks.

I glanced over to the window to see a darkened sky outside, and searched blindly around the bed until I found my phone underneath me. It was just after four in the morning. I hadn't slept more than three hours at a time since before Declan's accident, and couldn't remember when I'd slept nearly twelve.

Ever since that night, my body had always stayed so on alert—afraid that I'd get a call worse than the one informing me of his accident—that it was usually impossible to sleep long.

That, and sleeping in a chair in a hospital room wasn't the easiest thing to do.

I rolled off the bed and stretched my stiff body as I walked into the bathroom, then turned on the shower and stripped off my clothes. After quickly rinsing my body off, I hurried to get ready for the day, grabbed a book, and was out of the apartment within twenty minutes of originally waking up.

I drove with the windows down, and enjoyed feeling the cool predawn air of late summer whip through my car, stirring up the pieces of my hair that had fallen out of my bun.

The drive felt so routine that I wondered if I could have done it in my sleep. Every turn of the wheel felt like I was doing it out of habit, as if my body knew what to do before I even registered that I was turning onto the next street, ordering my usual drink from my favorite coffee shop, and pulling into my normal spot in the hospital.

In what felt like seconds, I was sitting cross-legged on the trunk of my car, and leaning back against the window so that I would have a perfect view of the sunrise.

I drank my coffee slowly, and when the sky lightened enough to allow me to read, pulled my book out of my bag and opened to where I had left off.

This had always been my favorite time of day because it was quiet and beautiful, and what better time to get lost in another world than when your world shifted around you?

But I had come to live for the mornings since Declan's accident . . .

There is that phrase: The darkest hour is just before the dawn. It was something I'd heard my whole life. People had tried to tie it to their lives in so many ways to give themselves hope. And I'd never understood why they would cling to a saying just to make themselves feel like they could get out of whatever situation they were in.

I understood now.

Because there is so much unknown in the darkness, and the unknown can be terrifying. Like our futures . . . like Declan's. Every day had been full of unknowns, and even though yesterday had been a small miracle, today would still be unknown. But the next day always brought with it possibilities, and though I hated to think in clichés, *hope* . . . but it was more than that.

Because it was never just the light of dawn washing away darkness that I saw; it was the beautiful transition of darkness to light, of the terrifying unknown to the promise that one day all would be okay.

And I knew as the sky filled with purples and pinks and oranges . . . I knew that no one would ever be able to find that kind of beauty without the dark.

Life wasn't supposed to be easy. Life wasn't supposed to

be all light. There needed to be a balance. Just as the world needed night, we needed our trials.

And I was going through the trial of my life.

I was struggling to find the beauty in my life with everything that was going on—but the beauty that was surrounding me gave me hope that one day I would.

I stayed on my car reading until the sun finished rising and my coffee was gone, then carefully slid off the trunk and walked across the parking lot and into the hospital. I waved to a few of the workers I'd come to recognize over the past three weeks as I made my way to Declan's room, and rummaged through my purse to find my phone charger as I got close.

Three weeks and I already had such a routine that starting school tomorrow would feel odd. Or maybe it would help. Maybe staying in his room most of my days wasn't healthy.

I sucked in a startled gasp and stumbled backward when I stepped into Declan's room and found a tall guy standing just inside.

My heart instantly took off. The pounding was so hard and loud to my own ears that I was sure he heard it when he quickly turned at my not-so-graceful entrance. "Jesus, Jentry!"

His mouth tipped up at the corner in a small smirk, but fell quickly. "Where have you been?"

My brow furrowed as I walked around him, ignoring the way his intoxicating smell filled the room, and the way I was craving to turn around and move into his arms. I focused on plugging my phone in so it could charge, and continued to avoid his stare as I sat down. "What do you mean?"

"I was getting ready to go for a run when you left this morning; that was hours ago."

I finally glanced up at him when I heard the underlying panic in his tone. "I've been here."

Jentry's face fell into a mask of frustration. "No. I went running, showered, and have still been here for over an hour. When you left, I figured this was where you were coming. When I got here and you weren't here, I tried calling you. It went straight to voice mail."

"My phone's dead; it died on the way over here." I wanted to ask why Jentry had taken it upon himself to know where I was at all hours of the day, but his tone and expression kept the comments from escaping. He wasn't acting overprotective or bossy; he seemed genuinely worried and frustrated even though I was sitting right in front of him. "I didn't know you would try to get a hold of me."

He took a steadying breath in and clenched one of his hands into a fist before letting it relax.

"Jentry, what is wrong? I'm right here. I've been at the hospital this whole time. I do this almost every morning. I was in the parking lot reading on my car. I read and watch the sun rise."

"What's wrong is that my brother is lying on that fucking bed in a coma. The last time I called someone I love and it went straight to voice mail, he'd gone for a drive and ended up here." He blew out an exaggerated breath and scrubbed his hands over his face. When he spoke again, he sounded exhausted. "I just thought you would have been here. I couldn't think of anywhere else you would have gone that early in the morning. When you weren't here—when your phone . . ."

"I'm sorry," I whispered, and stood to walk over to him.

I hadn't even thought of doing it. I hadn't thought of moving toward him, into his arms. I was just there suddenly with my head pressed against chest and his arms wrapped around me, in a place I fit perfectly.

"I'm right here."

His chest moved with a silent laugh, and a weighted sigh left his lips. "I see that." I felt his lips pass across the top of my head before he released me and took a few steps away, and watched as he scrubbed his hands over his face again. "Now that I know you're okay, I need to step outside for a few minutes."

My lips twisted into a grimace. "I wish you'd stop."

One of Jentry's eyebrows rose, and that wicked smile I had missed so much crossed his face. "Are you sure about that?"

"Am I sure that I want you to stop smoking? Yes, Jentry, I'm sure. It's bad for you."

He stepped closer and placed his knuckles under my chin to tilt my head up. Once we were just an inch apart, he whispered, "You think I don't catch the way you take that first deep breath when you come near me? I already know you like the smell, Aurora; don't think I've forgotten."

My eyes widened in horror as I wondered if I did actually do that, then narrowed. "I still wish you'd stop. As you pointed out, Declan is lying right behind us in a coma. You've already been deployed four times and came back alive. Stop doing something stupid that could hurt or kill you." I hadn't meant for so much emotion to pour through my plea, and from the shocked look on Jentry's face, he hadn't expected it, either.

Seconds passed as Jentry studied my face. His thumb brushed against my lips once just before he dipped his head and stepped away. With one last look, he turned and walked out of the room.

I let out a shaky breath and turned to really look at Declan for the first time. "Morning, Dec," I whispered as I walked past him, trailing my fingers over his as I did.

I went to where my phone sat on the chair on the opposite side of the bed, and tapped on the screen until I was calling the familiar number, and listened as it rang and rang until Declan's voice mail filled my ear. My gaze shot over his still form as I listened to his voice, and when it ended, I hung up and pressed my fingers to his forehead.

"Where are you, Dec?" I curled my other hand around his and said, "I know you're lost, but you don't have to be. Just find your way back. Come back, okay?"

I sat back and started grabbing for my book, but paused when Jentry walked back in. My brow pinched in confusion, but he didn't say anything about coming back so quickly, just grabbed one of the other chairs and moved it so it was on the other side of Declan.

Before he could sit down, I noticed that the small bulge that was normally in his pocket from his cigarettes was gone, and that his intoxicating smell wasn't any stronger than when he'd left.

I dropped my head to hide my smile, and pulled my book out of my bag. Just before I began reading, I risked one more glance at Jentry, but he wasn't looking at me; he was watching Declan. His eyebrows were pulled together tightly as if he was lost in thought, but something about the look in his eyes made me worry about just what those thoughts were.

19

Present Day

❦

Aurora

"How long do you think my mom will last before she says something about you being at a family dinner?" Jentry asked in a teasing tone as we sat there staring at the hospital that evening.

I tightened my grip on the dish holding the precious dessert, and turned my head enough to attempt a glare in his direction, but my mouth kept twitching up into a smile at the reminder of Linda's not-so-subtle hints that I'd intruded on family time last month at the beach. Funny that I would miss *that* Linda, the one who ignored me the majority of the time because she'd heard me screaming her son's name in pleasure. But I did. I would give anything to have that Linda back rather than the one I'd faced the past weeks.

I took in a calming breath and held it for a few seconds

before releasing it, and eyed the entrance to the hospital warily. We'd been having family dinner at the hospital the last three Sundays so that we could eat near Declan—all part of Linda refusing to believe that there was anything wrong with him—and were there again.

Family dinners without Declan had been difficult to get through, made worse by the unwelcome feeling that radiated from his mother, but tonight's left a particularly anxious feeling in my stomach. Linda was setting me up to fail. I knew she was, and I knew I should avoid anything that would give her an opportunity to tear me down, but for some ridiculous reason I had played her game once again.

Some stupid, irrational part of my mind still craved her approval, I guessed.

Jentry and I had still been sitting in Declan's room that afternoon when Linda had texted me. She'd informed me that she expected me to redeem myself from my first "disastrous attempt" at making her white chocolate bread pudding, and Jentry had watched as dread and panic settled over my features once Linda's words had sunken in.

We had left my car in the hospital parking lot, and Jentry had driven me to the grocery store since my poor attempt at hiding my panic had him on edge, and he refused to let me out of his sight while he tried to figure out what was wrong.

But I'd remained tight-lipped, too nervous to do much more than make sure that this dessert was perfection in a casserole dish

He'd put it together that whatever was wrong had to do

with Linda, but I hadn't told him about what had happened at last week's family dinner with that same dessert. It felt wrong to bring Jentry into what was going on between Linda and me. I knew he would try to put a stop to it, knew he would get in the middle of it, and I couldn't do that to him.

Another calming breath, and I reached for the handle on the door. "Okay, let's go."

We walked into the hospital and down the halls toward the kitchen area, where we'd been setting up family dinners the last few weeks. Technically it was for staff only, but Linda usually got her way, and seeing as how she made enough for the staff to eat as well, they had always been willing to let us use it.

"Are you sure you don't want me to carry that?"

I pulled the dish closer to my body, and Jentry's husky laugh rumbled from his chest.

"Sorry I asked."

Kurt rounded the corner not far from us, and after a quick word, Jentry turned back around with him to go grab food out of the car.

My eyes darted around the kitchen area when I finally got there, and I bit back a curse when I realized Declan's sisters weren't there yet. With one last deep breath, I forced a smile on my face and said, "Hi, Linda!"

Linda looked over her shoulder from where she was setting up a stack of plates and silverware, and like I had just done, her eyes darted around the kitchen area. When she realized I was alone, she let out a huff. Her tone was curt. "Rorie."

I allowed my smile to falter for a second when she turned back around. "Uh, where would you like the dessert?"

"Good God, child, did you actually try again?" she drawled. "Well, bless your sweet little heart; at least no one can say that you give up easily. Should I give it another taste test, or just throw it in the trash now?"

"Why don't you tell me, and I'll save you the trouble?" I murmured back.

She turned fully this time to face me, her eyes wide and unblinking. "Excuse—what did you . . . ? How dare you speak to me that way. After everything I've done for you. After everything *you've* done to this family!"

I ground my teeth at the reminder.

Linda's eyes darted over my body, and she flicked her hand at me, almost as if she were shooing me away. "And what on God's earth are you wearing? There is no hope for you, Rorie Wilde. None. I've told you time and time again, in order to keep a man happy you need to be able to be the wife that God intended us, as women, to be. Wives need to know how to cook, clean, and raise the kids. And we need to take care of ourselves while doing it. You can't seem to manage taking care of yourself without all the rest of it added on."

She stepped quickly up to me and yanked the dessert from my hands, and though I was expecting her to either dig through it or toss it in the trash, she set it roughly on the counter and walked slowly back toward me.

I held her stare and waited, because I knew she wasn't done, and I knew she needed this. But as my body shook from the rage that had been building over the past three weeks, I had a feeling that I needed this, too. She could give me whatever she wanted, because I was ready to give it back. Because for the first time, it was just Linda and me. There was no one else in there to get roped into our feud or try to stop it.

She gave me a well-practiced sympathetic look, and her voice dropped. "You are just letting yourself go. I swear, every time I see you, you are getting pudgier and pudgier. Honey, my sweet boy ain't gonna want a wife who doesn't love herself enough to take care of her own body. And what's to keep his eye from going back to Madeline? She's Miss North Carolina, you know."

A humorless laugh trickled up my throat at the memory of Madeline's tiara from the day before. "Hard to forget."

Linda looked pointedly at my stomach for long seconds, clicking her tongue over and over again as she did, pretending as if I hadn't spoken. "I don't know how many times I can say it, but you need to do something," she finally said, then murmured, "I would say you shoulda worn a dress that maybe could have hid your stomach, but then you would have just looked like a confused little boy."

I had the strongest urge to suck in my stomach, but fought it. I knew there was nothing to suck in. I knew, once again, she was just doing this to be hateful and drive me crazy. My mind flashed back to the way Linda's words had made me feel so insecure when I'd seen Jessica the day before, and anger simmered in my veins.

I opened my mouth, but Linda spoke before I could.

"Honey, you're just fat, and we need to fix it!"

"What did you say?" Jentry said in low, terrifying tone from somewhere behind me.

The edge in his voice was enough to make Linda and me stiffen for a few seconds before Linda's head snapped up and she turned on her mom charm. "Oh, you know how ladies are, always standing around gossipin'. Go on now, son, just put the food anywhere."

He set the large dishes down on the counter closest to the door, then took slow steps toward us. "What the fuck did you just say," he demanded again; this time it was no longer a question.

"Jentry, don't," I pleaded as he neared us.

"Young man!" Linda said in a horrified tone. "I am so very disappointed in what has come out of your mouth this weekend. I raised yo—"

"Raised me better? Is that what you were going to say?" Jentry huffed as he took the last few steps to place himself between us.

"Really, *don't*," I said through clenched teeth, and rocked forward so I could reach for his arm to pull him away, but he held a hand out behind him to stop me.

When he continued speaking, his dangerous tone was laced with disappointment. "In a few days I've seen more than enough from you to know that you aren't the woman who raised me. The woman who raised me wasn't so threatened by her son's girlfriend that she'd pretend she wasn't there. The woman who raised me wasn't so heartless that she'd tear down the same girl every chance she got just because she was hurting. We're all hurting. Rorie's fucking hurting, too."

"She has ruined this family!" Linda seethed; her entire frame shook from her anger.

Jentry took a step back toward me. His hand was still outstretched, but now looked like it was reaching for me. "You know, I've been going crazy trying to figure some things out since I got home, but I'm starting to put a lot together just from this conversation. The woman who raised me also taught me to respect women. And I do. I respect women who deserve it, and *Rorie* does. Because she loves Declan, too. She's grieving, too. And throughout everything you've done, she's never said a word. She wouldn't tell me what you were doing even when I figured out that it was you, and when I did, she said it was deserved. What kind of woman makes a girl think she deserves the bullshit you've put her through?"

Jentry grabbed on to my forearm and pulled me close to him as he took another step back, away from Linda, toward the door leading out of the kitchen area.

Linda watched our movements with a mixture of emotions. There was shock and hurt at Jentry's words, but whenever her eyes flickered back in my direction, anger unlike anything I'd yet to see from her burned there.

Jentry turned us around and came to a halt when we found Kurt standing just inside the doorway holding two dishes, staring at us in shock and confusion.

"Do you want to tell me why you're talking to your mother that way?" he asked.

Jentry's head tilted to the side. "No."

"No?" Kurt's tone was rougher and rang with authority as Jentry began leading us out of the room.

"No," Jentry confirmed. "Because if I tell you now, I'm gonna say a lot that I'll regret."

Jentry never once released me as he hurried us down the halls of the hospital, and didn't speak though I tried to get him to countless times.

"Do you understand why I never wanted to tell you? I didn't want you involved!

"She's your mom, Jentry! She's angry, and she needs someone to take it out on."

I looked around us in surprise when we were suddenly in Declan's room, and sucked in a sharp inhale when Jentry released me just as abruptly, causing me to stumble over myself.

He hissed a curse and caught me. "I'm sorry, I'm sorry." Once I was steadied, he released me and scrubbed his hands over his face as he turned to pace in the room. His body was vibrating from his anger, and his dark eyes were filled with a deep disappointment that made me ache for him.

"Jentry . . ."

"You should have told me."

"No, I shouldn't have. This is between Linda and me."

He stopped pacing and gestured toward Declan's bed. "It doesn't matter what happened to Declan, Aurora. What I walked in on should have never been said. What she did with Madeline yesterday should have never been done. The guest room—I already fucking figured it out. And you'd just let that go?"

A weighted huff forced from my chest, and it felt like I deflated. "No, but what could I do? I told you, it's deserved—"

"It's not," he said through gritted teeth.

"—I've known that she needed someone to be angry with. But at first, it was just . . . I don't know, it wasn't that bad. In the last week it's gotten a lot worse, and in the last week I've had a lot more trouble holding back from saying anything to her."

"You shouldn't hold back!"

"You don't understand!" I nearly yelled, and paused to take a few calming breaths. "Jentry, you don't understand. Please try to grasp the fact that to me it has *felt* deserved, and know that every time Linda has said anything to me, there has been at least one other person with us. Holly and Lara, Madeline, Taylor . . . always someone. We've never been alone for more than a minute at a time. Someone always comes in. You and Kurt came in the night you moved back. She left the room when you left us in the guest room. You walked in just now. And I do not want other people to be pulled into what is going on between Linda and me. Can you understand that?"

A muscle ticked in his jaw, and his eyes shut as he dropped his head. He rubbed at the back of his neck for a second before nodding. "Yes, but you should have made it a point to get her alone long before now. I've seen more than enough in just a few days, and you already went through it all as if it wasn't new—as if it just kept adding more weight to your shoulders. And from what I heard today, what she said to you, she's *been* saying to you. You should have put an end to it when it first began."

"It's not that simple." The exhaustion of the past three weeks was evident in my voice, and my body shook with the need to sit down, as if the weight of every emotion during that time had built up and was now crashing down on me. "You forget that she's your mom . . . she's Declan's mom. You forget what we're going through."

Jentry suddenly ate up the distance between us in long strides, and captured my face in his hands, holding me as if I were breakable.

My breath escaped me, and my hands automatically clung to his forearms to keep myself standing.

"I haven't forgotten, but it doesn't fucking excuse what she's said," he said.

Hard and soft. Always.

His piercing black eyes roamed my face and fell across my lips over and over again. Even though I knew I should pull away, even though Declan was lying just a few feet away from us, I was silently pleading with him to press his mouth to mine.

"You are beautiful, Aurora," Jentry said. Just like it did every time he said it, something stirred in me listening to his deep voice say my name. The way it rolled off his tongue like a caress, and each time a breath softer than the rest of his words, made me crave to hear it again. "There is no part of you that isn't beautiful. Don't ever let anyone make you think otherwise—especially Linda Veil. Do you understand?"

I hesitated, then nodded slowly, still trapped in the haze that his eyes always put me in.

"Beautiful Aurora," he whispered, as if to himself, then slowly stepped away from me. Then, as if he was unable to stop himself, he reached back out and cupped his hand around the base of my neck. In a move too quick to stop—not that I would have tried—he pressed his mouth to my jaw, then turned and left.

Jentry

Though I tried to push it away, my frustration at the situation only built with each step, and by the time I stormed through the door to the kitchen area again, my entire body was vibrating with barely controlled anger.

"Mom!" I barked when I spotted her going on as if nothing had just happened. My adopted sisters and their husbands were there now, and she was entertaining them as if it were just another night.

"Jentry, honey!" Mom called out after a quick look behind me to make sure I'd come in alone. "Come make a plate."

"Are you kidding?"

Mom dramatically held a hand to her chest and let out a low gasp, like she was offended by the few words I'd said.

Considering it didn't compare to what I'd said just minutes ago, I didn't buy it.

After Dad received a pointed look from Mom, he turned

and stared me down. "Now, I don't know what's going on with you today, but you can't just go running out of here, then come storming back in with that kind of attitude. You may have been gone for a long time, and things might be a little tense right now, but we are still your parents, and this is still family dinner. You will treat it as such, and treat us with respect."

I scoffed, and didn't take my eyes from Mom as I replied to him, "I told her that I respect women who deserve it. Last I heard, she didn't."

"I beg your pardon!" Mom drawled.

"I can't believe Declan let all that time pass without saying a word to you about the way you were ignoring Rorie, and I can't believe she let you treat her the way you have been the past few weeks. Who the hell do you think you are trying to ruin her life when it's already been destroyed?" I yelled, and Dad took a step toward me.

"Watch your mouth, young man, that is your mother."

"Fat," I stated with a grave laugh. "Mom's been making Rorie think she's fat. A girl who could stand to gain weight. She tried to make her think that Dec would go running back to Madeline—fucking *Madeline* of all people—because Rorie was letting herself go." I turned my glare at Mom again. "Are you out of your goddamn mind?"

For once, Dad didn't have anything to say to me. He just turned to look at Mom with a questioning look.

She looked horrified—no, worse; she looked like *I* was hurting her.

"Mom took all the stuff out of Rorie's guest room so that

it was completely bare when I moved home, and then the next morning brought it all back and acted as if she had bought it. And that's only what I've figured out in the days that I've been home. But I know that this shit has been going on since Dec's accident."

"Language, Jentry," Dad said in warning, then asked softly, "Linda, is this true?"

Mom instantly burst into tears. After a few loud sobs, she calmed enough to ask me, "How can't you see it? How can't you see what that girl is doing to our family? First Declan, and now you? I'm losing my boys because of that trash!"

"You didn't fucking lose Declan because of her. It was an accident! But you will lose me if you keep treating her the way you have been. Rorie is the— God, Mom she has the best heart, and you're treating her like she's evil!"

She threw her hands out and gestured around. "Look at what she's done to us! She is! All I've ever done is try to be there for her, to help her, and she goes off spreading these wild tales to turn what remains of my family against me."

"She hasn't said shit, and that's why you've gotten away with it until now!"

"Jentry," Dad said in a sharp tone, but Holly spoke up.

"Mom, you weren't nice to her at the family dinner last week. We were all there; we heard and saw everything. You continued to criticize and tear her down, then dumped her entire dessert in the trash."

A bitter laugh sounded in my throat as Aurora's panic that afternoon finally made sense.

Dad let out a slow, disappointed sigh and dropped his head to stare at the floor.

"I heard what you said yesterday about Declan and Madeline, Mom, and I let it go then because she begged me to and because I didn't know it was this bad. But this?" Exhaustion and disappointment dripped from every word when I said, "I've watched her destroy herself in the small time I've been home because of you, and I'm done. I'm so fucking done." I turned to leave, but just before I walked out of the room, I warned Mom, "Don't go near her again."

20
Present Day

Aurora

The look on Jentry's face when he walked back into Declan's hospital room a few minutes later made me wish that this night could have gone a dozen other ways, just so long as he would have never had to see that side of Linda.

He shut the door roughly behind him, and groaned as he ran his hands over his head and down his face. I watched as frustration and tension poured from him from where I sat next to Declan, but didn't say anything, just tried to give him his space in the small room.

He stood facing away from me with his fingers laced together on top of his head. His body vibrated subtly despite the way he was methodically breathing, trying to calm himself.

After a couple of minutes, he spoke low, but didn't turn

around. "You said everyone eats in here during family dinners?"

"Yes," I said warily.

"Then I should go. I don't think it would be a good idea for me to be in a room with my mom right now."

I sighed dejectedly. "Jentry, I don't want this for you. It's something that Linda and I will have to talk out one day, but I don't want it to affect your relationship."

His head shook as he turned to look at me. "Just trust me when I say it wouldn't be good for us to be in the same room right now. Not after what I just said to her."

I opened my mouth, ready to tell him that she would probably get over what he had said, but then a sinking feeling hit me. My face fell and I inhaled audibly.

There was no fresh wave of that intoxicating scent I loved but had come to hate.

"Jentry, no . . ." I trailed off, my voice barely above a breath.

My eyes lingered on the angry set of his face, and the way his body twitched with his aggravation, worse now than when he'd walked in. I had thought when he'd left that he was going to smoke and had only just remembered that he'd thrown away his cigarettes that morning.

"Jentry, what'd you do?" I asked, my voice just as soft.

His head tilted to the side, as if he was preparing for me—or maybe daring me—to get upset by what he was about to say. "She had to know that what she was doing wasn't okay."

"No . . . Jentry, no. I told you that it was between her and me!"

"Aurora, I can't know about this and not say anything!" He swung his arm out toward the door as he said, sneering, "I walked into that room and she acted like nothing had just happened. *To me,* she acted like that *to me.* Which tells me that she had no intention of stopping any of that bullshit because she didn't feel bad for it. I don't know if what I said will even make a difference, but she needed to know that people are aware of what she is doing."

"But they were never supposed to be!" I said, my voice louder than I intended for it to be.

"I get it, Aurora, I swear to God I do. This needs to end with the two of you—and I'll gladly let it," he said, closing the distance between us as he spoke. "But whether or not you wanted other people to be pulled in, Mom's been pulling people in by letting them be around when she's said things to you, and for whatever reason, they've let it go on, too."

I knew he was right. I knew I needed to be thankful that he had stood up to Linda for me when no one else had. But I never would have wanted *this.* I never would have wanted Jentry to stand up to his mom, of all people.

His voice dropped and his dark eyes stared into mine. "Aurora, I love you. You can't expect me to see you hurt and not do something about it. You hurt, I hurt."

A warm shiver danced up my spine at his words, and without thinking, I reached out for him.

At the last second before my hand could touch Jentry's, his eyes flickered behind me and widened, his body stilled.

When he spoke, his tone was a mixture of disbelief and shock. "Dec?"

I whirled around in my chair to find bloodshot green eyes staring at us in confusion. "Declan?" My tone matched Jentry's, and then melted into a whispered cry. "Dec!" I reached for his hand as tears began falling down my face, and I choked out a cry when his fingers slowly curled around mine. "Dec, you're in the hospital, but everything's fine. You're going to be fine." My words were muffled by my sobs, but my words couldn't have been truer. For the first time, I *knew* he was going to be fine.

"No, no! Don't!" I pled when he reached for his breathing tube, his confusion bleeding into panic. "Just leave it."

Jentry was already rushing out of the room, and I vaguely heard him yelling something before his voice trailed away. Seconds later, two nurses came hurrying in and talking quickly, and I was being pulled away from Declan and pushed out of the room by one of them.

"Wait, I need to be in there!"

"We'll inform you when you can come back in, sweetie," the woman said sternly. "You know how this goes; please wait in the waiting area."

I stood there in shock for an unknown amount of time as I tried to figure out what to do. In that time, a doctor walked calmly into Declan's room, and I heard the three people talking loudly. To Declan or each other, I wasn't sure. All I could focus on was the fact that Declan had woken up.

I finally turned and began walking down the hall in the direction of the waiting area, and halfway there, heard a bunch of people talking frantically, and numerous hard, quick steps. I turned another corner and saw Jentry and the Veils nearly running toward me.

Their voices rose when they saw me, and Jentry broke away from them to get to me first.

"What happened? Why are you out here?" he asked quickly, and reached for me.

The way his long hands wrapped tenderly around my arms seemed to ground me enough to remember how to speak or discern time, but the excitement that hung in the hallway made it so that neither Jentry nor I realized that we shouldn't be standing so close. That he shouldn't be holding me.

"I don't know. Nurses came in and told me I had to leave. A doctor went in. They said we had to stay in the waiting room until they came and got us."

"Did something go wrong?" someone asked urgently in the Veil group.

My head shook quickly. "No, no. They just came in."

"I told them his eyes were open," Jentry added just as fast.

"His eyes followed you," I said, and looked back up at Jentry. "His eyes followed you. And then they were watching me. He curled his hand around mine. He's really awake. He's awake."

Jentry crushed me in an embrace that felt as though it should have lasted for the rest of time.

But eventually it ended, as all things do. As more things would. Because Declan being awake meant more than just finally having him back. It meant we would have to relive that night. It meant that whenever Declan decided to announce it, the rest of the family would know about my past with Jentry. Would know that I had turned down Declan's proposal and had planned to leave him. Would know that I was in love with someone else entirely, but someone just as close to the rest of them.

And as we all waited anxiously for the chance to see Declan again, I knew Jentry had realized the same thing. His eyes kept flashing over to mine, worry set deep there, and anxiety radiating from his body.

When we were finally allowed back to see Declan, Jentry kept himself close enough to me that if he reached out, he'd be able to touch me, but far enough away that when Declan saw us again, it wouldn't look like we were together.

The doctor was explaining things to the family, but I wasn't hearing him. I was watching Declan watch me with a blank expression. For a while, I wondered if he didn't know who I was at all, but after a few minutes of staring at me, he turned his hand over, palm up.

I stepped closer and slid my hand into his, and marveled again when his fingers immediately curled around mine.

"Hey, Dec," I said softly. "Glad you found your way back."

He didn't speak—I wasn't sure if he even could—just continued to watch me blankly.

His family spoke to him around us, but he never looked

away from me or acknowledged in any way that there was anyone else there.

I looked uneasily up at Jentry, and his dark eyes glanced over to me for a second before darting back to Declan.

I followed his line of sight when Dec tapped on my finger, and smiled down at him. "What is it, Dec?"

His face pinched in pain as he worked his throat a few times, and I heard his mom and sisters gasp in surprise when he spoke. "Ring."

My eyes widened and mouth fell open in amazement at hearing his voice. "What?"

"Where's your ring?" he croaked.

I glanced down to look at the finger he'd been tapping on, and his question finally made sense. Sort of. I stared at the third finger of my left hand for long seconds, and looked at Jentry again to see him watching us in confusion and horror as he caught on to what Declan was asking, and what he thought.

"We're engaged," Declan said roughly, slowly. "Aren't we?"

21

Present Day

Aurora

My stomach fell and the air in my lungs forced out with a rush, the rest of the family went silent and still. I stared at Declan's green eyes, knowing my expression must have matched Jentry's in that moment. I had to have looked horrified.

What was I supposed to say to him when he had just woken up from being in a coma for more than three weeks? How was I supposed to tell him that we weren't engaged when he obviously, clearly remembered asking me, and he had *just woken up*?

I don't know how much time passed after his question, but I was thankfully saved from answering at that moment when a nurse came in.

"I know this is a very exciting time, but there are some

things we need to do. I can allow one or two of you to stay for a while, but not all of you."

Even if Linda hadn't spoken up in that moment, I knew she and Kurt would have been the ones to stay. This was their son.

"I'll be back," I promised Declan, and slowly slid my hand from his. Running my hand over his forehead, I whispered, "I'm so happy you came back."

I kept my eyes on the floor and managed to keep the horrified cry from escaping my chest until I was out of his room and around the corner.

Jentry was there, as he always was. He wrapped an arm around my waist and pulled me close against him when my knees weakened and it got too hard to stay standing.

"Don't," I protested weakly when he turned me around and his free hand slid up to cradle my face. Someone could walk around the corner at any second, and then—of all times— wasn't the time to have to explain about us. But any objection I might have had fled my mind when I looked up.

His face was etched with pain and the confusion I felt, but he still pulled me against his hard body. His hands were holding me like I was breakable, but he was clenching his jaw like it was taking all his strength to refrain from making me his again.

Hard and soft, I thought, then let myself get lost in his eyes. Those dark eyes seemed to look straight into my soul.

"What was I supposed to say?" The words tumbled from my lips before I could stop them, but from the slight shift in

Jentry's expression, I knew he'd been expecting them, and didn't have an answer for me, either.

"We're going to get through this," he said so softly that I wasn't sure if I just thought I could hear his voice. "Let's just focus on the fact that he's awake; we'll figure out everything later."

I wanted to. I wanted to go back to how it had been during the hours we'd waited to see Declan again after he'd first woken. The excitement that had been thrumming through the waiting room had been palpable, making the nervousness coming from Jentry and me get lost as it wove its way between the two of us.

I wanted that excitement back. I wanted to fall to the floor and thank God for helping Declan find his way home.

But the only thing running through my head now was that we had so much more to worry about than Declan publicizing my past with Jentry. Telling Declan about Jentry had been hard enough the first time; I couldn't imagine doing it again. And this time, it would be done while Declan thought we were engaged.

"He thinks we're engaged," I mumbled needlessly.

Jentry's face pinched slightly, but smoothed out as he brushed his thumb over my cheek. "Yeah. That's something we'll have to figure out." He exhaled through his nose slowly, then asked, "After everything that's happened in the past few weeks, have you changed your mind?"

My face fell and chest constricted. "What? I don't . . . what?"

"Losing someone—or almost losing them—can make you realize what they mean to you."

"Jentry . . ."

"If that's how you've felt with Declan, if you've regretted not saying yes to him, then this might be good for you."

Seconds slipped by while I stared at him in shock. "Are you honestly asking me this right now? Are you really standing here trying to figure out if I want to be with him?" I gently pushed away from Jentry and backed up a couple of steps until I was pressed against the hallway wall.

His brow furrowed in frustration as he watched me, but I knew it was frustration with himself. He rubbed at his jaw in the way he did when he was wasting a few seconds in order to calm down, then said gruffly, "You can't fault me for asking. I know you loved him—I know you still do. I can see it, and it wasn't like I expected you to stop. You were the one who was here for him the most, and I know it wasn't out of guilt or obligation."

"And so in your mind that all translates to me thinking I made a mistake?" I asked.

"No, but I have to give you that chance. You struggled to choose between us once because you were with him, and now things have changed. The last thing I want is for you to feel stuck between Declan and me again *because* of me."

"You are so stupid, Jentry Michaels," I whispered slowly. "Do you have any idea how much—" I abruptly stopped when Lara rounded the corner.

"There you two are," she said. "The nurse said that they

weren't going to allow visitors for the rest of the night so Declan could try to rest once Mom and Dad leave the room. We already packed up all of the food and we'll drop it off at Mom's on our way home unless you want to take it back to your apartment."

I glanced at Jentry for guidance, and watched as he shook his head.

"We're fine without it. Do you know what they're doing in there?" he asked, and nodded in the direction of Declan's room.

Lara shrugged, but smiled with relief. "No. They said there would be someone here working with him starting tomorrow to make sure he remembers everything, even how to eat. It'll be a process, but at least he's awake now."

We both murmured our agreements as she hugged us good-bye. Once she rounded the corner, I spoke before Jentry could. "We should go home."

The hospital wasn't the place to continue talking, and now that the majority of the stress and worries from the past weeks was gone, I was exhausted and wanted to try to relax before my first day of school the next day.

Jentry didn't respond other than turning to leave when I did, and remained quiet all the way through the parking lot.

We came up on my car where I had parked it early that morning, and I wondered at how everything that had happened that day had been forced into just one day. It felt like it had been days since I'd sat on the trunk reading, not hours.

Jentry held my door open as I slid into my car, and studied me with the same expression he'd worn when watching Declan after he'd woken.

I reached out to press my hand to his chest and whispered, "Whatever you're thinking, stop."

His mouth twitched up into a brief smile as his eyes searched mine. "Be safe. I'll see you soon."

I watched him walk toward his car before I pulled out of the parking space and heading to the apartment, but Jentry wasn't there when I arrived.

I changed into sleep shorts and a tank top and fixed my hair back into another mess of blond waves on top of my head, but there was no way for me to relax. I'd expected Jentry to be there, and after our short and confusing conversation in the hallway of the hospital, I was worried about why he wasn't. A half an hour after I had gotten home he still wasn't back.

I paced nervously through the living room as I tried to hold off calling him, and had almost given in when I heard a key in the lock.

I rushed to open the door before Jentry could, and was already reprimanding him before it was fully opened. "Just this morning you nearly lost your mind because I wasn't where you—" I cut off quickly when I found Jentry weighed down with bags. When I spoke again, I was calmer. "After what we went through this morning, you didn't think to let me know that you weren't coming home?"

Another twitch of his lips for a brief, apologetic smile. "I'm sorry, but I brought dinner since we didn't eat."

I grabbed the bags of food from his left hand when he shifted his body to hide what was in his right, and turned to go sort out everything in the kitchen.

My body tingled when he entered the kitchen behind me, but unlike so many times before, I allowed myself a quick glance over my shoulder to look at him. "Thank you for the food."

He dipped his head and looked away. "I don't know how much time you'll have now that you're going to be working . . ." I listened as his footsteps approached where I was standing. "But I noticed you were almost done with that book you've been reading, and I wanted to make sure you had something for the mornings."

I turned, my face was already pinched in confusion, but quickly morphed into excitement when he held out the next two, and final, books in the series I was reading. "Jentry," I whispered in amazement as I stepped forward to take the books from him. "Thank you. Wait—how did you know?"

He gave me an amused look. "You've been reading that book since I got home."

"Right, no, that's not what I—" I shook my head and exhaled quickly as I tried to steady my thoughts. "But you've seen my boxes of books. How did you know that I didn't already have these?"

Jentry just watched me for a few moments, then lifted an eyebrow in response.

At that look, my eyes narrowed in suspicion. "I understand you are always taking in your surroundings and don't miss much—if anything—but those books are in my closet," I reminded him.

He didn't falter.

"Good to know," I whispered mostly to myself, then studied the books in my hands again. "Thank you, Jentry. This is—this is incredibly sweet of you, even if I do find it creepy that you've probably searched my closet and drawers."

"I wouldn't go that far," he said with a short laugh, "but I do want to know why you buy physical books."

I shot him a confused look as I set the books down and walked toward the food again. "I like being able to hold the books," I said slowly, not understanding why it mattered.

"But then you just store them away in your closet."

"Oh," I said when it finally made sense. "Uh, well, when we moved in here, I couldn't find shelves that I liked that I could afford. Besides, I have these very specific shelves in mind, and couldn't find anything that came close to them. I tried leaving some of the books out around the apartment. . . ." I stopped short of telling him how much Linda had hated it. "It just didn't look right."

He nodded slowly as he looked around the living room and I went back to divvying up the food.

"So what will you be doing while I'm gone all day?"

"Searching your closet," he said immediately.

A smile spread slowly across my face as I shook my head. "Anything else?"

The energy in the kitchen shifted as he walked toward me and leaned his back against the counter once he was next to me. "I want to go through the police academy. I'll start looking into when the next class begins, what I need to do."

I blinked quickly in surprise. "You do?"

My surprise caught Jentry off guard. "Is that not something that Dec ever mentioned?" When I shook my head, he continued. "That was always my plan. Go into the Marine Corps, then become a police officer."

"Why such dangerous jobs? Are you one of those people who like to do life-threatening things, like skydiving?"

He laughed, but his face was serious. "No, uh . . . no, that's not me. I just want to protect people."

"I see that," I said softly, and my cheeks burned with frustration with the man next to me. "Jentry, what you said back at the hospital—"

"You didn't understand why I wanted you—"

"I do," I disagreed, cutting him off. "I do. You want me to be sure I'm making the right choice. There's been the time of having you gone, and then time thinking we were all going to lose Declan, and throughout both of those, I was choosing someone. But from day one, it was never a choice with you, it was a need." My cheeks burned even hotter. "There is nothing without you, Jentry. You told me yesterday that you fell in love with me that first night; is it so impossible to believe that I did the same?"

I could tell from his expression that he wanted my words to be true. "But Declan—"

"—would never be you. On paper, he's perfect for me, but I still tried to force him to be you nearly every day of our relationship. In nearly a year, I have never felt for him a fraction of what I feel for you." I placed my hand on his cheek and said, "For a time, things are going to be about Declan. They have to, even more now that he's awake, and I know you know that and agree with it. Nothing can be about us right now, and like I told you yesterday, being close to you physically makes remembering that too difficult, but don't for one second think that I will ever stop needing, wanting, or choosing you."

Jentry

I watched Aurora walk to her room that night after we quickly finished our dinner. My arms stayed folded tightly across my chest so I wouldn't reach out for her and bring her back to me as she turned from my sight. I lingered there for a second before turning and walking slowly toward the guest room in the apartment, letting the day wash over me.

Mom's hatefulness toward the girl I love.

Declan waking up.

Aurora. Always Aurora.

I rubbed at the back of my neck, hoping to relieve some of the tension there, and loosed a slow breath as I entered the hallway. My footsteps slowed, then stopped.

The guest room door was cracked and the light was on. I had left the door closed and light off. I always did with my rooms.

My breaths slowed to a stop so I could listen to every little

sound around me, and within seconds, awareness slid over
my skin like a disease. I hissed out a curse as my hands automatically curled into fists and my body began vibrating with
frustration and expectation.

"How the hell did you get in here?" I asked, then slowly
turned my head to glance over my shoulder.

Jess lifted an eyebrow as if she didn't understand why I
hadn't expected her, then shouldered past me to walk into the
room.

Once I had followed her in there and shut the door, she
let out a long, dramatic sigh that ended with a psychotic-
sounding laugh. "This is incredible. Really, I don't know what
to do with myself now that I have this information." She ad-
mired her nails as she plopped down on the bed and made
herself comfortable. "How long has this been going on, Jent?
Because it sounded like it was longer than the few days that
you've been home."

"What are you doing here, Jessica, and how did you get in
here?"

She rolled her eyes and grumbled, "Fine, boring questions
first. I told you I needed a place to stay for a—"

"You said that yesterday."

"And I found a place to sleep last night . . . obviously." Her
lips curved up in a slow grin and her eyes faded to somewhere
other than this room. "But the invitation wasn't open for tonight. So here I am. And do you really need to ask how I got
in here? How do I get in anywhere, Jentry?" she asked, but I
knew the question was rhetorical, so I kept my mouth firmly

shut. "I got bored waiting for you when Little Miss Perfect came strolling in here, but then you finally came back, and boy oh boy did I get an earful."

The way she laughed maniacally set me on edge; always had. It reminded me of our mother. Of *her* mother.

Once Jessica stopped laughing, she speared me with an excited look, and her face contorted as her smile twisted into something sinister. "How you feelin', Jent? You worried about what I know? Worried about what I'll say? Worried about how dear ol' Declan will react when he finds out about you and his precious girlfriend?" She spouted off her questions softly, but rapidly, and I could see it in her expression that she was getting excited about the prospect of pissing me off. "You gettin' mad? I bet you are. You feel it? It's inside you, always inside you. Does your precious *Rorie* know about your sickness?" she asked, sneering Aurora's name. "Does she know how you'll ruin her?"

Despite the anger coursing through me, I didn't move or speak. I knew it was what Jessica wanted, and I refused to give it to her. But as she continued to taunt me, I no longer heard her words, but our mother's . . . and soon those words turned into my own.

Words I had said a year ago to Aurora, words that had never been truer, and words that had haunted me more than ever in the last few days.

"I see it, I see you getting mad. What does it feel like?" Her eyes widened in anticipation, and I wanted to throttle her for it.

She always asked what it felt like, and every time it made me feel worse than ever. Made me feel dirty somehow.

"Come on, Jent, hit something," she goaded, and her excitement slowly faded when I forced my arms over my chest.

"Let me guess: don't want the precious Rorie to hear? What is it about this bitch anyway? I don't see anything special about her. She looks like a doe-eyed freak." Jessica scoffed and went back to studying her nails. "What Declan ever saw in her . . ." She trailed off and shook her head.

Breathe in. Breathe out.

Breathe in. Breathe out.

My jaw was starting to ache from clenching it so tight, but I knew I needed to fake my calm until she left. "You need to leave, Jess. You know when you can come back."

She let out a soft, melodic laugh with just a hint of madness woven through it. "Why, you don't want to be seen with me? Don't want Rorie to know about me? Too late, Jent. Besides, I have nowhere else to go."

"I'm sure you can find somewhere."

"Like Declan's bed? I'm sure he needs company now that he's awake," she hinted suggestively, and for the umpteenth time since finding Jessica in the apartment, I forced myself not to lash out at her. "And I bet he's gonna need *all kinds* of company once he finds out that you've been taking care of his girl for a long, long time."

I shut my eyes briefly as I focused on just breathing, and rubbed roughly at my jaw. "*Out.*" My demand came out louder than I meant it to, but no less harsher.

She pouted pathetically and sprawled out on my bed, as if she had no intention of leaving. "You said I could always come to you."

"Yeah, and you know when. Now is not the time; you're only coming here to piss me off. Go back to your house."

"What house?" she asked bitterly, giving me the first glimpse of something other than the chaos that our mother had engrained in her.

"Where are you staying?"

"What does it matter? You don't care!" she mocked, but like a light had been flipped on, that wicked smile came back, and she swayed as she sat up on the bed and sang, "As long as we stay away from you, nothing can go wrong in Jentry's perfect world because he's in denial of who he is and what's inside him."

"When you want help, I'll fucking help you, Jess. But you don't want help! You want money when you don't get enough from whoring yourself around, or because you spend too much on drugs for Mom," I hissed as I closed the distance to the bed. "So until then, get the fuck away from me. I've tried to help you too many times, and in return, all you do is try to ruin what's in my life before you take off running again."

She lurched forward until there were only inches between us, and eyes as dark as mine glared back at me. "Me ruin your life?" She laughed haughtily and shoved her hand against my chest. "You ruin everything you touch, Jentry. Don't forget that. You see your best friend lying in that hospital? What was that I heard tonight about why he got in the accident in the first place?" She smiled knowingly, then sneered, "That's what I thought. You had a hand in that, didn't you? How long until your so-called family knows about that, huh? And how long until Little Miss Perfect isn't so perfect because you've destroyed her?"

"Leave," I said on a growl. "Now."

She shouldered past me as she got off the bed, and turned as she reached the door. "I'll be waiting to watch you burn in your own flames, *brother.*"

I followed her out of the room, and my stomach dropped when I saw Aurora standing halfway across the living room with a look of shock on her face.

"Well, well, well," Jessica began, but I cut her off.

"Jess." Her name rumbled in my chest and shouted its warning, but Jessica had never cared about my warnings. She had always pushed against them, hoping to watch me explode.

"If it isn't the cheating whore herself—"

"Fucking leave!" My voice boomed through the apartment, and I caught a glimpse of Aurora jerking away from the sound just before Jessica started on a fit of uncontrollable, frantic laughter.

"I just wanted to meet her." She jutted out her bottom lip in a mock pout, then let her mouth curve into a wry grin. "After all, *Rorie* and I have taken a trip or two around the same cock."

"Jessica!"

She lifted her hands in surrender, and giggled. "I meant block. Watch out for this one," Jess said to Aurora in a sing-song voice as she continued backward toward the front door, swaying and pointing at me the whole time. "He's a bomb, and he's about to go boom!"

I slammed the door shut as soon as she was outside, muffling her last words, and stood there staring at the door as my body shook with a rage that Jessica always brought with her.

Minutes passed with my back still to Aurora, my hands on the door as if Jessica might come barging through even though I'd locked it, before Aurora spoke. "What . . . what just happened? I heard you yelling and was coming to see what was going on, and that's when I heard her, and then you were walking out of the room."

"I told you to promise me that if you ever saw her again you would stay away from her. She's crazy. You saw a glimpse. Literally, a *glimpse* of what she can be like."

"Why was she here?" Aurora's hand pressed to my shuddering back, and I let out a harsh breath at her touch. "Jesus, Jentry, why are you shaking?"

I turned and looked at her confused and worried face, and wanted nothing more than to take her into my arms and assure her that everything would be fine. But I couldn't. Not after what had just happened, and not after Aurora had told me just an hour before that being close to me was too difficult.

I ran my hands over my face as I groaned, and tried to calm myself. "She was already here when we got back. She was here when you got back. I don't know how she got in, but she has a knack for sneaking into places."

Aurora looked horrified, but there was no point in lying to her about Jessica.

"This is what she does. She sneaks into where I live and waits so she can talk to me. That's how she'd always done it until I went into the Marine Corps, then she started stealing my number from Declan's phone."

My explanation seemed to remind her of something. Her blue eyes searched my face and her mouth opened and shut twice before she hesitantly asked, "What did she mean . . . what did she mean about—just, what did she mean?"

My head shook slowly. "She said a lot, Aurora. You have to give me more than that."

"She *is* your twin," she stated, as though she was confirming. When I nodded, she blew out a harsh breath. "Then I'm going to assume that whole part after she said she 'wanted to meet me' had to do with Declan, unless she just said it because she thought it would upset me."

I watched her expression closely as I confirmed, "They have a past."

Instead of looking hurt, Aurora's face showed disgust. "I might actually prefer Madeline for once."

If I hadn't still been shaking from the aftermath of my sister, I might have laughed. "Declan didn't know who Jessica was at the time. He hadn't seen her in about ten years because if Jess came looking for me before then, she made sure none of the Veils were around. I—" I quickly cut off from telling her too much at that time, then said, "It didn't go over well when

I found out. He's avoided her ever since, but that doesn't mean she's stopped searching him out."

Aurora nodded, but she didn't seem to realize she was doing it. "Is she dangerous?"

"No. She wants money, but she won't just take it. She'll wait until you give it to her, because she knows that *we* know she'll just keep showing up until we do give her money. What she really wants is attention, but she won't hurt anyone or steal anything. But the way her mind works, Aurora, there's no talking to her like a normal person. It's like trying to reason with someone with multiple personalities, even though they are completely sane."

She looked at me blankly. "I don't—I don't understand."

I hesitated for a second, then said, "I can't explain it all right now. Just know there's no way to keep her out of here, but if you see her, stay away from her. She'll get into your head and I can't let that happen. But, Aurora, she was here tonight, so she knows about what led to Dec's accident, she knows about us, and she will do *anything* if it will make me mad."

Her face slowly fell as she backed up a step, and then another. When her eyes met mine again, she breathed one simple word that seemed to fit this situation so well. "Shit."

"Yeah."

PART V

That Night . . .

H<small>E RELEASED HIS</small> hold on my hair, and let his hand trail down as I leaned forward to place my hands flat on the wall. The touch was soft and caressing, and my body came alive as I waited for the hardness that I knew would soon follow. Because it had to follow.

"Not a sound," he reminded me.

I looked over my shoulder at him, and nodded. I kept my eyes locked with his as I waited. I'd known he was trouble the second I'd seen him downstairs—his body screamed it. But his handsome face, which had hinted at the bad boy underneath, had transformed here in the bedroom. Control made him intoxicating to look at.

He pushed slowly into me, and I bit back a whimper. I'd thought before was incredible, but feeling him in this position was all new and too much. Too deep, too full. It was taking my breath away in the most erotic way. His hands moved over my hips, and his fingers tightened against the skin there before releasing. With that wicked grin, he pulled out just as slowly, and I cried out when he slammed into me again and again.

I dropped my head between my arms and clawed uselessly at the wall as I tried to hang on. I felt it building deep inside me, and stopped clawing at the wall to push against it, and closer to him. Each stroke felt deeper than the last; each felt like it was taking me to a place higher and higher—and soon I was going to fall.

"Oh God!" I hissed when he grabbed my hair and arched me back. My body trembled violently as he pushed inside me, and my mouth popped open with a soundless moan when I shattered against him.

This was too much. I was arched so far back that I wasn't even touching the wall anymore. My head was resting on his shoulder, and he was moving so perfectly inside me that one orgasm faded into another. The arm holding me up tightened around me for a split second before both hands released me, and I just barely caught myself against the wall as his pace quickened until his ragged breaths and movements stopped when he came with a low curse.

He leaned over so his body was resting above me, and his chest moved roughly against mine for those few seconds before he placed soft kisses on my back and moved off the bed.

A husky laugh came from him when I shakily fell to the mattress, but I didn't try to comment on it. My body was still trembling, I was still out of breath, and even though all I wanted to do was fall asleep . . . I wanted all of it all over again.

This overwhelming, body-numbing experience . . . I wanted it again and again. As long as it was with him.

I rolled to my side and smiled against his kiss when he climbed back onto the bed, and easily curled against his body when he lay down and pulled me close.

"What, you're not going to give me a chance to leave?" I teased.

His dark eyes were smiling, and his fingers were gently pulling through my long hair. The tenderness after the rough pleasure just before made me smile and stupidly crave more time with him. Time that stretched into days and weeks and months—time we couldn't have.

With a shake of his head, he said, "You decided to stay; there's no way I'm letting you leave until tonight's over."

"And when this night is over . . ." I trailed off and met his knowing stare. "What can I remember you by?"

One dark eyebrow rose, and as his hand completed another pass down my back, he pressed our lower bodies closer together in a silent answer.

I held back a smile as goose bumps covered my skin. There was no question that I would never forget the incredible heights of pleasure this man had already brought me to, but that wasn't what I had meant, and from the way he seemed to be contemplating something, he was fully aware of the fact.

"Just tonight." His tone held a hint of uncertainty for the

first time since we'd entered the room, making his words sound like a question.

I nodded slowly. "Just tonight."

He let out a long breath and his eyes drifted to the side. "Jay." After a moment's hesitation, those dark pools of obsidian found me again. "Just remember me as Jay." His hand moved slowly up my body until it was cupping my cheek. He leaned close, but stopped just a breath from my lips. "And you?"

"Aurora."

22
Present Day

Aurora

"Y ou need anything?"

I turned around and glanced up, bringing myself back into my classroom, and focused on the other kindergarten teacher, who was popping her head into my doorway. "What? No. No, I'm gonna be heading out of here in just a minute."

She cocked her head to the side and squinted her eyes at me. "You sure? You look a little . . . overwhelmed."

I let out a soft laugh that hinted at some of the stress I'd had resting on my shoulders over the last month or so. My head shook slowly as the words begged to be released to this woman I barely knew. To vent to someone who had no emotional connection to anyone involved in what was happening in my life.

The principal of the school had been aware of the situation with Declan in case anything happened once the school year began, but I hadn't felt it was necessary to tell anyone else. And since we'd started getting our classrooms ready after Declan's accident, and my mind had been on dozens of other things, I hadn't made the time to get to know the other teachers much.

I sent her what I hoped was a reassuring smile and said, "I'm fine, must have just zoned out for a second there."

"Kids can be exhausting, but it gets easier." She smiled warmly and stepped away. "See you on Monday!"

"Bye," I called out a second too late, and looked slowly around my classroom. What I had been counting down the days until, what I had once been so excited for, now felt like nothing more than a place where I was hiding from all of my problems.

In the five days since Declan had woken up, there hadn't been time for anything more than working and worrying. When I had been able to get over to the hospital, either there had been a nurse or therapist in the room working with Declan, he'd been sleeping, or visiting hours had ended. The nurses hadn't cared to enforce visiting hours while Declan was in a coma but had decided they needed to now that he'd pulled through.

For the first time since Declan's accident, I had gone more than two days without seeing or hearing from Linda, not that I was about to complain. But I also hardly saw Jentry.

Jentry had decided to continue to work for Kurt until he went through the academy, and with our new schedules, we only saw each other in the evenings for maybe an hour before I started falling asleep. But even that time was strained, and we hardly spoke. Something was bothering Jentry, and I couldn't figure out what it was.

I finished getting my room ready for the next week then grabbed my things. With one last look around the room, I shut off the lights and left. Not really paying attention to where I was going as I walked to my car or drove to the hospital, just thinking, worrying, stressing, and wondering . . .

Wondering how I had gotten here. How I'd gotten myself into this mess, and thinking of what I could have done differently.

I walked the familiar path in the hospital until I was at Declan's door, and was prepared to be asked to come back at another time, but instead opened the door to find the room much as I would have a week ago: Declan alone in his bed, the rest of the room empty.

Only now, Declan was awake. And instead of lying flat on the bed with tubes and wires running everywhere, he was sitting up, and free of anything connecting him to a machine.

I faltered for a second at the door, and had to steady myself with the handle when the sight of his green eyes threw me off balance. For some ridiculous reason, I wanted to cry.

"Hey!" I said with a pained whisper, and finished walking into the room. "It's gonna take a while to get used to walking in here and find you looking at me," I said as I hugged him gently, then took one of the seats near his bed. "How are you feeling?"

For a long time, Declan didn't say anything; he just sat

there watching me. If I hadn't heard him speak that first day, I would have worried that he couldn't remember how.

"I'm sorry I haven't seen you since Sunday. I've tried to come but every time—"

"I know," he whispered, cutting me off. He smirked for a brief second. "They don't let you see me, doesn't mean I don't hear you."

"Yeah, I guess I didn't think about that. I still would have tried to come more often if it weren't for school."

Declan looked at me blankly for a second, then blinked a few times. "School? Wow. I, uh, they said how long . . ." He ran a hand through his hair and exhaled uneasily. "Still weird. To me, you start school in a couple of weeks, you know? But I guess . . ."

When a minute had passed without him continuing, I urged him to tell me everything that I had missed in the last five days. "What are the doctors saying? Therapists?"

"I'm weak, but I can walk across the room before I have to sit down. I broke a couple of ribs. I guess you would know that."

I smiled, but didn't interrupt.

"I don't know, they just keep saying I'm lucky, Rorie."

A startled laugh escaped me. "Yes. That is such an understatement, Dec. You went straight into a huge tree. No one could believe you'd survived the way you'd hit. With your coma, they told us to expect you not to know how to speak, or walk or write or eat. You're so lucky, we're all so lucky that you're okay."

He just nodded absentmindedly for a few moments, his eyes never leaving mine as he did.

"What is it, Dec?"

"You're still not wearing your ring."

I froze at his sad, confused statement. Seconds ticked by as I tried to figure out the best thing to say, the best way to handle this. Because there was still Jessica, and I didn't know what she would say, if she would say anything; but I knew that I wanted to be the one to tell Declan and his family. But at that moment the last thing I wanted was to hurt Declan all over again, and I didn't want to stress him out when he was already so confused.

But then I remembered the drive here, and how I had wondered what I could have done differently to keep myself from getting in this mess. And I wondered if tomorrow, when I looked back on today, I would wish I had done things differently in this conversation.

Keeping that in mind, I took in a slow, deep breath and steeled myself.

"Declan, what do you remember from the night of your accident? Between us, I mean."

"We got engaged," he said immediately, robotically. "Then next thing I know, I was in this bed and looking up at you and Jentry."

My stomach churned and heart clenched painfully. "You remember getting engaged, or remember asking me to marry you?"

His eyes never wavered from mine. "Asking, I guess. Why?"

The door to the room opened, and I turned to follow Declan's line of sight when his face went blank.

My heart took off when a pair of obsidian eyes met mine, and it took all of my strength to stay in my seat and maintain my expression when I was actually yearning to find strength and take comfort in his arms.

"Hey," Jentry's husky voice rumbled. "Mom and Dad will be here in a bit. Do you want me to wait and come back with them?"

I opened my mouth, unsure of what would come out, but Declan's voice filled the room instead. "No, man. Come on in."

Jentry took slow steps into the room as his eyes darted between Declan and me, staying on me longer and longer each time. "How you feeling, Dec?" he finally asked as he got closer to the bed.

"Be better if I could figure out why my girl doesn't wear her engagement ring," Declan joked as he reached forward to take my hand in his, but his voice fell flat.

When I looked back at Declan, he was watching Jentry the same way he'd been watching me earlier. I risked a quick glance at Jentry's still form, and wished I hadn't.

It was Sunday all over again. Jentry had the same look in his eyes that he'd had that day, the one that had worried me. His body was rigid, as if he was waiting for something, but for some reason, I had a feeling he wasn't waiting for me to tell Declan the truth. It felt like Jentry was waiting for me to tell *him* something he didn't want to hear.

I shook my head slowly, trying to push away the confusion that Jentry's presence had brought, and cleared my throat. "Um, Dec . . . a lot happened between you asking me and your accident. I didn't—"

A quick knock sounded on the door before it opened, revealing a smiling nurse with a cheerful voice. "Okay, time for your exercises!" She walked around the room, moving certain things, oblivious to what she'd just walked in on. Without looking at Jentry and me, she said, "I'm sorry, but you'll have to come back later. However, I'm not sure if Declan here will be up for visitors once we're done."

I looked at her back blankly, and without realizing I was speaking, asked, "Could we just have a few more minutes?"

She turned and squished up her face with fake sympathy. "No can do. I already gave ya an extra five minutes because I knew you were in here. You can come back tomorrow!"

"Come on," Jentry said softly, but firmly.

I stood to leave, and after gently removing my hand from Declan's, brushed the tips of my fingers over his arm. "I'll be back," I assured him as I turned, but stopped abruptly at his confused tone.

"I apparently missed a few weeks, but what else did I miss that you're just gonna leave without kissing me?"

My wide eyes snapped up to Jentry's, but he gave nothing away with his expression. After a few seconds, he looked over my head toward Declan, then turned and walked out of the room.

I turned back to Declan, and guilt ate at me when I met his clear green eyes as I approached him and placed my hand against his warm cheek. "There is so much we have to talk about, and I swear we'll go through all of it the next time I'm here." I pressed my lips to his forehead and whispered, "I'm so glad you came back."

Before he could respond, I turned and left the room.

I found Jentry walking slowly down the hall with his hands intertwined on the top of his head. I hurried to catch up with him, but didn't look at him once I did.

"Don't—"

"I only kissed his forehead," I said, cutting him off.

He released a harsh breath, as if relieved, but continued walking for a few seconds in silence. "It doesn't matter."

My body jerked in surprise and my head snapped up to look at him, but he remained facing forward. "It doesn't matter? What do you mean, it doesn't matter?"

Jentry turned suddenly and crowded me in the small hallway. "Because he loves you. My brother is *in love* with you, Aurora. Because he thinks you're his goddamn fiancée. Because I still hate myself for doing this to him. Even more now than before!" He hissed, then stepped away and settled against the opposite wall.

"Do you think I've somehow missed all of that? Do you think I somehow stopped hating myself?" I asked. "And yet, *I* am the one who is left having to break Declan's heart . . . *again*."

"I can't be the one to tell him that you aren't engaged. That has to be you. If you go through with it, then I will gladly do the rest for you."

"Why do you say it like that? What do you mean *if* I go through with it? And why is it that lately it seems as if you're hoping I won't?"

"Because—" He cut off quickly, and pressed his fist against his mouth, as if it would help keep his words from escaping. When he spoke again, they were nearly inaudible. "Because a part of me is still praying that you'll be smart enough to leave."

And I knew . . . I knew who he meant. I knew that after all this time, after all our heartache, after all our hard decisions, he was still giving me chances to leave him.

I searched his dark eyes. "Why do you do this? Why can't you—God, Jentry, why can't you *see* you the way I do?"

When he removed his hand, his face was blank. "Let's not talk about this now."

"Right," I said sarcastically, "because it's something you'll have to explain later. Something that will help me understand you, something that I so desperately need. But that *later* will never come! Will it?"

"Aurora . . ."

"No, don't," I said through clenched teeth, and closed the distance between us. Pressing my hand roughly to his chest, I said, "I hurt, you hurt . . . right? Right?" I gritted out.

"Aurora, you don't—"

"Then can't you feel what you're doing to me?" Not waiting for his response, I turned and left the hospital.

Jentry

I dropped my head back against the wall and stared blankly up at the ceiling until the fluorescent lights became too much to handle. I pushed from my spot on the wall and took a step in the direction that Aurora had just left, then froze.

That girl clouded every one of my senses to the outside world, while heightening their receptiveness to her. Everything dulled around me until all I knew was her, what she made me feel, and what I needed and wanted from her. Nothing else mattered when Aurora was near. Nothing else existed.

I had learned far too well how little I noticed of our surroundings during our time together at the beach, and was reminded of it that weekend when I hadn't realized that Jess was in the apartment with us. I should have reminded myself to pay more attention today.

My stomach fell as I turned back to look at the two people I had caught a glimpse of, but didn't have to wonder long about what all they had heard. Their shocked expressions said more than enough.

For the first time in all the years I had known her, Mom was speechless.

She lifted a finger and started to point it at me, then stopped and dropped her hand.

Seconds ticked by, and all that passed between us were confused or disappointed looks, and a few head shakes from my dad.

"How could you?" Mom finally said, her voice just above

a whisper. "How could—what have you done? And with that . . . that—"

"Don't," I said in warning, cutting her off. "Whatever you're about to say, don't." When neither of them said anything else, I asked the question I didn't want the answer to. "How long were you there?"

Mom huffed, the sound bordered on a shocked laugh.

Dad pointed behind them as if he didn't realize he was even moving. "We had been talking with the doctor. We knew Declan was about to have physical therapy, so we went to catch up with the two of you when we saw Rorie leave Declan's room. You have a lot to explain, but this isn't the place."

I nodded once, but still spoke. "This goes a lot deeper than what you just saw—and Declan knew. Before his accident, he knew."

Mom shut her eyes and held up her hand in a silent plea for me to stop talking. "Declan would have never done something like this to you. I can't—I just can't believe you would do this to him. And with *her*."

"Linda," Dad said softly, but his tone still rang with authority.

I opened my mouth to respond, but shut it and shook my head, knowing I would once again say things I might regret. Knowing they would follow, I turned and walked out of the hospital, and kept going into the parking lot.

"We need to talk about this, Jentry," Dad called out when I continued toward my car.

"We will, but I don't know how to talk about it when Mom

already has it in her head to hate her for no reason, and then is using this to hate her even more when she doesn't even know what the hell is going on!"

"She has ruined this family and is now trying to tear you and Declan apart," Mom nearly yelled now that we were out of the crowded hospital hallways. "What more do I need to know?"

"Everything, and nothing, because you don't deserve to know all of it!"

"Jentry," Dad barked.

I took a calming breath and ran a hand over my head and down my face. "I'm sorry, but I know that Mom won't believe any of what I say because she already hates her." Keeping my eyes on Dad, I explained, "I met her before Dec ever did. I fell for her before Dec ever knew she existed. Dad, I fell in love with her in a way I didn't think was possible. I'm *in love with her.*"

"Oh, Jentry," Mom scoffed, and looked away, shaking her head with disappointment.

"If it was anyone else, and any other situation, I know you'd be reacting differently. Mom, try to look at it from my perspective. From Aurora's."

"Oh, is she *Aurora* now?"

"Mom . . ." I was begging with her to understand, to just listen. From the way her eyes were watering, I knew she wanted to but didn't know how with what she had seen and what she knew now. "Mom, think of it this way: I met and fell in love with a girl I thought I would never see again. I thought

I was crazy to fall for her like that, but for nearly a year, she was all I thought about. Then Dec picks me up and takes me to the beach, and I'm about to meet his girlfriend he's talked nonstop about, and it ends up being the same girl. She only met Declan because she went back looking for me."

"So then she'll be with just anyone!" Mom cut in, frustration leaking through her tone. "Anyone who gives her the time of day. When one guy leaves, she looks for another!"

I could tell Dad thought the same thing.

"It wasn't like that. I—I thought that too at first, but it wasn't like that; you just have to trust me. I'm not going into the whole thing, but you have to know that she really does love Declan. We fought . . . we fought a lot about what was happening, about what we meant to each other, and about what we were going to do."

"What you were going to do." Dad's aggravation was obvious. "You should have stepped aside because Declan was with her."

"I fucking tried! She tried! But would you want her to stay with Declan even though he isn't who she wants? Would you want her to keep lying to him?"

"She's an immature girl who isn't ready for a commitment and goes with whatever is new at the time!" Mom said. I groaned in frustration.

"See, there's no point in even trying to tell you. You won't understand because you won't try to hear me out! You're making Aurora out to be someone like Madeline, and she's the furthest thing from that. This has been killing her. It destroyed her to try to choose one of us, but she eventually did. She had finally told Declan about us, the night of his accident. Her guilt over that night has been greater than anything you can imagine. But she still loves him, and I love him, and I hated knowing that I would take her from him because she *is* mine. And after telling him, he now doesn't remember any of it, so we're right back where we were! So while you stand there acting like she's doing this for fun, let me tell you this is the hardest thing we've ever fucking been through!"

I was met with silence and more disappointed looks after my outburst. After a minute of us all watching each other, Mom spoke. "Then I'll make it easy for you. . . ."

23
Present Day

Aurora

I finished unloading everything from my car into the apartment, and set the music channel on the TV as loud as I could stand it so it would drown out my thoughts.

Unfortunately, it was futile. My thoughts screamed louder.

I laid out the large poster paper, paints, and glitter to make a few remaining signs I had realized during the week would be useful in the classroom for my students, then searched the apartment for a pencil. It wasn't until I was going from the kitchen to the living room again that I realized I was stomping.

It didn't matter. Anger was better than tears. All I did lately was cry, and I was so tired of crying.

I stopped short when that thought crossed my mind, and rolled the pencil between my fingers as I let the words coast through my head again.

A defeated laugh bubbled past my lips when I wondered how many times during this month I had told Taylor, or thought to myself, that I was tired of crying, yet continued to do just that.

I had never really thought of myself as an emotional person, but then again, I wasn't the kind of person who lacked emotions, either. It irritated me in books when the heroine was heartless just as much as it did when she was a sobbing mess, but at the moment, I would have given anything for a few days of nothing.

Just nothing. No pain, no confusion, no heartache. No guilt, no worry, just . . . nothing.

It sounded like heaven.

But my life was still turned on its side, as it had been for weeks, and everything and everyone were unknowns. And emotions tend to run wild when life is full of unknowns.

I made one last attempt to clear my mind of everything that had happened at the hospital and focused on nothing but the words of the songs flowing through the apartment, and the signs I needed to make as I settled onto the floor again.

Two signs later, and I was singing and swaying along to the music. I pulled the third and final piece of paper in front of me, and stopped to stretch my back and arms before bending back over the paper. I picked the paintbrush up and dipped it into the dirty, inky water, but my movements slowed as I moved to dip it into a color. Slowly, I straightened as I had when I'd stretched, and looked across the apartment.

There, in the corner and taking up most of the far wall, were huge shelves. Filling about a quarter of those shelves were books.

I sat on the floor with the paintbrush still in hand hovering over the black paint, just staring at the shelves as immeasurable time passed by. I knew they hadn't been there when I'd left for work this morning, but at the same time, they looked as if they'd been there for so long.

I stood to go study the new furniture, and cursed when I knocked over the cup of dirty water. I grabbed for the cup to stop everything from pouring out, but a good amount of the inky water had already spilled out and spread across the last piece of poster paper until it was ruined.

If I hadn't just noticed the bookshelves, it probably would have bothered me. But at the moment, I didn't have time to care.

I steadied the half-filled cup, then walked slowly across the living room and into what was supposed to be the dining room—but I'd never cared to use it as such since we had the kitchen table. Instead, half was an office-type space, and the other half I'd wanted to turn into a reading corner, complete with bookshelves.

I'd just told Jentry about what I'd originally wanted to do with it—but had never had the money for—the night that Declan had woken up while we'd eaten dinner.

Awe filled me as I lightly trailed my fingers across the shelves and along the perfect designs subtly carved into the wood. Swirls led into knots that were etched deep enough into the wood to catch your eye, but not enough to look gaudy or take away from the overall shelving or books.

It was exactly what I would have picked out for bookshelves: huge, sturdy, stained dark, and with an incredible amount of room for books.

I couldn't begin to imagine how much the entire set had cost or where Jentry had found it, and I couldn't figure out why he had done it at all.

I turned expectantly when I heard a key in the door, and just stared at him when he stepped into the apartment.

His dark eyes found mine instantly, but fell away as he walked toward the guest room without saying a word. In that brief second there had been so much pain he'd tried to hide, pain I couldn't begin to understand.

He was keeping something from me, I knew. Something I assumed he wanted to keep from me in order to make me leave. As it had for so long, it felt like he was tearing my soul in half.

After a moment's hesitation, I followed him into his room and shut the door behind me to quiet some of the loud music filling the apartment.

He stood with his back to me, his head hung low and hands clasped around the back of his neck. He looked more beaten down than I'd ever seen him, and considering Declan was awake and going to be fine, it didn't make sense.

"What's wrong?" I asked cautiously.

Jentry let his hands fall limply at his sides and lifted his head, but didn't turn to look at me. He let so many minutes pass without responding that I thought he wouldn't. I had started walking toward him when he finally spoke up.

His voice was strained with whatever was weighing on him. "I think you should stay with Declan."

"What?"

He sighed and slowly turned to face me, but he wouldn't meet my eyes. "I think you should stay with—"

"No, I heard what you said, I just can't believe that you said it, and don't understand why you did! What is going on with you lately? Why are you pushing me away after days of pulling me close? Do you know how confusing you are?"

He laughed, but there was no humor behind the sound. "I'm sure I can understand."

"That's it? Nothing else?" I asked when he didn't continue, my frustration and confusion apparent in my tone. "Why are you pushing me toward Declan suddenly? Even if you stopped wanting me, you know that I couldn't go back to a life with him. I told you what it was like for me before you ever entered my life again. I can't do that to him again. It wouldn't be fair!"

Jentry's face pinched as I spoke, as if he wanted to deny something, but he kept his mouth shut.

"Why'd you do it?" I gestured behind me to the shut door. "Why'd you buy the shelves? Why do you keep doing things like that and acting like you care, only to pull away and shut down on me?"

"I do care!" he shouted, and flung his arms in exasperation. "What I care most about in this world is you, Aurora, but I'm trying to protect you and everyone else I love! And protecting you means making sure you'll be okay, and *Declan* means you'll fucking be okay!"

I placed the tips of my fingers to my temple as I tried to understand his words, and a frustrated laugh burst from my chest. "Do you hear yourself? We agreed that it would be too hard to have a relationship that we had to hide from Declan and your entire family while Declan was in a coma, and recovering. But how could a world where we aren't together ever be okay?"

"They know, Aurora. My parents know about us. They were at the hospital; they heard us!"

My stomach felt as if it had fallen through the floor. The blood drained from my head, and I felt like I might faint. "What?"

"They know," he said calmly. "I tried to explain it, but they don't understand. They just—they don't get it. We ended the conversation with Mom saying they would more or less disown me if I did this to Declan."

I stumbled back until I hit the wall, and used it to help keep me upright. "What?"

"I've been driving around for the last hour thinking about what they said, and thinking about Dec. As much as I love them, that threat wouldn't keep me from you, because they *are* my family, and I know they'll always be there no matter what my mom said today. But I can still keep me from you."

I shook my head slowly. "I don't understand."

"As much as it kills me—and it fucking *kills* me, Aurora," he said through gritted teeth, "I know this is what's best for you. Declan can give you what you need. A life with a guy like me isn't what you deserve."

"Why?" I asked, sounding just as crushed as I felt. "You talk about yourself in this way that—Jentry, I don't understand. Help me understand you." I pushed from the wall and walked shakily toward him. "From that first night you told me that you shouldn't be allowed to *stain* my good. Do you know how many hours I have turned those words over in my mind, trying to figure out what you could have meant by them? And then to find I never even understood the depth of them until you came back into my life. But every time you say something about yourself, it destroys something inside me. You are breaking my heart! Why do you view yourself this way?"

As he had so many times before, his face morphed into a mask of practiced indifference.

"Why can't you tell me?"

"Why won't you drop it?" he asked quietly, and his eyes met mine before darting away.

"Because I am missing something crucial, and I know if I know this then I will finally understand so much about you that has confused me for so long. I *need* to understand, Jentry!"

"You know all you need to," he said. "Guys like me—"

"No, don't start that again! The worst part of all of it is that you believe what you're saying. What could have happened in your life to make you think that you don't deserve something *good*? What could have happened in your life to make you push me away like this when I can feel how much you need me?"

Jentry's eyes were looking past me, but I knew he wasn't seeing anything in that room. Whatever he *was* seeing haunted him.

"Because I see you, too, Jentry. I see what you refuse to," I continued, "and if I can't understand what you are trying to force me to see, then I can never show you how wrong you are. I can never begin to show you that your soul is—it's just—it's beautiful," I said exasperated, unable to find a better word.

He huffed through his nose, but didn't respond otherwise, and his body slowly stilled until he looked like he had been carved from stone, then finally murmured, "Jessica . . . I told you I didn't grow up with her."

I nodded, prompting him to continue.

"My biological father was abusive. There wasn't a time in my childhood that I remember the abuse starting; it had just always happened. My mother, Jess, me . . ." He trailed off. "He was uncontrollable when he was mad. Nothing stopped him until he felt like he'd had enough. My mother did drugs, and they made her crazy and paranoid. One day when Jessica and I were eight, we came home from school and our mother told Jessica that it was time; that they were finally leaving. I thought that meant me, too."

I covered my mouth when it fell open, already knowing what he was about to say. "Jentry," I mumbled into my hand.

His chest pitched from the force of his nearly silent, mocking laugh. "My mother screamed when I started following them. Just *screamed* as if I was hurting her. When she stopped, she asked why I thought she would try to save me when I would only turn into my father. 'It's inside you,' she'd said. 'You can't escape that evil. Any good you touch will be tarnished; you're just like him.'"

My mind raced and chest ached. I couldn't believe a mother could leave her child, let alone in a home with a man like that, and I couldn't believe that her words had stayed with Jentry all this time. "Jentry, she was on drugs; she didn't know what—"

"I'd already had anger problems, I believed her," he explained. "Kids made fun of Jess and me because we had bruises or the same clothes for a week at a time, and I would go off on them the way our father went off on us. I was the disturbed underprivileged kid. *Hopeless.* That's what one of my teachers called me. The night my mother and Jess left was—" Jentry stopped abruptly and shook his head. "I started locking myself in my bedroom at night. Shoving the dresser and everything I could in front of the door. When that didn't change things, I started hiding out in the library at school and sleeping in there just so I wouldn't have to face him. Declan found out a couple of weeks later what I'd been doing. Mom marched into the library that same afternoon with Dec trailing behind her, and dragged me out of there by my ear, demanding to know why I hadn't told someone." His mouth curved up into a fond smile, and I found mine doing the same. "She went to the police department that day after I was settled in at their house, and officially adopted me later that year. I still have *his* last name, but the *Veils* are my family."

I understood then—not Jentry or why he thought of himself in such a horrible way—but why he had been so surprised by my feud with Linda. She had saved Jentry, and she loved her family fiercely, just as they loved her. "And your biological parents?"

Jentry's eyes hardened again, and he shrugged. "Father might be out of jail by now, I don't know. According to Jessica, my mother is still alive somehow. Still on drugs. That's why Jessica is so psychotic; she grew up with only our mother and took on her personality. There's nothing wrong with Jess, but she's . . . Well, when my attempts to help her went bad time after time, I just learned that it was better to stay away from her. She's too unpredictable and toxic. She knows I want to help her; she knows she can come to me when she wants it, but she never wants it. She just wants money."

I nodded absentmindedly and placed my hand on his shaking arm. "Your life started off bad—extremely bad—but why would that determine what you do or do not deserve now, Jentry?" I asked hesitantly.

"My biological mother was—is . . . *is* crazy. What she said back then, it was just her paranoia. But that doesn't mean that it didn't scare me *then,* that it didn't make me vow to live a certain way. It also doesn't mean that I haven't learned that she was right."

I exhaled heavily. "She wasn't!"

"I told you I had anger problems before. Because of what she said, I swore to myself that I wouldn't turn into my father, that I wouldn't be a violent person. But it's there, deep down, always burning and building, just waiting to snap."

"Because you're afraid of it!"

"Ask Declan," he said uneasily, and his dark eyes met mine for a moment. "Ask him what it's like to watch me snap, because he is one of two people who have been on the wrong end of it."

His admission surprised me, and I wondered what they had been fighting over in the first place, but I let it go when he continued talking.

"I vowed to myself that I would protect people instead of hurt them. That's why I became a Marine. That's why I plan to go through the academy to be a police officer. But the smallest thing could still set me off. Do you know what it feels like to constantly have anger simmering in your veins?" he asked. "It's sickening, and it's dark. So, yes, my mother was crazy, but she was right. It wasn't until one night at a party with the most beautiful girl I have ever seen that I realized that, and finally understood what she meant. Because this anger inside? It's dark. And you, Aurora? You're good and you're light, and I knew that from the moment I saw you; just like I knew what would happen if I was allowed to touch you." Like he had that first night a year ago, he pressed his hand to my chest and whispered, "My dark would stain your good . . . but I couldn't walk away from you."

I placed my hand over his, and said, "You're more afraid of your anger than I ever could be, even knowing what I do now."

Jentry looked like he was going to disagree, so I pressed harder against his hand and spoke over him.

"Do you see me?"

His eyes searched mine. "I've always seen you."

I released his hand to place mine on his chest, and whispered, "Just as I have always seen you. Nothing about what you told me has changed anything."

The corners of his mouth lifted, then fell. "It doesn't matter, because we both know what happens from here."

"You want me with Declan to protect me from you." It wasn't a question. "All of this . . . all of this pushing me away has been you trying to protect me."

Everything I always felt from him swirled between us: love, need, passion. And all of it he was trying to hinder. His face pinched like he was in pain before he admitted, "I can't ruin you, Aurora."

My eyes shut as a shaky breath forced from my lungs. The war my heart had been in since Jentry had stepped back into my life was coming to an end. I could feel it. My body, mind, heart, and soul were all so exhausted from fighting each other.

A few difficult words would lead me back to a certain future, one my entire being rebelled against, but one Jentry was set on me living.

A few easy words would send me to an unknown future. One I craved with every piece of me, and one that would undoubtedly be the biggest struggle of our lives.

"Don't move," I told him gently, and turned to make sure he was still standing there before walking out of his room and into the living room, where my craft projects were still laid out.

A lump formed in my throat as I walked over to what I needed, and knelt down on the floor.

My eyes followed what I was doing with rapt attention, as if I was afraid to miss a single second of the process in ending this final battle.

Futures are uncertain, unpredictable, like the inky water that had spilled across the pure, white paper. Nearly imperceptible ripples had moved and flowed until a unique stain formed. The ink was permanently, irrevocably embedded in the surface.

From that very first night, Jentry had been a tidal wave of ink branded into my soul, staining me with our complicated, devastating story.

And it was beautiful.

If only I could make him see it that way, too.

When I finished, I moved back through the apartment slowly as I let the weight of my choice wash through me, but I knew in my soul that this was right.

We had pushed and pushed—trying to force each other back or away for one reason or another. But even though futures were uncertain, I knew that a future without Jentry wasn't a future at all.

"Take your shirt off," I demanded as I rounded the corner into his room again. My voice was hoarse with emotion, so there was no force behind my demand, but Jentry still shrugged out of his shirt.

His brow furrowed when his shirt fell to the floor and his dark eyes darted over my face quickly. "What—"

Before he could continue, I stepped up to him and pressed my right hand to his skin, transferring a layer of paint from my hand to his chest, just over his heart.

He tensed for a second before relaxing. His tone was a mixture of amusement and confusion when he asked, "What are you doing?"

"We're done. We're done pushing each other away, and you're done trying to get me to leave. You have to see that by now nothing you can say will make me go." I looked up into his eyes when I took my hand away, leaving a white handprint on his chest, and said, "Stain me, Jentry; I don't care. I'll do it right back."

The words were barely past my lips before his mouth was on mine. My hands slid from his shoulders up to his neck in a feeble attempt to hold on to him as he forced me back toward the bed.

Our movements were frenzied and uncoordinated as we hurried to remove our remaining clothes, all the while we fought for control of the kiss and to stay upright as we crawled onto the bed. But like our first night together, all time seemed to slow once the last piece of clothing had fallen to the floor.

We stayed kneeling on the bed, watching each other and refusing to let go of one another as our rough breaths filled the room.

What could have been seconds or minutes later, Jentry asked gruffly, "You understand what you're doing?"

I couldn't help a brief smile. "I've known from the beginning."

"Then you know what this means." He leaned forward to pass his lips across the base of my neck, and a small shudder moved through my body.

When I spoke, my words came out breathy and soft. "It means you'll stop trying to make me leave."

A laugh rumbled in his chest. "I swore if I ever got another chance, I would never let you go. We do this, I'm not letting you go for anything."

Another smile touched my face as my gaze darted over the white streaks of paint from his neck down to his torso. Lifting my hand, I pressed it to the original handprint. "You know, that sounds like another chance for me to leave," I whispered teasingly. "I'm not worried about my heart, Jentry. I gave it to you long ago and I've never regretted it. We do this, I'm showing you why you deserve everything."

He captured my mouth in an unhurried kiss as he wrapped me up in his arms and gently laid me on the bed, and my body tingled in anticipation as he slowly moved to hover over me. Because every touch and movement and brush of his lips and stroke of his tongue against mine was soft, soft, soft . . . and I knew him.

I had always known him.

And I knew what came with his soft.

Our kiss never faltered as he settled his body between my legs, and I moaned into his mouth when he pressed his hard length against me. His hands ran down my body lightly, tenderly; every few inches his fingers tightened for a brief instant in a way that promised what was to come . . . that made me want to beg for it.

He spread my legs more, then wrapped his large hands around my hips and slowly, oh so slowly, tightened his grip as he pressed the tip of his length against my entrance.

My fingers curled against the comforter as I fought to keep my pleas silent, but his name flew from my lips when he pushed into me quickly, roughly.

His dark eyes held mine as he moved inside me, alternating between hard and fast pounding, and long, slow strokes. All of it made it hard to remember how to breathe and sent warm shivers down my spine.

I had fantasized about this man and this time with him for a year, and now that it was here, I was worried I would wake up.

But no matter if my eyes were opened or shut, all I saw and felt was Jentry and this moment. The way his breath felt against my skin, the way he felt moving inside me, the way his fingers felt gripping me—as if he was afraid to let go—the way his eyes pierced mine and demanded every unspoken word. All the soft with the hard. And all of it, *everything*, was perfect.

He released his firm hold on me and curled over my body; his hips slowed and movements became more controlled, but no less powerful. His hand slid tenderly across my skin to cradle my neck as the other clutched at the bed beside me.

His eyes searched my face as he lowered his mouth to mine.

"Keeping you forever, Aurora." His lips brushed against mine once, twice . . . "Need you to fucking breathe."

I whimpered against him, against his kiss, and slid my hands around his head to feel his buzzed hair under my fingers when he deepened it.

If he only knew how much I needed him—but he was currently taking my breath away.

I broke from the kiss, but didn't move away. I pressed my forehead to his and held his stare as I fought to catch my breath . . . and prayed that this moment wouldn't end.

My body trembled and stomach tightened as each thrust brought me closer and closer to the edge. I was on fire, and soon it felt like we would both be consumed in the flames we had created.

Those dark, dark eyes burned with so much passion when my mouth fell open with a soundless moan and my body shattered beneath him.

When my shaking calmed, he pressed a soft kiss under my jaw and whispered, "Beautiful," as his pace quickened again.

I wove my arms around his back, and held on to the man I loved as tightly as I could, and tried to memorize the feel of him beneath my fingertips. Tried to memorize the way the muscles in his back gently bunched and relaxed as he made me his, then tensed and shuddered when he found his release inside me.

Jentry hovered above me for several seconds then slowly lowering himself onto me, and something about the weight of his body made all of this real. Made it final. I knew later we would have to deal with all the difficulties again, but in that moment they didn't exist.

I trailed my fingers lazily over his shoulders and back, then up to his buzzed hair and back down again.

"I have waited so long for you and for this, Jentry Michaels."

He lifted his head so his dark, smiling eyes were piercing mine. "Would've waited forever."

"Yeah. But you also would've kept talking yourself into reasons to make me leave."

"Of course I would have," he said honestly, then rolled off me, but pulled me with him until we were on our sides. "I wouldn't know how to let you go now, Aurora, but the thought that I could hurt you will always haunt me."

"You won't—"

"You can't know that," he argued gently.

"I can."

He smiled sadly as he trailed his fingers along my jaw. "Even then, that still means Jessica . . ."

"And dealing with Linda and facing Declan and the rest of the Veils after everything that's happened for the rest of our lives." I laughed softly and searched his eyes. "I know, Jentry. Falling in love with you was the easiest thing I've ever done, but figuring out how to start our lives will be the most difficult. I knew that when I chose you."

Jentry's hand paused for a second, then his thumb brushed across my lips. "Again."

I thought over his short demand, but his meaning made

sense soon enough. And though I tried to keep a straight face, my mouth kept pulling up into a smile. "I think I fell in love with you the first time you tried to make me leave you."

His body shook with his silent laughter. "Yeah?"

"No." I gave him an amused look as I thought back to that night. "No, it was that first time you told me that you weren't letting me go."

Jentry's eyes swam with regret. "If only we had been talking about longer than that night, we could have skipped a lot of bullshit."

"It would have been easy," I said as I curled closer to his body, as if I needed the protection his arms and this room could bring. "But life isn't meant to be easy."

24
Present Day

~❦~

Aurora

I glanced at the bookshelves as Jentry and I hurried to leave the apartment the next morning, and asked, "Where did you find those? They're beautiful."

His face fell, and for a while he didn't respond to me. It wasn't until we were in the car on the way to the hospital that he finally murmured, "One of the guys on Dad's crew helped me make them."

I turned quickly in my seat to look at him, and stared blankly for a few seconds. "You made those. The bookshelves."

Jentry nodded slowly. "I used to work for my dad when I was in high school. Dec did, too. He could have built shelves if you'd asked him to. Declan only deals with the business side now and hasn't done any of the manual stuff since we graduated from high school. Neither had I, which is why I had help."

"Jentry . . . thank you." I didn't know what else to say. I wanted to go over every detail of the shelves, but couldn't seem to figure out how to now that I knew that Jentry had done all of that for me. "Just, thank you."

He shrugged nonchalantly. "You needed shelves so your books wouldn't just stay boxed up in the closet."

"But those . . ." I trailed off and shook my head. "Those were exactly what I described, and they're—" Jentry's phone began ringing, and I watched as his face fell into an unreadable mask when he pulled it out to check the screen.

His eyes darted up into the rearview mirror, and then the side mirrors before focusing on the road again.

I didn't have to ask who it was when he ignored the call and dropped his phone into the cup holder, but my suspicions were confirmed when his phone started ringing again a minute later.

"Have you heard from her since you made her leave the apartment last week?"

Jentry's nod was faint. "Every day. Just after I get to work, and right before I get back to the apartment. It's possible she's waiting somewhere around the apartment or my dad's office, but I don't know. It's not like Jess to stay in one place for long unless it's around our mother. She can't afford it, and she can't afford to follow me like that. She needs— She just can't."

"Have you answered any of the calls?"

"She's just taunting me. She'll get tired of it when she doesn't get what she wants."

I waited for a minute to see if he would continue. If he were anyone else, I wouldn't pry. But this was Jentry and I needed to know what to expect with Jessica and their relationship. "Why do I have a feeling it's not money that she wants this time?"

"She wants me to get mad."

"Oh."

"Like I said, it isn't like her to stay in one place, and she can't afford to follow me. But if she wants me mad, she'll do what she thinks she has to, which is why I'm not ruling it out."

"You said that the other night, that she wanted to make you mad. I don't understand why—"

"You don't?" he said with a laugh. "After everything I told you last night? About my biological father, about what I'm so afraid of? Jessica uses that against me. She acts like I think I'm better than her; says I've been running away from who I am because I didn't end up where she and our mother are. My anger . . . she loves it. It fuels her sickness because it makes her think we're on the same level. She gets this twisted high just seeing me get mad." There was a short pause before he softly admitted, "Jess was there when I found out about her and Declan. I can still remember the way she kept laughing as I beat the shit out of him. Egging me on, asking if I was going to hit her, too, like she wanted me to."

"What . . ." I stared at Jentry for a moment, then turned straight ahead, but I wasn't seeing the road in front of us.

I couldn't imagine the girl Jentry was describing. It didn't fit with the girl I had first run into, or even the one from this past weekend. Who, after being abused, would try to pull that same kind of anger from their brother? Who would try to turn their twin into their abuser?

"Jentry, she's—"

"Insane?" he offered with a sarcastic laugh.

"Are you sure she isn't on drugs, too?"

He nodded slowly. "I was around our mother and her friends enough that even being that young, I knew the signs. The drugs that they do, they take a toll on you. They would take a toll on Jess, and she's too obsessed with the way she looks to let that happen."

"Why is she this spiteful if you've tried to help her? Why hasn't she let you help her?"

A weight seemed to settle over him from my questions, and for a while we just drove. "I don't know," he finally said. "I don't know if it's because Jessica feels responsible for our mother, or not. But I know that in those kinds of houses with those parents and those lifestyles, the kids either work to get away from that situation, get sucked into it, or embrace it. Jessica fully embraced that life, thrives in it, and spits in my face when I try to help get her out of it. Honestly, most of my life it's been easier to try to forget she existed." He rubbed his hand along his jaw, and let out a harsh breath. "I can't believe I just said that."

"I'm sorry, I can't imagine how difficult that must have been growing up, and how hard it must be now. I never even had a sibling to fight with, let alone one who tried to do what she does."

"I have only ever considered the Veils as family. I still wasn't okay with walking in on my best friend and twin sister, even if I hardly see her. But they're the only ones who have treated me like family, and the only ones I've ever cared about. You know, that first day I was back here and Mom had dropped all my stuff off at the apartment in that big pile, it threw me off for a second. Because that house was the first place I'd considered home, and suddenly all my shit was just sitting in a pile somewhere outside that house, like she was throwing me out." He laughed humorlessly as he pulled into a parking spot at the hospital. "And now she's disowning me."

"Jentry," I said uneasily, "I'll fix this somehow."

"Aurora, she's not going to, no matter what she says."

I grabbed his arm and waited until he was watching me. "You said you did, but are you sure *you've* thought about this? Linda hates me. Even if we get past the initial shock and anger with everyone, you have to remember that your mom will probably always hate me. And your relationship with Declan might never be the same."

"I would've hated Declan for having you if you'd chosen to stay with him, but I would've always loved him as a brother and best friend. I know once the hurt fades, he'll feel the same. As for my mom, she doesn't have to love you. I do. She'll still love me, and she already knows I won't put up with what she's been doing to you. Besides, this way she might not bother us that much."

I laughed softly. "I wouldn't be so sure about that. I saw her more than ever once she started hating me."

"Then I guess we'll have to get her to at least like you,"

he said simply, then leaned forward to press his lips to mine. "We're gonna figure it out, Aurora, because it's always gonna be us."

Jentry

W hat's happen—are we in the wrong room?" Aurora asked slowly as she looked at the empty room just minutes later.

Declan wasn't just out of his room . . . the room was completely cleared, as if he'd never been there.

I touched Aurora's arm as I backed out of the room into the hall, and looked around for the first nurse I could find. "Excuse me, can you tell me where—"

Recognition lit in her eyes when Aurora joined me, followed quickly by confusion. "Oh, Mr. Veil? I'm surprised you hadn't heard the news yet, or that you weren't here. He was released yesterday evening."

"He was released," Aurora echoed dully. "He went home?"

The nurse simply smiled. "Yes, poor thing didn't want to stay in for another weekend. Who could blame him?"

"Thank you," I mumbled, and waited until she'd walked away to start pulling Aurora back out of the hospital.

"I don't understand why they wouldn't tell us," she said once we were back in my car and I was pulling out of the space.

"My parents are mad."

"But why wouldn't Declan have told us that he was getting out? He doesn't remember that night; he would have called me to tell me, wouldn't . . ." She trailed off and sank into her seat as my worries hit her. "They told him."

I tilted my head slowly to the side. I wanted nothing more than to deny it, to take away everything that was weighing on her. But I knew I couldn't; knew there was no point in lying to her for the sake of keeping her at ease now. "They had to have."

"This wasn't how it was supposed to happen," she whispered to her window, then remained silent for a while. "I say that," she went on with a dull laugh, "but I didn't try hard enough to make it happen any other way. You were right; I was lying to your family by not telling them the truth of that night. If I had, I would've had more time to tell Declan once he woke up. Or maybe I should've just waited at the hospital until they let me see him and told him that first night, gotten it over with right away instead of letting a week pass."

"No. That . . ." I blew out a slow breath and shook my head. "I don't know when the right time would have been, but you were right not to do it that first night. You have to remember that you had already told him. How were you supposed to figure the right time to tell him again after he'd been in a coma and forgotten the first time? Not to mention that it was damn near impossible to even get a second with him. I went to see him every day after work this week, and the two times I actually saw him, I only got about five minutes total before I was kicked out again. So how do you lay something like that on him when you know you're about to have to leave him alone in a hospital?"

"Those were some of the same things that went through my mind that kept me from saying anything, that kept him thinking things about us that weren't true. But this . . . this is so much worse and makes me wish I'd just done it."

The only reason I wanted to agree with her was because I wanted what was coming next to already be over. But no matter how much I'd hated seeing Declan think that Aurora still belonged to him, and no matter how much his words had amplified my need to keep Aurora a safe distance from me and my demons, no time in the hospital would have been a good time to tell Dec the truth about their relationship, or ours.

"Oh my God," she said when we pulled up to my parents' house.

I bit back a curse when I looked around the driveway and street. There were other cars, indicating my sisters and brothers-in-law were there, and what looked like Mom's parents—I'd never gotten close with them.

"*This* makes it worse," she said, sounding dejected. With a sigh, she unbuckled herself and opened the door to step out of the car.

She didn't wait for me to catch up with her, just walked determinedly toward the front door with a grave expression on her face.

Once we neared the door, I stopped her. "Say the word, and we're gone."

She looked up at me with an amused expression. "Swear?"

I grasped her chin with my fingers and turned her head until she was looking up at me. "I mean it, Aurora."

"I know you do. But I've been preparing myself for what's about to happen inside this house for the past ten minutes, and if I keep looking into your eyes and don't walk through that door right now, I'm not sure I'll still have the strength to go through with it."

She tore her eyes from mine and began pulling away from me, but at the last second, turned back and pushed up on her toes to press her mouth to mine. Her lips moved in sync with mine for a moment before she breathed, "I love you," against them, and forced herself away and into the house.

Aurora

I held my breath while I walked quickly into the house, afraid to wait for someone to answer the door, or even for Jentry to open it. I needed to do this before I talked myself out of it, because the disastrous climax that waited for me in one of those rooms would only continue to wait. Only continue to haunt me and taunt me.

I already had Jessica doing one of those things. I didn't need an entire family added on to that.

I walked through the entryway into the kitchen, somehow still holding on to my false bravado, but felt it splinter and crack when I heard nothing but excitement coming from the living room.

My footsteps faltered and slowed, and Jentry's brief, reassuring touch on the small of my back was all that kept me going.

The final step, from the kitchen into the living room, seemed to freeze time.

The scene wasn't what I had expected to find, and I just managed to hold on to my waning confidence until I caught sight of Declan's face. He looked like he was seeing the sun rise for the first time. His excitement would have been contagious if it hadn't seemed so out of place among my fears and worries.

I felt Jentry's confusion as if it were my own, doubling what I was feeling and trying to understand. He didn't speak, didn't move, hardly breathed . . . but I knew he was studying every single person in the living room, taking it all in.

"Aurora . . ." Jentry's whisper was nearly inaudible to me, and I knew no one else had heard him, but that one word seemed to push Declan into action.

He stood slowly from his spot in one of the recliners, his face showing his pain before he was able to control it, and then he was walking toward us.

His grandma, sisters, and their husbands all watched him with rapt attention as he walked; all with smiles on their faces.

Linda and Kurt were the only ones watching me. Their glares said more than they were able to in that moment.

"Didn't think you'd be here just yet," Declan said as he got closer to where Jentry and I were standing. His clear green eyes flashed over to Jentry for a moment, and in that moment, his face went cold. But it happened so fast I wasn't sure if I imagined it.

"Uh, we . . . well, we went to the hospital . . ." I glanced quickly at everyone again before asking, "Why didn't you tell us you'd been released?"

A mischievous smirk lit up Declan's face, and for a second it was hard to believe that any of it had happened. The coma, the heartache, the worrying . . .

"Wanted to surprise you," he responded simply, vaguely.

"Surprise me? By letting me go to the hospital to find you gone?"

Declan's smirk turned sheepish, and his eyes darted down for a second. A soft laugh flowed from his chest. "At least now I know why you haven't been wearing your ring."

"Dec . . ."

He pulled the ring he had proposed to me with out of his pocket—the same ring that was supposed to be in my jewelry box in our apartment—and grabbed my left hand.

Gasps of surprise, shock, and excitement filled the room, followed by one from his mother that was very clearly horrified.

For once, Linda and I were on the same page.

"Rorie Wilde," Declan began, "will you marry me . . . to-night?"

"What?" My voice came out soft, but the dread I felt leaked through the word.

Declan's smile didn't waver; he remained as still and silent as Jentry although everyone else in the room immediately began moving and speaking.

"What?"

"Tonight!"

"Oh, that's so sweet!"

His family's voices bounced around the room, mingling with Linda's as she tried to hold on to some semblance of calm. "Declan, let's think about this! You haven't even been awake a whole week!"

"Rorie and I nearly lost each other once, Mom. There's no point in waiting."

I looked from Declan's parents back to him. This wasn't happening. Not now, not in front of everyone.

Like before, Declan's eyes darted to Jentry, and his expression faltered and went cold again for a split second before he could control it. I knew if I had still been looking at his parents, or even if I had blinked, I would have missed it.

And I knew if Jentry hadn't been watching me for my reaction, he would have seen it, too.

Declan placed the ring at the tip of my finger and asked, "So what do you say?"

Just as he began sliding the ring onto the third finger of my left hand, I jerked my hand from his grasp and took a step away.

Silence filled the room and felt like a living, breathing thing, weighing down upon us, just waiting to see what would happen next.

"I can't," I whispered, and took another step back. "I can't—Declan, I can—I need to talk to you."

My eyes were burning with unshed tears and it suddenly

became hard to breathe, and I wondered how I would get through this as I left the room. Just the thought of telling Declan the first time had felt impossible, but this—this made the first time seem laughable.

That time, he hadn't been in a coma just a week before. I hadn't known he'd even planned on proposing; I'd thought we were growing apart anyway. And now, all of that had happened, and he had proposed again in front of his entire family, asking me to marry him *that night*.

I would rather have died than told Declan the truth in that moment.

I didn't walk far, just into the kitchen, because I didn't know how far Declan could walk without getting tired, and it wasn't long before Declan followed me in.

A mere second later, Linda began screaming at Jentry.

A sob burst from my chest and the tears finally began falling.

Declan didn't speak or move; he just waited.

"I can't marry you," I finally said.

He nodded slowly. "I figured that out." His mouth opened, then shut quickly, and he went back to waiting.

But I couldn't figure out where to begin, because I couldn't understand Declan. There was a sadness deep in his eyes, but he didn't look as if I'd just rejected his proposal. He didn't look like the girl he'd thought was his fiancée had just told him she couldn't marry him. He looked as if he had been waiting for this conversation.

"Why, Rorie?" he said pleadingly. "Why won't you?"

"I'm sorry, Dec. I'm so sorry. I never wanted to hurt you,

but I—" I sucked in a sharp breath, as if my body was rebelling against voicing the truth to him again, then forced out: "I fell in love with Jentry."

He winced in pain.

"It was before I ever met you. I just didn't know who he was. I didn't know who he was to you, and didn't think that I would see him again! I'm sorry! I didn't mean for this to happen, but I couldn't continue a relationship with you when my heart belonged to someone else. It wasn't fair to you. You have to understand than I never wanted to hurt you; *he* never wanted to hurt you."

Declan's lips formed a sad smile after a few moments. "God, that hurts just as much hearing it the second time."

25
Present Day

Aurora

My eyes widened as Declan's words registered. "Wh-what? What did you say?"

"Hearing that, hearing you admit you love him, hurts just as much now as it did the first time."

"What do you mean?" I nearly yelled in a mixture of shock, anger, and confusion. "You knew? You *remember*?"

He took a step toward me and held his hands up as if he was going to reach for me, but I stumbled away from him as Jentry hurried into the kitchen.

Declan didn't spare a glance for him, just moved one of his hands in Jentry's direction as if silently asking him not to speak, then admitted hesitantly, "Yes, I remember that. I remembered when I woke up because it felt like just seconds after."

Jentry looked at me questioningly.

"Declan already knew about us," I choked out. "He knew when he woke up."

Jentry tensed and slowly looked over at him. "Dec, how could—do you . . . do you have any idea how much she has agonized over telling you *again*? And this whole time you've just been—Christ, you've just been pretending not to remember? And for what?"

Declan's head dropped and shook slowly as he spoke, but he still wouldn't face Jentry. "Man, you've already taken her from me," he growled in a low tone. "The least you could do is give me some fucking time alone with her."

"The least *you* could do is give me some time to come to terms with the fact that you used your coma to your *advantage* and have let me believe that you thought we were engaged," I seethed. "Do you know how sick that is, Declan?" Without waiting for his response, I turned and walked from the house.

The humid air shouldn't have felt as refreshing as it did. I gulped down deep breaths of the heavy, midmorning air, letting it wash over and through me, and tried to imagine it calming me.

But that crushing weight now felt like heavy, sickening anger. That churning worry now felt like the most confusing betrayal—because I hadn't just been betrayed. We'd all betrayed each other.

I had been sitting on the top step of the Veils' porch for only a couple of minutes when I heard the front door open again, and I knew without turning around who had followed me out there. Because there was no yelling, no demands to know what had just happened, and I couldn't feel his presence . . .

My head snapped up and I automatically reached out to help Declan when he groaned in pain as he tried to sit down beside me, but as soon as he was settled, I released his arm and went back to staring out over the large field I had run across just a week before when I'd tried to escape everything.

Declan sat by my side in silence for a while, but when he started to talk, each word was slow and filled with pain, as if he were reliving it. "I remember asking you and watching the way your face fell, like I'd just crushed you. I remember you started telling me everything about you and Jentry, remember it like you'd been thinking it for a long time and it was finally just pouring out. And I remember thinking I needed to leave, that I needed to get away from you because I couldn't look at you anymore."

"Dec . . ."

"It was like going from one moment to another," he continued. "The last thing I honestly remember was storming out to my truck. I don't know why I don't remember getting in it or driving, or even this wreck everyone keeps asking me about. But I was heading for my truck, and then the next thing I know, I'm looking up at you and Jent. It felt like a split second between the two. But then . . . then there are times when I try to think back to see if I can remember more, and I swear I remember you, Rorie. I remember you . . ." He trailed off and laughed edgily. "God this sounds stupid, but I remember you talking to me. I remember your voice. *Only* your voice. I remember you asking me where I was and begging me to come back. But it seems like a dream."

I clamped my hand over my mouth to muffle the sob that rose up my throat, and shut my eyes at the onslaught of tears.

"Rorie?" he asked softly, and reached for my arm.

"Not a dream," I choked out.

"What?"

"That wasn't a dream." I wiped furiously at the steadily falling tears, and tried to calm myself enough to speak. "I kept thinking that you were lost, and if you could just find your way back, you would wake up."

"So I heard you?"

I nodded quickly. "I must have called you hundreds of times just to hear your voice, whether I was sitting next to your bed or somewhere away from the hospital. And every time I would wonder where you were, and I swore that the time you finally answered me, I would apologize for what I had done to you. Because I knew you wouldn't have been lost if it hadn't been for me. Dec, I'm so sorry!" I sobbed. "I never meant to hurt you!"

"Come here," he murmured, and pulled me into his side. "I can't let you apologize to me."

"Yes, you can!"

"Rorie, look at me," he said gently, and lifted my tear-streaked face until he was looking me in the eye. "I can't let you apologize. I tried to keep you when I knew you weren't mine." His voice wavered during the last few words, and his green eyes watered. "I knew during that weekend at the beach. I didn't know *what* was going on between the two of you . . . but I knew. I could see it. I was so afraid of what would happen when he moved back that I tried to do everything I could to keep you before that could happen. Tried to do everything I could to keep you from pulling away and going to him. *Especially* to him. Jentry has girls for a night before he forgets all about them; that's how he'd always been. I knew he would do the same to you, and I wanted to prevent that and keep you with me."

I watched him in shock as he told me everything, unsure if I was breathing or not as I realized that weeks of heartache and worry could have been avoided.

"But that night . . . I'd never expected what you told me. Because even though I didn't believe him at the time, Jentry had said on the way to the beach that he was hung up on someone he never expected to see again. And it didn't take a lot to connect what both of you had told me and realize that it had been you all along. And when you told me where you met him—damn it, Rorie, do you realize that I nearly walked in on the two of you that night? I never took you back to the frat house, but I didn't realize that you'd already been in my room."

I dropped my face into my hands as that night came flooding back when Jentry went to talk to someone at the door, and mortification set in.

"And how pissed off I'd already been at the thought of you looking for someone, only to realize that it was my brother. When all of that came pouring from you and settled in, I didn't know what to do. I was livid and sick and so damn torn up that I didn't know how to even look at you anymore. But I knew I'd already lost you to him before I'd even met you. I hated him, I hated you, I hated myself . . . and I just had to get away from you. And then . . ." He laughed sadly and shifted on the step. I looked up at him to find him staring at me as if he'd lost everything. "And then I woke up and saw you standing there with him and didn't understand what was going on or how I'd gotten there. But once things were explained to me, I thought I could try again. I was selfish enough to think I had a second shot at keeping you. So please do not apologize to me."

I gently leaned over, trying not to jostle him, and laid my head on his shoulder. "But I *am* sorry," I whispered. "So incredibly sorry. Hurting you . . . I never wanted to hurt you."

Another sad laugh left him as he wrapped his arm back around me. "Rorie, if there's anything I'm sure of in the past year, it is that you didn't want to hurt me. Doesn't mean it doesn't hurt."

I wanted to apologize again, but kept the words back. We stayed like that for a few minutes before I asked, "Knowing what you know, what did you think would've happened if your plan had worked?"

"I just would have prayed to God that Jentry would eventually do something to make you hate him," he responded immediately.

I laughed softly. "You're lucky you broke a couple of ribs." The amusement quickly faded from my face and voice when I said, "What you did, the way you tricked me, that wasn't fair. But our relationship wasn't fair to you because even if he'd never come back, I would've never belonged to anyone else. I'm sorry for all of it."

"I'm not," he said honestly. "I had an incredible year with you, Rorie Wilde. I'm . . . I'm not happy for you or for him. I don't know how to be. But I know we're over. I've known from the second I heard you two out on the beach that one night. I just didn't want to admit it."

My body stiffened. "You heard us?"

Declan sighed uncomfortably, and unwrapped himself from me to straighten up. "Yeah, our bedroom windows had been open. I couldn't hear what you were saying, just heard you. But people fighting like that aren't fighting over someone smoking."

"Taylor?"

"Found me just as I'd started storming out of the bedroom. I wanted to die when I saw her because she looked so panicked, and it confirmed what I'd already been thinking; so I pretended not to know where you were."

My head shook absentmindedly as I looked back at the field while I let Declan's words sink in. "I think back on it and wish I would have done so many things differently. Told you differently, or just at a different time. Sooner. But nothing ever felt like the right time because I do love you."

"Do you?" he said in playful awe. "Hey, I got a ring and a pastor. Wanna get married?"

"Even though I'm happy knowing you didn't lose it, your humor isn't appreciated right now, Dec." But even as I said the words, a smile began covering my face.

"Just needed to see you smile again."

I rolled my eyes and rested my head on his shoulder again. "I would like to know how you got that ring back. I had it in a jewelry box."

"Really? I found it in my room with a bunch of stuff when we got here last night. When I found it, my mom said that they'd given it to her with my belongings after the accident. She kept saying it must have fallen off your hand."

I sat back and looked up at him, and knew by the look on his face that he was telling the truth. "No, they gave *me* your belongings because your mom was filling out paperwork. I put the ring away when I went back to the apartment the morning after your wreck." I sucked in a quick breath then released it slowly when I thought about the one time I knew for sure Linda had gone through our apartment. "Never mind, I . . . never mind."

"What—"

"Trust me that now is not the time to hear about all of it."

His brow furrowed, and he looked like he was going to push the issue, but he sighed instead. "I'll wait for you to tell me if you do me a favor."

I lifted an eyebrow in question, and his green eyes searched mine for a second in silence.

"I know that no matter what, I'll be standing by Jentry's

side at his wedding as his best man. So if it's you . . . If you marry him, don't ask for my permission. Don't ask me to give you away. I'm already doing that by letting you go."

I nodded faintly and whispered, "'Kay."

"It's going to be hard to find someone like you."

"Good, then you'll be able to find someone better," I said, and leaned forward to press my lips to his forehead. "Love you, Dec."

JENTRY STAYED CLOSE enough behind me that I could have leaned against him as Declan told his family what he really remembered from the night of his accident, but was being considerate enough to Declan not to actually touch me.

Declan explained everything once he was seated back in the recliner: what he'd figured was happening between Jentry and me, what his plan had been before the accident, and what his new plan had been when he woke up. And when it was necessary, Jentry and I filled in the blanks in the story—*our* sides of the story.

Kurt remained quiet, as did Linda's parents—though they looked thoroughly shocked. Lara, Holly, and their husbands varied between shock, confusion, and disappointment throughout it all. Linda was the only one who remained completely impassive and still as stone from start to finish.

I had a feeling that beneath her blank exterior, she was fuming.

"Well," Linda said once it was all over. "What happens now?"

I glanced across the room to where Declan was sitting, then met the eyes of the rest of his family as we all waited for someone to say something.

"You can't expect us to just go on acting as if this had never happened," she continued. "You couldn't honestly think we would be okay with you going from one son to another."

"Mom—" Jentry began, but Linda cut him off.

"No, she has done enough. Rorie, it's time for you to leave now. I know most of my family agrees with my request that you never set foot in this house again."

But instead, protests of "Linda," "Honey," and "Mom" sounded throughout the room.

Her lips pursed and she gave me a stern look. "Get going before you ruin my family some more."

"She goes, I go." Jentry's deep voice rumbled behind me. "Or is that what you're still expecting, since yesterday that was your ultimatum? If I stayed with Aurora, you were disowning me."

Even though I had explained that I'd given Jentry my full name when I'd first met him, Declan hadn't heard him use it, and I didn't miss the way his head snapped up when Jentry said it, either. A small pit of guilt formed in my stomach, but I tried to push it back.

Linda's face fell. "Of course not. I didn't honestly think you would choose her over your brother, but no matter my disappointment in your choices, you are still my son! And as my son, I do not approve of—"

"Mom, do you think it's easy for me to look across the

room and see Rorie standing with Jentry?" Declan asked, his voice thick with emotion. "She's supposed to be here," he said firmly, and gestured to the side of the recliner. "But you don't hear me asking her to leave, and you won't."

"Honey, she played you and she's gonna do the same to Jentry."

"No, she didn't. Didn't you hear us explain it? The three of us got caught up in a hard situation with bad timing, and we all worked through it in different ways. She could have gone about things so differently, and I would have gladly been the one forcing her out of the house, but she didn't. This is how it's going to be from now on. If I can live with it, you can, too."

With those last words, Linda snapped. "I refuse to allow this trash into my family."

"What is it, Linda?" I demanded forcefully. "What is it about me that you don't like?"

"Aurora," Jentry said softly behind me; his tone neither a warning nor encouragement, but some odd mixture.

"No, it's like you said, she always wants to bring everyone into it, so I'll stop waiting for it to be just us. We'll finish it with everyone." I set my gaze on Linda and gritted my teeth as I said, "Your family has always told me how *sweet* and *loving* you are, but you chose to let me see sides of you that your family didn't know existed, and for what purpose?" I laughed, but there was no humor behind the sound. "You know, I thought you, if anyone, would be happy about this because all you've ever wanted was me out of the picture so that Madeline could have a chance to come back. Madeline.

Madeline, who cheated on your son with *multiple* other guys for *years*. But for some reason Madeline is a better choice than me any day. For some reason you've called *me* trash more times than I can count! Just the thought of hurting one of your sons guts me, and Madeline has never cared to apologize for sleeping with Declan's friends. But she wears an obnoxious tiara everywhere, and she's Miss North Carolina, so it's okay, right, Linda?"

I hated that tears were welling up in my eyes, but these were words I had been thinking of and wanting to say for weeks, emotions I had been keeping back, and they were finally bursting from me.

"So what is it?" I asked again when she didn't respond, only this time my tone had turned pleading. "Is it that I love your sons, and that scares you? Is it that I knew I was forcing one into a life he shouldn't be in, so I tried to get both of us out of it so I could be happy and so that he could have a fair chance at finding someone worth his love? Or is it that I care about your entire family so deeply that I will put up with every hateful thing you throw at me because loving them means I love you, too? When Declan was in a coma, I knew you were scared and hurting, and needed someone to hurt back. And you did! You hurt me over and over again, but I'm still here. When will it be enough?"

Still she didn't say a word.

"Maybe you weren't threatened by Madeline because she never loved Declan," I assumed softly. "Maybe that was it all along. Maybe you saw that I did love your son, and that scared you. Sons usually leave, daughters stay, right? Isn't that what people say?"

Kurt smiled for a moment at that; Linda's face tightened.

"I've never once tried to take Declan from you, and I'm not going to try to take Jentry from you. I moved here for *you,* I've been to every family dinner with and without Declan for *you.* I'm here, and your sons aren't gone. Can't you see that?"

Linda just stared at me for long moments before lifting her chin and curling her lip. "Get out of my house." Without waiting to see if I would, she turned and walked from the room.

26
Present Day

~~~~~

Aurora

"How is it that it isn't even noon yet, and this day has already felt incredibly long?" I asked Jentry a couple of hours later when we were back at the apartment and walking into the master bedroom.

We hadn't stayed much longer at the Veils' after Linda had walked out of the living room, since it was clear she wouldn't be coming back as long as we were there.

Declan told us that he planned to move back in with his parents—that it would be easier since he still needed to go through some physical therapy and couldn't go back to work yet—but none of us had mentioned what would happen with the apartment after.

It was a place that Declan and I had picked out together, and a place that had never started to lose the prisonlike feeling even after Jentry had moved in or Declan had woken up. And even though neither of us had said as much, I knew Jentry and I both felt a little uncomfortable there knowing that it had been my space with someone else. The lease wouldn't be up for some time, but we would figure out what to do later. For now, the day had already been exhausting enough.

I crawled onto the large bed once Jentry was lying on it and leaning back against some pillows. I rested my head on his stomach and looked up into his dark eyes, and an overwhelming sense of contentment and peace flooded through me as I watched him watching me.

This was it; this was my sunrise.

"I see you," he murmured roughly, and lifted his hand to trail it through my hair.

I nodded, because I saw him, too. I saw his love and his happiness—matching my own—just the same as I saw his pain and his fear. I didn't need to ask about the pain, because I had no doubt it was linked with Declan's and mine, but the fear . . . "Before this week, I would have sworn you were fearless. Does your anger scare you that much?"

Jentry looked amused that I'd even known he was thinking about it, but the amusement faded. "Yes and no. I try not to focus on it. The more Jessica is around, the more I do because she will never let me forget about it. And when I look at you . . ." He trailed off and just stared at me for a moment. "When I look at you, Aurora, I see everything I've ever wanted. And as much as I hate it and try to push it away, that makes me hear my biological mother, and makes me terrified of what I could do to you. The thought of ever hurting or ruining you haunts me."

I opened my mouth, but hesitated.

"Say it," he prompted gently.

"You told me that you vowed to protect people instead of hurt them, but the way you are—you don't protect people because you feel like you should or you have to. It's your natural instinct to. The possibility of what you could do when you're angry is what fuels your fear of it. Anyone can do something horrible when they're angry. The difference is that you've lived it. You've felt it. You grew up in it, but you got away, and that isn't your life even if Jessica wants you to believe that it is."

"You haven't seen me when I just . . . when I lose it."

"No, but I know you," I said firmly. "And I think anyone would beat up their best friend if they found him with their twin sister."

Jentry's face pinched as he held back a laugh. "I don't know about that, and I don't want that image in my mind anymore."

I moved so I was on my knees, facing him, and ran my hand over his head until I was cupping the back of his neck. Pressing my forehead to his, I brought my other hand up and trailed the tips of my fingers over his lips. "This," I said softly. "You can think about it and find it funny. Not because you snapped, but the whole situation." I worried my bottom lip, and kept my tone hesitant when I said, "You told me that you've gone off on two people. Was she the second?"

"No," he said quickly. "No, that . . . that was something

else. It still had to do with Declan, though. Told you I got back here as soon as I could when I found out about Dec, and that I couldn't leave before that." Jentry's dark eyes glanced to mine before looking away.

I blinked quickly as I tried to understand exactly what he meant. When it seemed like he wouldn't elaborate, I reminded him, "I've been asking you ever since you came back what kept you away for those three weeks."

For a long time, he just stared at nothing as silence filled the room. "I was already so upset over Declan," he said, as if he was defending whatever he'd done.

"Your anger doesn't scare me, Jentry," I whispered.

"Remember when I told you that you couldn't think about the ifs, or try to take the blame for something you had no control over?" When I nodded, he continued, "One of my NCOs . . . he and I have had bad blood between us for a while. Years. His buddy died during an ambush on my second tour, and he's always blamed me even though I know I couldn't have stopped it from happening." His eyes flashed to mine. "That doesn't mean I didn't agonize over what I could've done differently. It doesn't mean I didn't blame myself for a long time."

My eyes fluttered shut as my chest ached for Jentry and for the people affected in that ambush.

"When I got the phone call from you about Dec's accident, I immediately tried to get leave. But the request had to go through that NCO first, and he saw it as his last chance to piss me off before I got out, and denied it. Tore the request up right in front of me. I was going to wait until the morning and take a new request straight to the commanding officer, but he kept saying shit about his friend and about Declan until I lost it. Three guys had to pull me off of him." Jentry's tone was hard, but still so quiet I could barely hear him. "He tried to have me arrested, but the commanding officer lessened it. He put me on restriction until my contract was up."

"What's that?"

"It's like being grounded. Can't leave; have to do extra duty. I couldn't get back here, but it was better than the alternative."

My head shook slowly, absentmindedly. "Jentry, I'm sorry."

"You're sorry?" he asked, his tone full of disbelief. "Did you not hear me? It took three Marines to pull me off him. He tried to have me arrested, Aurora. Do you see why this scares me?"

"He was pushing you."

"That doesn't excuse it."

"I see you. I see the protector you are. Declan's been on the receiving end of your anger, and he never once mentioned being worried about that for me. He was worried you would *leave* me. Your commanding officer must have seen what you did to that guy, and I doubt he would have only put you on restriction if he thought you had serious problems with your anger. And if you really thought you were like your biological father, I don't think *you* would have trusted yourself in the position you had in the Marine Corps, and I don't think you'd trust yourself to potentially be a police officer."

"There are men in those positions who are like him."

"But they aren't you," I whispered, and pressed my mouth to his to stop any other arguments he may have had.

I removed my shirt, then cradled his face in my hands to deepen the kiss when he pulled me over so I was straddling him. When his fingers went to the clasp on my bra, I pulled away far enough so my lips continued to brush against his when I spoke.

"From the beginning, you've been trying to protect me from you, Jentry. Protect me from something that isn't there." When my bra fell to the floor, I grabbed one of his hands and placed it on my chest, and sat back to look directly into his eyes as I asked the question I had so long ago. "Should I be scared of you?"

His dark eyes blazed, but he didn't speak.

"You said no then, and I knew that I could trust you. It doesn't matter what kind of past you've had, what your mother told you, or what your sister wants you to believe. *You* are good. There is nothing inside of you that could ever hurt me."

I released his hand to place mine against his chest as I had the day before. "Now do you understand?"

We sat like that for long moments, and though he didn't respond, I watched as the internal struggle played out in his eyes and on his face. Every part of him wanted to believe what I was saying, and he was beginning to, but it wouldn't be so simple. I knew that no matter what I said today, and no matter what he believed in that moment, Jentry would have to be the person to push his fears away for good. He had to be the one to decide that he wasn't going to allow his past to continue to haunt him for the rest of his life.

"Now tell me," I pleaded against his lips as I slowly pulled his shirt off his body. "What scares you the most right now?"

"Waking up tomorrow in a desert without you. Not knowing who you really are or if I'll ever see you again." Jentry lifted me off his body and laid me flat on the bed, and rolled over until he was on his knees so he could take my shorts and underwear off. His eyes never left mine, even when he stepped off the bed to finish taking off his own clothes. "But you're here," he began when he knelt back on the bed between my legs, and bent to kiss his way up them. "I can touch you and taste you."

A shuddering breath left me when he pressed a slow kiss to my sex, and then continued up my stomach and chest.

When he was hovering above me, he gathered my hands in his and whispered, "I can see you, Aurora, and you're so damn beautiful. And you're finally mine."

I only had enough time take a breath in before Jentry slammed my hands straight out to my sides onto the bed, and pushed into me. The same breath I had just inhaled forced back out of my lungs with a powerful rush; my mouth fell open as my body stretched around him.

His fingers intertwined with mine and dug into the comforter, pinning my hands to the bed as he held himself over me. Each thrust was rough, exuding power and control, and was oh so perfect.

He released my hands and slowed the movement of his

hips when I wrapped my legs around his waist, and his fingers trailed gently up my arms until he was tenderly cupping my neck with one hand, and burying the other in my hair.

Slowly, his hand fisted in my hair and pulled down to expose my neck to him. Goose bumps spread across my skin and a warm shiver ran down my spine at the slightest hint of stinging across my scalp. Heat flooded low in my belly when his thumb softly moved over the front of my throat.

Hard and soft. And I knew this was just this beginning, and would be so different than the night before.

His head dipped so he could place soft, slow kisses across my chest and between my breasts, and my already uneven breathing turned ragged when he moved to focus on my nipple. His hips began moving faster and faster, and just when he started to slow again, the teasing licking was replaced with a swift bite that forced a cry from my mouth.

Soft kisses were placed on, and around, the area where he had just bitten down. The hand that was still tenderly cupped around my neck moved to trace faint shapes along my throat. My body shook with the need for him to continue *this,* and the need for more of the *other.*

Jentry's hand suddenly tightened in my hair, forcing my head back more. I tried to reach for his head in hopes that I could keep him where I wanted him, but another jerk in my hair had me arching so far against the bed that I had to grab hold of the comforter at my sides again. My legs tightened around him, and it was all I could do to try to hold on as each jolt of pain sent a shock to my core, and was immediately followed by the sweetest *soft*.

My body was so tightly strung that I knew . . . I knew whenever the next blissful *hard* came I would come crashing down around him. And I wanted to so badly. Each time he backed away left me ready to scream for more, ready to beg for that much-needed end, yet all that left my mouth were whimpers and moans.

He removed my legs from him and pulled away from me, but just as I was about to protest he slid down my body and covered my sex with his mouth. Within seconds of his teasing, the tightening inside me became too much, and my body began trembling, and suddenly it felt like I was weightless as warmth surged through my veins.

I was still struggling to catch my breath, slowly coming back to earth and the bedroom when Jentry flipped me to my stomach and pushed me up onto my knees. Keeping my chest on the bed, he took both of my hands in one of his and rested them at the small of my back as he roughly pressed into me again.

"Jentry!" I breathed; my body shook fiercely as my second orgasm took over the first.

My legs trembled. I was barely able to keep myself up as he pushed into me over and over, nearing his own release.

He abruptly released me and curled over my back, his body tense and tight against mine. One of his arms wrapped around my stomach to keep my body pressed against his; the other shook as he struggled to keep both of us up, his hand planted firmly on the bed inches from my face.

His chest moved roughly against my back as he slowly lowered me to the bed, and every inch of my skin covered in goose bumps when he lowered himself enough to press his lips to the base of my spine, then higher and higher until he was covering me again, and his mouth was at my shoulder.

Hard and soft. I knew I would never have one without the other, and I wouldn't want it any other way. Because this sweet, tender side of him was just as incredible as the body-numbing sex.

He gently rolled me onto my side and curled his body around mine so that he was facing me, but I was so physically and emotionally exhausted, I could barely keep my eyes open.

"Sleep," he said gently. "Just know that when you wake up, I've got a year to make up for."

I smiled lazily and ran my fingers across his forehead and down his cheek. "We have a long, long time to make up those months lost, Jentry."

"I don't plan to spend the rest of our lives making up what I've already lost with you. I've got a lot to look forward to with you, so give me a week or two, and then it's only present and future."

My eyebrows lifted and a startled laugh escaped me. "You want to make up for a year in a week or two?"

Dark eyes dipped down my bare body, making me feel too warm, and somehow, impossibly, I wanted to feel him again.

"Aurora . . . yeah." His husky growl had me biting down on my bottom lip.

"And what happens when these two weeks are over, and you have to actually talk to me?" I asked teasingly. But even as I said the words, I moved closer to brush my mouth across his.

Jentry held my face away from his to study me for a second. "You didn't have to take your clothes off for me to fall in love with you. If you had changed your mind in that room and all we'd ended up doing was talking to escape the party, we still would have ended up right here."

I curled my hand around one of his and stared at him in wonder. After a few moments, I whispered, "Thank you for not letting me go."

His eyebrows pulled together as confusion settled over his face.

"If you had ever truly let me go, we *wouldn't* be here." I leaned forward to kiss him soundly, then settled down with my head against his chest. As I had the night before, I drifted off to sleep listening to Jentry's beating heart while he slowly pulled his fingers through my hair.

27
Present Day

Jentry

I just, I can't—I don't know how to handle this," Aurora said in frustration the next morning. She stopped loading up the box in front of her and leaned against the wall.

"Well, unless you plan to write 'fragile' on it, I don't think you need to handle with care," Taylor mused sarcastically.

"Funny." But Aurora sounded defeated, and when she saw me take a step in her direction, she put a hand up in a silent plea for me to stay. "I'm fine, this is just throwing me off. In my head . . ." She trailed off, and looked sadly at all the boxes around the room. "I obviously know that Declan is okay, and that we're just moving his stuff back to your parents' house," she said to me. "But I keep starting to feel this overwhelming heartache, and I start to panic. Because when Declan was in a coma, I was terrified of having to box up his stuff for Linda if he never woke up. So doing it now is making that come back even though that isn't the case. And—I don't know. It's frustrating and I can't make it stop."

"Do you want Taylor and me to finish this?"

"No," she said quickly. "No, we'll be done in a minute or two. It's just weird. I don't know how that fear is even able to slip in. I feel like I'm devastated, and then I remember that he's fine."

"Well," Taylor said, "if it makes you feel any better, I don't know how to handle the fact that I've been here for two hours, and Linda hasn't shown up to say something ridiculous to you." She sighed longingly. "I like bitchy Linda. She's easy to make fun of."

"Taylor . . ." Aurora didn't try to continue, just shook her head and went back to packing.

If I hadn't seen the way Mom treated Aurora firsthand, Taylor's words would have bothered me more. "Still my mom," I reminded her as I finished closing up a box.

Taylor widened her eyes as she picked up her box to leave, giving me a look as if she didn't care. "She's still super-rude."

"Enough." Aurora gestured in the direction Taylor had gone. "I'm sorry. You already know about her—"

"No filter," I finished for her, and smiled. "Aurora, it's fine."

"But she is the best."

"Of course I am," Taylor said from the doorway. "I'm gonna make a coffee run. Rorie . . . usual?"

"Please. Extra shot of espresso," Aurora mumbled from where her head was buried in the box.

Taylor glanced at me and mouthed, "I'll make it two." Then louder, "Want anything else while I'm out?"

I looked over to Aurora, who was shaking her head. "I'm fine. Just get me whatever you're getting Aurora."

"Want me to take the boxes over to Declan so there's no awkward moments? Yes? No?" Taylor asked, drawing out the word.

"No, I'll do that later," I answered. "Let me get my wallet for you."

"Well, isn't that sweet. Except I already have someone who funds my caffeine addiction, so we're covered." She blew Aurora a kiss and said, "Don't have a panic attack if I'm not here to watch it. Love you!"

Aurora rolled her eyes and shouted, "Back!"

I waited until I heard the door shut to say, "Even if I had never met you, I would have run screaming from Taylor that first night at the beach."

She laughed softly and closed up the final box. "She's fun."

"She's something," I corrected.

Her smile slowly faded as she looked around at the three remaining boxes in the room, her head shaking distractedly. "So weird. He's fine; I know that."

I walked across the room and pulled her away from where she was pinned between the wall and a box, and into my arms. I pressed my lips to the top of her head and kept them there when I said, "He's doing PT at my parents'. All of his stuff will be gone in a couple of hours, and if you want to come so you can see him, then I want you to."

Before she could speak, the front door opened and shut. Aurora cocked her head to the side and called out, "What'd you forget, Taylor?"

My arms tensed around her when I heard the responding voice.

"My, my, my, my, *my*. We sure don't waste much time around here, now do we?"

Aurora's face fell. "Is that—"

A wild laugh came from the front of the apartment, answering her question before she could get it all out.

"Poor little Declan," Jessica began as Aurora and I hurried from the bedroom. "I could always go play nurse for him. Looks like he needs someone to take care of him now that Miss Perfect has moved on," she sneered, her eyes raking over Aurora as she spoke.

"Leave," I demanded.

"Whatcha gonna do if I don't, Jent?" She smiled wickedly, and turned in slow circles as she made her way back toward where the other two boxes of Declan's things were. She popped open the top box and looked inside. "What do we have here?"

"Jess, leave. I won't keep asking you."

She curled her lip, but didn't look up at us. "You're no fun anymore. Hey . . . remember when you used to say that if I wished real hard, the bruises would disappear? You lied," she said sullenly, and pulled her hair back to show faint fingerlike bruising on her neck.

"What happened?"

"Who cares? Not you!" she hissed. "Oh wait, do you? You

gonna go defend your whore sister's honor?" She laughed loudly and began advancing on us. "You gonna go get mad? You gonna hit someone?"

"Tell me what happened."

"Why?" she snapped.

"God damn it, Jessica, *let me help you*!"

"Help? You can't help? You'd only make things worse! You would ruin me; *he* ruined me. He ruined *her*!" Her wild eyes were still on me, but she was suddenly pointing at Aurora. "You're going to ruin her! It's inside you! You will hurt people if you keep running from who you are!"

The way she was screaming and looking at me was so like the way our mother had all those years ago. I could feel my anger simmering in my veins and my chest's movements growing more pronounced.

Just as my hands started to clench into fists, Aurora slipped her hand into one of mine and squeezed tightly.

"I see you," she whispered from beside me.

And in that moment, I could see what Aurora had tried to tell me. Because I could feel it all—but I could also feel her.

And that anger *was* there, and it *was* simmering in my veins, but it was growing hotter and hotter because I *was* fucking terrified that there was a possibility that Jessica could be right.

I squeezed Aurora's hand back, and waited until I knew I wasn't going to yell at Jessica—something I knew she wanted so badly.

My chest was still rising and falling roughly, but my voice was calm when I finally looked my sister in the eye and said,

"The only thing I could ruin is my life if I let you stay in it. You know when you can come back. Until then, I don't want to see you again. Leave, Jessica. Now."

Jess waited, seemingly unfazed, though I knew better. The way she was holding herself showed her hurt and disappointment, but after a handful of seconds, she smiled wickedly and turned toward the door. She swayed the entire way out, as if she didn't have a care in the world, all while singing, "Someone's gonna go boom."

Aurora exhaled roughly once she was gone, and tightened her grip on my hand. She twisted so she was in front of me, her head already shaking sadly. She didn't need to say anything, I already knew. Everything she was thinking was clear in the way she was looking at me.

She was proud of me.

She loved me.

She was worried about what would happen with Jess in the future.

"We just need to get through one tough situation at a time," she said warily after a minute of us just standing there holding each other.

"Yeah. I'd like to say that one's done, but I have a feeling she'll be the last."

"We'll figure it out." She buried her head into my chest, and didn't move until the door burst open again a while later.

Taylor came in already talking, and stopped walking abruptly when she saw us. She pointed at us with the drink carrier. "What's wrong? Did I miss something? If y'all were about to cozy, you can just wait, because it's Taylor time and I have my fuzzy socks."

"Oh, Taylor." Aurora laughed, and for the first time in too long, it looked like she was free of all the weight that had been pressing down on her. After pressing a quick kiss to my chest, she winked at me and turned. "Let's just say Linda has nothing on what you just missed, and other than that, it is completely unexplainable."

Aurora

I woke up sometime after Taylor had left that morning to an empty bed even though Jentry had been curled around me when I'd lain down, and it took a few seconds to realize I heard the shower running. A quick glance over my shoulder at the open window confirmed the sun was just getting to the high point in the sky, but my body felt tight, as if I'd slept for hours.

I stretched out my arms as I climbed off the bed, and had just started pulling off my shirt to join Jentry when I heard a noise from outside the bedroom, and wondered if that was what had woken me.

I pulled my shirt back on as I ran through the apartment to the front door, and didn't take the time to look out the peephole before opening it.

"Linda," I said in surprise, and after a short pause, opened the door wider to let her in. "Hi." I glanced around the entry-way quickly, even though I knew I wouldn't find any boxes there. "Um, we finished packing up Declan's things this morning. Everything's in Jentry's car; we were going to bring it by later."

She didn't speak or look at me as she entered the apartment, just walked slowly toward the living room until she got to the first couch. Instead of sitting on it, she turned to face me, and my initial surprise at her arrival multiplied when I found her eyes filled with tears.

"Are you— Did something happen?"

A shuddering breath left her before she could cover her mouth with her hand, and a few tears slipped down her cheeks.

"Lin—" I cut off abruptly when her arms suddenly engulfed me in a hug.

It was the first time Linda had willingly touched me, and it was the first time she had hugged me. For a moment, I stood there frozen before my arms slowly wrapped around her back as she cried on my shoulder.

"Don't take this the wrong way, but this is scaring me more than any other meeting with you has," I said softly, and felt her laugh between her sobs.

"Mom?"

Linda quickly moved away from me and turned so her back was to Jentry, and set about wiping at her cheeks.

"Mom, what's wrong?" Jentry asked, his tone full of alarm now.

I sent him a meaningful look as he approached and shook my head slowly, and was glad to see that he had put clothes on even though his skin was still dripping with water.

"She okay?" he mouthed.

I shrugged, because I honestly didn't know, and whispered, "Can you give us a sec?"

He looked from me to Linda, then reached out to graze the tips of his fingers along my hip before walking away.

Once he was gone, I asked warily, "Can I get you some sweet tea?"

Linda's shoulders bounced with her amused huff when she turned back around. "Please, yes, this old girl could use a glass or two."

Her response shocked me so much that for a few moments, I just stood there watching her to see if she would start laughing condescendingly. When she didn't, I backed away slowly, then turned and hurried into the kitchen to get a glass and fill it with the tea I had made earlier that morning.

Linda was sitting on the couch when I returned, and before she even took a sip, she studied the glass and sighed.

I held my breath.

"You know, it has bothered me from that first day you moved in here." She lifted the glass, as if to show me what she was talking about, then took a long drink. "Anyone can make sweet tea, but few people can make it right. And Kurt's mother . . ." Linda trailed off and tsked. "Rorie, she made it right. She taught me how to make it just right, and I taught my kids."

"And Declan taught me," I added quietly, and then smiled at the memory. "We'd been visiting my parents one weekend during the school year. Turns out I added too much water and not enough sugar; I couldn't believe he could make it better. But he did."

Linda nodded. "I knew that recipe from the first sip, and it scared the hell out of me. Everything you did scared me. Not to mention that I was not okay with what I had heard."

My cheeks burned with embarrassment.

"You know, Declan hadn't brought Madeline over to meet us until they'd been dating for two years, but he wanted us to meet you right away. I knew . . . a mother always knows." She sighed heavily, then said, "Yes. To everything you said and asked yesterday. Yes."

I blinked slowly as I tried to think back to what I had said, but could only remember yelling at her. "Linda, I don't—I don't remember what I said. I was mad, and I—"

"I'm scared of you because you love my sons. I was scared that you would take Declan from me, and I'm scared that Jentry has already chosen you over us. It's easier to want Madeline because she's superficial and I know she would never last in this family. She was never a threat, but you always have been." She set the glass shakily down on the coffee table and covered her mouth with her trembling hand when her eyes filled with tears again. "I wanted to hate you and blame you for letting Declan drive away after you two had fought . . . for letting him get in the accident. But I knew that's all it was, an accident. And you were always there. Always willing to do whatever anyone needed you to. So it was easier to hate you for being there at all. To hate you for still loving and caring for Declan while he slept. Taking care of him is supposed to be my job, and I hated you for the fact that I knew he was okay as long as you were there. There was just so much hate and pain building up inside of me for those weeks and it felt like I was drowning."

I reached out for Linda's free hand when a soft cry escaped her chest, but remained silent, knowing she wasn't done and just needed time.

"You were right, Rorie. I was hurting so much that I needed to make someone else hurt. I needed you to hurt with me. And as much hatred was inside me, as much as I wanted you—this threat—gone from my family, I couldn't seem to stay away from you. I needed to see you just to know you were still there. But then the vicious cycle would begin all over again, because there you would be, ready for whatever I needed, and I would hate you for it and need to see you hurt. Need to see you show the pain that was suffocating me. I've never been more ashamed of my actions than I am of the way I have treated you the past weeks. I could say that I am sorry and apologize a thousand times, and it would never make up for the things I have done or said. But I am sorry, and I need you to know that nothing has ever been true. Everything has been a cruel attempt to make you leave."

I nodded and smiled sadly as her words from the past month flew through my mind too quickly for me to focus on any specific insult.

"I am sorry, Rorie," she said, her voice shaking. "Or . . . Aurora?"

"Rorie. No one calls me—well . . . just Rorie."

Linda nodded. "I'm sorry."

"I know you are," I said, "and I know you were hurting. It's funny listening to you explain everything from your side because all I wanted was for you to show some of the pain that *I* was feeling. The way you acted like Declan would walk through the door at any second drove me crazy, and I just wanted you to acknowledge what was happening and show that it was hurting you the way it was me. But I guess we all get through difficult times in our own ways. We do what we have to in order to survive when it feels like we won't."

"Right," she agreed softly. "This situation the three of you are in now."

"I didn't want it to happen like this."

She nodded slowly, then shrugged. "Life doesn't always happen the way we want it to. Just do what you can to keep my boys close. And please, don't take Jentry from me. I may not have given him life, but he is my son."

"I'm still here. Jentry's still here. We aren't going anywhere. He loves you and he loves Declan; and from what Dec said yesterday, there's nothing that's going to keep them apart."

Linda gave me a watery smile, and reached out to brush some of my hair away from my face, then cradled my cheek with her hand. "Thank you, Rorie."

I stood when she did and followed her to the door, and after another brief hesitation, accepted my second hug from her.

"Linda?" I called out as she walked out of the apartment, and waited for her to look back. "I forgive you, you know . . . for all of it."

Her steps halted and her eyes widened as my words sank in. "If I got to view you as a threat for the rest of my life, I would consider myself a very lucky woman."

I wasn't surprised to find Jentry leaning against the entryway wall when I shut the door and turned. "What just happened?" I asked as I walked toward him and fell into his arms.

"I think you just met my mom."

I narrowed my eyes at him and scrunched my nose. "I meant the way she sort of told me she would be happy with me being in the family, but I should have known you'd listen to the whole thing." I looked up at him in awe, and couldn't stop the smile that formed on my face. "That was incredible. So that's Linda?"

Jentry dipped his head in acknowledgment. "What do you think about everything she said?"

I thought for a few seconds before saying, "It made sense. When she said it, I could see it even though I could vividly remember how miserable she made me. But I think things will be better for us now. I think having a better relationship with her will make what's going on with Declan a little easier. One tough situation at a time?"

He made an affirmative grunt, and the corner of his mouth lifted in a crooked smile as he pulled me tighter against him. "But until the next situation, I still have a year to make up for."

"Do you?" I asked breathlessly when he dropped his head to trail the bridge of his nose across my neck.

Another grunt sounded deep in his chest.

"Are you sure you want to—" My question ended as a soft moan when he bit down on the base of my throat.

"Aurora," his rough voice rumbled against my skin. "Yeah."

Epilogue
Two Years Later

Jentry

Yeah. Mom, we're gonna be there," I said, trying to talk over her. "I got held up on a call for a little bit, but I just got home and changed."

Mom tsked at me. "I have got to get that girl fed, Jentry."

I laughed softly. "We'll only be thirty minutes late. She'll eat. And I'm sure she's kept herself fed today with all the food that's in the house."

"All right now. See you in a bit."

I ended the call and walked back through the house to find Aurora, and smiled to myself when I smelled the white chocolate bread pudding she'd made for the family dinner that night. I didn't know why Mom worried. If Aurora got hungry enough, she would've just eaten that.

"You ready to go?" I called out as I walked down the hall.

The smile that began when I saw her standing in the living room fell when I noticed her rigid stance and blank stare.

Her arms were folded protectively across her swollen, six-month-pregnant stomach as she stared straight ahead at the couch.

"Aurora, what—" I cut off abruptly, and faltered for only a second before I continued walking to place myself between my wife and my twin sister. "Jess."

"Officer Michaels," she murmured teasingly, then held her hands up. "No need to arrest me today."

"She was just sitting on the couch when I came back out here," Aurora said from behind me.

Jessica sighed. "Okay, well there *is* that. But it's a hard habit to break, and I didn't think she would let me in."

"*She* is standing right behind me, and has reason not to let you in here," I said tightly.

Her eyes slowly moved down to look past me; pain flitted across her face. "You didn't tell me you guys were going to have a baby last time I saw you."

"Last time I saw you I'd just arrested you for prostitution. It wasn't one of our best moments—and not the time to talk to you about what's going on in Aurora's and my life."

Eyes identical to my own darted away. "Yeah, maybe not."

Silence engulfed the room as Aurora and I stood there watching Jessica, waiting for whatever would happen this time. In the two years since Aurora and I had been together, we'd only seen Jess a handful of times. I saw her more often now that I was a police officer and she was still doing things

I hated in order to pay for our mother's drugs. Even then, I hadn't seen a trace of her in two months, and I'd had no idea that she knew about this house.

Then again, Jessica could find out anything she wanted to.

I finally sighed, and said, "I don't know why you're here or how you found us, but coming in like this isn't okay. Coming here at all isn't okay. You can call me if you need something, because I know you still have my number, but I can't have you bringing your life into our home anymore. Not now that we're going to have a baby. Jess, you know when you can come back, but for now you have to go."

Instead of moving or laughing, or doing any number of the things that I would have expected her to, she stayed still. "That's . . . that's kind of why I'm here."

I studied her for a few seconds, but her solemn expression never changed. "Why now? What happened?"

Her eyes drifted to Aurora, who had moved a step to the side to be able to look at Jessica, and a soft smile touched Jess's face. "Just . . . things that I never understood before." She nodded absentmindedly, and her eyes got a faraway look. "Still trying to understand them completely, but I'm getting there. And I know you aren't sure if you should believe me, and have somewhere to be," she said with a sigh as she stood.

"Jess," I said quickly to stop her from leaving. "If you're serious, then stay and we'll stay. We don't have to leave."

She waved a hand between us and said, "This can be enough for now, because just saying that felt big, and I don't think either of us is ready for more. I have a lot to say . . . I think, and I know I have a lot to apologize for. And I know how to let myself in, so you can't really keep me out." She smiled with her reminder. "I'm ready, Jent. I'll be back."

"Do you think she's being serious?" Aurora asked after I'd shut the door behind Jessica. "I mean, there wasn't any laughing or taunting or . . . anything."

"I know," I mumbled, and tried to push down the hope that had started building. "I won't know until the next time I see her. She can play any kind of role she wants to, but she can't hold on to it for long. I'll ask around, see if she's been buying for our mother, or if she's been on the streets. If she hasn't, then we'll see what she has to say the next time she shows up."

Aurora nodded and blew out a harsh breath. "I just hope she knocks next time."

I bent down to pass my mouth across hers and said, "You should have yelled, at the very least. The fact that you just stood there when you found someone as crazy as Jess in our living room scares the shit out of me. Next time you see her, whether she knocks or not, make sure you put more distance between the two of you, and that I'm somewhere within that distance." After another kiss, I straightened and turned to go collect the dessert Aurora had made.

By the time we made it to my parents' house, we were forty-five minutes late, and Mom had called again during our drive over there to make sure we were still coming, and that Aurora was okay and not starving.

In the last couple of years, they'd grown so close that I was sure Mom thought Aurora had been the one she'd adopted into the family instead of me. And ever since Aurora had found out she was pregnant, Mom had tried to attach herself to Aurora's side.

It had been a long pregnancy already . . .

I planned on changing the locks soon just so I could have a few days with my wife in peace.

We had barely set foot inside before Aurora was pulled away from me and ushered to a chair in the dining room.

"I'll get a plate for you. How's my grandbaby today?" Mom asked as soon as she had Aurora seated.

"He's kicking away," Aurora said softly, and placed a hand low on her stomach as her face lit up.

"Oh, sweet girl, you both must be just starving. Can't believe my son made y'all late for family dinner." She sent me a glare at that, but kissed my cheek on her way to the kitchen.

Declan rounded the corner into the dining room and placed a swift kiss on top of Aurora's head on his way over to me. "Man, that is a big baby belly," he said with a smile. "Sure there aren't five or six of them in there?"

I rolled my eyes, but couldn't contain my smile when I looked over at Aurora.

She'd turned in her seat to watch us, and her smile was breathtaking and contagious. "Right?" she said with exasperation that didn't match her excited expression. "It just popped out this week out of nowhere."

"You look like you're about to pop," Declan corrected.

Her eyes narrowed playfully, but then her shoulders sagged. "I feel like a whale."

"Aurora . . ." I shook my head slowly, but knew there was no point in arguing. I'd found that out quickly over the last few months. If only she could've seen what I was looking at.

She'd said something to that effect every day that week, ever since her stomach had gone from slightly rounding to looking like she was about to give birth to twins at any moment. Her feet may have disappeared from her view suddenly, but in that time? God . . .

My wife was always beautiful, but that *glow* they talk about with pregnant women? Yeah, that had shown up over the last week, along with her huge stomach, making it nearly impossible to stop looking at her.

Declan sucked in air through his teeth. "I wasn't gonna say anything."

I smacked his shoulder, but he was already laughing.

"You look gorgeous, Ror. I promise."

"I hate you," she said flatly.

He held a hand to his chest, then held it out toward her. "You don't have to lie just because Jentry's standing here."

Her tone didn't change. "No, I kind of hate you right now."

"Wait until someone feeds you, then decide if you hate me or not."

At that moment, Mom came rushing in with a plate for Aurora. "Everyone will be in here in a minute. Don't bother waiting." She snapped at us as she went walking away. "Boys, you are grown; come get your plates."

Aurora took a big bite of food and kept her eyes on Declan as she chewed. With a shrug, she said, "Still hate you."

Declan made a face, then turned to look at me. "She doesn't hate me."

"I know, Dec."

Their exchange didn't bother me. They hadn't since the day Declan had gotten out of the hospital. I knew who Aurora had chosen, and why, and I knew she would never waver in that choice.

It had taken a while for the three of us to be near each other, and have things be normal—much longer than if just Declan and I were together, or if he was with Aurora—but eventually, we had figured it out. Aurora and I had never thrown our relationship in Declan's face, and we were mindful of the things we said or how close we were whenever he was around.

That being said, the announcement that we were getting married had been hard for Declan. When we told the family the week before the wedding that Aurora was pregnant, he'd quietly left dinner, and we didn't hear from him until the rehearsal. Setbacks in the progress we had all made, but Aurora and I had expected them. And I knew with one hundred percent certainty that Declan was happy for us now.

He was still my best man in the wedding, and he even danced with Aurora during the reception.

"Hey," Declan said quietly, and held a hand out to stop me when I began walking toward the kitchen. "So I wanted to talk to you without Mom trying to overhear."

I glanced at the entrance into the kitchen, then back to Dec. "You say that as though Mom likes gossip."

Declan lifted an eyebrow, and I held back a laugh.

"What's up?"

"I met Rorie, and I thought it was forever. . . ."

My head tilted to the side when he didn't continue. "Where are you going with this, Dec?"

"I see it between you two, but I didn't understand what could be different between the two of you, and what she and I had." A smile lit up Declan's face even though he tried to hide it. "I get it, man."

It took a second before *I* got what he was saying, then I asked, "You met someone?"

"Never thought I would have this, Jent. Not after what happened, and just—just because I didn't know it *could* happen."

My smile matched his, and I nodded, because I knew what he meant. Meeting Aurora had been like a dream that I constantly struggled to stay in even after she'd been gone. "Well, that's awesome, Dec. I'm happy for you; Aurora's going to be, too. When do we get to meet her?"

"I don't know." He paused, as if he was actually considering that, then his smile turned wry. "She likes contractors in ties, so I'll probably have to keep her away from you."

I barked out a short laugh and nodded in Aurora's direction. "You're safe, Dec. I have everything I want."

"Soon," he assured me, then turned and headed for the kitchen, and I moved toward my wife.

Her eyes darted in the direction Declan had just left before meeting mine again. "Everything okay?" she asked softly.

I had a family, and there was a possibility that Jessica was ready to turn her life around.

I had a wife who could bring me to my knees with a smile, and she was pregnant with our son.

Okay was an understatement.

I placed my hand on Aurora's chest, and watched her eyes warm and dance with wonder and adoration.

My good. My light. My bliss.

"Perfect."

Acknowledgments

As always, thank you to my amazing husband, Cory. I wouldn't be able to do any of the work I do if it weren't for you.

Kevan, thank you for always being there and having my best interests at heart.

Tessa, I know, I know . . . you totally wanted a triangle! One of these days I'll get you one, I promise. But you have to admit that it was fun going from what this started off as . . . to what it is now.

Amy, thank you for being there through every step of this process, even when I was too confused to know what was happening in my own story. Ha!

About the Author

Molly McAdams grew up in California but now lives in the oh-so-amazing state of Texas with her husband, daughter, and fur babies. Her hobbies include hiking, snowboarding, traveling, and long walks on the beach . . . which roughly translates to being a homebody with her hubby and dishing out movie quotes.

31901060072446